In my mouth, Asa tastes the way a snuffed-out candle smells: charred fibers, smoke gummed against my teeth, the bald softness of wax cracking under a dusting of soot. I first taste it after checking into the inn just a couple miles' walk from the Grand Canyon's South Rim. Asa moves from the safe pocket between my gums and the inside of my cheek, rolling over my molars before pouring into the cradle of my tongue. It's not like in the other motels that dotted this journey, the nights she coated the back of my throat in a thick film the same as a seasonal sickness that sticks your lips together, something foul and faint and just out of reach. It's not like on the road, where she nestled in my sinuses and let me enjoy the blandness of stale french fries and endless cups of drive-thru coffee. In the privacy of my room, at the end of our journey, she wants me to taste her as she really is.

From "Every Form of Person," by J. A. W. McCarthy

THE CANTERBURY NIGHTMARES

Edited By David Niall Wilson

STORIES BY

MICHAEL BOATMAN · S.A. COSBY · AI JIANG
ERIC LAROCCA · J. A. W. McCARTHY · SCOTT J. MOSES
STEPHEN MARK RAINEY · JOHN B. ROSENMAN
ANNA TAMBOUR · TERENCE TAYLOR · STEVE RASNIC TEM

Meet the Authors

Steve Rasnic Tem is a past winner of the Bram Stoker, World Fantasy, and British Fantasy Awards. His novel *Ubo* (Solaris Books), a finalist for the Bram Stoker Award, is a dark science fictional tale about violence and its origins, featuring such historical viewpoint characters as Jack the Ripper, Stalin, and Heinrich Himmler. He has published over 500 short stories in his 40+ year career. Some of his best are collected in *Thanatrauma* and *Figures Unseen* from Valancourt Books, and in *The Night Doctor & Other Tales* from Macabre Ink. You can visit his home on the web at www.stevetem.com.

J. A. W. McCarthy is the Bram Stoker Award and Shirley Jackson Award nominated author of Sometimes We're Cruel and Other Stories (Cemetery Gates Media, 2021) and Sleep Alone (Off Limits Press, 2023). Her short fiction has appeared in numerous publications, including Vastarien, PseudoPod, LampLight, Apparition Lit, Tales to Terrify, and The Best Horror of the Year Vol 13 (ed. Ellen Datlow). She is Thai American and lives with her husband and assistant cats in the Pacific Northwest. You can call her Jen on Twitter @JAWMcCarthy, and find out more at www.jawmccarthy.com.

Scott J. Moses is the author of Our Own Unique Affliction (DarkLit Press). An Active member of the Horror Writers Association, his work has appeared in Cosmic Horror Monthly, The NoSleep Podcast, Planet Scumm, and elsewhere. His work has been praised by Laird Barron, Brian Evenson, and others. He also edited What One Wouldn't Do: An Anthology on the Lengths One Might Go To. He is Japanese American and lives in Maryland. You can find him on Twitter @scottj_moses or at www.scottjmoses.com.

Eric LaRocca (he/they) is the Bram Stoker Award®-nominated and Splatterpunk Award-winning author of the viral sensation, *Things Have Gotten Worse Since We Last Spoke*. A lover of luxury fashion and an admirer of European musical theatre, Eric can often be found roaming the streets of his home city, Boston, MA, for inspiration. For more information, please visit ericlarocca.com.

John B. Rosenman was an English professor at Norfolk State University where he designed and taught a course in how to write Science fiction and Fantasy. He is a former Chairman of the Board of the Horror Writers Association and was the editor of *Horror Magazine* and *The Rhetorician*. He has published over 200 stories in places such as *Weird Tales, Whitley Strieber's Aliens, Fangoria, Galaxy, Endless Apocalypse, The Age of Wonders*, and the Hot Blood erotic horror series. John has published two dozen books, including science-fiction-action-adventure novels such as *Beyond Those Distant Stars, Speaker of the Shakk, A Senseless Act of Beauty, Alien Dreams*, and the Inspector of the Cross series (Crossroad Press). He has also published a four-book box set, *The Amazing Worlds of John B. Rosenman* (Crossroad Press). In addition, he has published two mainstream novels, *The Best Laugh Last* (McPherson & Company) and the Young Adult *The Merry-Go-Round Man* (Crossroad Press). Recently, he published two science-fiction novels, *Dreamfarer* and *Go East, Young Man* that are the start of a new Dreamfarer series.

Two of John's major themes are the endless, mind-stretching wonders of the universe and the limitless possibilities of transformation—sexual, cosmic, and otherwise.

S.A. Cosby is an award winning best selling author from Southeastern Virginia. His book *Blacktop Wasteland* won the Anthony, Barry ,Macavity and ITW award for best novel and also was awarded the *LA Times* book award for Mystery or Thriller. His novel *Razorblade Tears* was a NYT best seller winning numerous awards as well and was selected for former President Barack Obama's summer reading list. He resides in Gloucester County with two cats, a squirrel, and a few good bottles of whiskey.

Ai Jiang is a Chinese-Canadian writer, a Nebula Award finalist, and an immigrant from Fujian. She is a member of HWA, SFWA, and Codex. Her work can be found in F&SF, The Dark,and Uncanny, among others. She is the recipient of Odyssey Workshop's 2022 Fresh Voices Scholarship and the author of Linghun and I AM AI. Find her on Twitter (@AiJiang_) and online (http://aijiang.ca).

In his civilian life, **Michael Boatman** has co-starred in shows like *China Beach, Spin City, ARLISS, Instant Mom* and, most recently, *The Good Fight*. He's also the author of the novels, *Revenant Road, Last God Standing* and *Who Wants To Be The Prince of Darkness?* His short stories have appeared in magazines like *Apex*, and in anthologies like *Tales of Capes and Cowls*.

Terence Taylor (terencetaylor.com) lives and writes in Gowanus, Brooklyn, with Shuri, his black cat and part-time muse. After years of comforting kids with award-winning children's television written for PBS, Nickelodeon, and Disney,among others, he turned to scaring their parents in print. His short story "Plaything,"appeared in Brandon Massey's *Dark Dreams*, the first horror-suspense anthology of African American authors. Terence's work was in the next two volumes, and his short stories and nonfiction essays have since appeared in *Lightspeed, Fantastic Stories of the Imagination, Nightmare Magazine, What the #@&% Is That?: The Saga Anthology of the Monstrous and the Macabre*, and more. His first novel, *Bite Marks*, was a modern-day Grand Guignol about the unintended but catastrophic creation of an undead infant. Graced with a starred review by Publishers Weekly that described it as "a gritty, screen worthy supernatural noir set in 1980s New York," it was followed by *Blood Pressure*. Twenty years later, a new menace endangers the humans and vampires that survived book one. Terence will soon conclude his trilogy with *Past Life*, set in 2027, as that rising horror threatens to end the world.

Stephen Mark Rainey has been writing professionally for over thirty years. He is author of numerous adult novels, including *Balak, The Lebo Coven, Dark Shadows: Dreams of the Dark* (with Elizabeth Massie), *Blue Devil Island, The Nightmare Frontier, The Monarchs*, and others. Currently, he is writing novels for *Elizabeth Massie's Ameri-Scares* series for young readers, with four already in print and several more on the publication schedule. In addition, Mark's work includes five short story collections; almost 200 published works of short fiction; and the scripts to several *Dark Shadows* audio productions, which feature members of the original ABC-TV series cast. For ten years, he edited the award-winning *Deathrealm* magazine and has edited the anthologies *Deathrealms, Song of Cthulhu*, and *Evermore*. His short fiction has recently appeared in the anthologies *Borderlands 7, Fright Train*, and *The Black Stone: Stories for Lovecraftian Summonings*. Mark lives in Greensboro, NC

Anna Tambour's latest book is the 2023 collection *Death Goes to the Dogs*, published by Oddness.

Editor's Foreword

I started this project with what I believed was a solid plan, born of a catchy title I conceived long ago. The plan was that I would style myself as the narrator, in the style of Chaucer, providing commentary along the way, and tie this into something clever. I can tell you, that is not what happened.

It was 2020. We—I—thought the pandemic was coming to an end, that things were looking up and that change would come swiftly. The world had different ideas. Still, I sent out my invitations. I laid out my plan to a number of very talented authors. Some turned me down, either over the theme, the timing, or the general malaise of the time. Those who accepted, those whose tales you'll find in this fairly slim volume, share one very important thing, and they share it with me, and all of you as well. They lived through one of the strangest, most difficult, and dangerous periods in American history, and for the most part, did so in isolation.

I asked them to write a story inspired by that time, by their own experience. I asked them to place that tale at the end of the pandemic, and for their characters to be meeting, accidentally, in groups, and individually at a non-extant motel on the last road into the Grand Canyon National Park.

I thought I would get a bunch of stories that were—not pastiches—but modern ghosts of the tales Chaucer told, but there is one truth about authors, and about stories. They are very hard to control, and every time you *try* to control them, you either fail, or it ends badly.

Another truth is that no two people experience the same things in exactly the same manner. I wrote a story once where the main character observed that we all live in our own tiny universes. Like a giant Venn diagram, they interlace, border, and blend with those of others, but they are never the same. The stories in this collection epitomize this. Some are directly inspired by the theme. Some only vaguely fit the theme, but are inspired by the time, situation, and spirit of theme. They were written and turned in over a period of more than two years. At least one story, by an author I greatly admire, was the first thing they'd been able to write since the pandemic started… the one story that broke the ice.

At least one made me uncomfortable enough that I discussed it at length with the author and it was slightly revised. There are old voices, new voices, new to *me* voices, different walks of life. At least two have become very famous since I started this project, and as bad as it all was, I have that period of time to thank for introducing me to them. I'm not going to go on, and on, and I'm not going to play Chaucer, I'm simply going to welcome you to *The Canterbury Nightmares* and wish you... pleasant dreams.

CONTENTS

The Old Man's Tale

By Steve Rasnic Tem

We all seek a kind of understanding. How the world works, and our place in it. It doesn't have to be true.

Dan heard a disturbance of birds, maybe some cats and maybe something else, deep within the dark shadows beyond the parking lot. It sounded harsh and desperate, and it was difficult to say what was going on. No one else seemed bothered. Perhaps they'd become used to commotion. An old-fashioned word—did anyone else still use it? He was a few months shy of seventy-four, so he figured he had a right to use an old word or two.

He was surrounded by people, although he couldn't see them in any detail: the dark silhouettes of fellow pilgrims and storytellers against the fading crimson light. He was determined to believe none of them meant him harm, which during these times seemed a major leap of faith. People were less trusting than they used to be, and far less kind. Lies and deception, hatred and fear, the worst in people had taken control. Dan was confused and angry most of the time. It was safer to hide your pain and suffer in silence. There had been numerous shortages this past year, but the most critical might have been empathy.

His eyesight had deteriorated in recent years, the decline accelerating over the course of this trip. This might have been a result of his diabetes and kidney disease, or something yet undiagnosed. He couldn't be sure if the things he saw were a symptom or a revelation. Dark silhouettes stood at the edges of things, making a Rorschach of the night. He thought he'd feel better if he saw their mouths.

The face a few yards away was that of the organizer. Dan had been skeptical—he never responded to either unsolicited mail or phone calls—but Jane had been so excited by the invitation and the possibility of finally seeing the Grand Canyon, and the last thing Dan wanted was to disappoint her.

He'd been afraid the stories from the other travelers might disturb her, but she insisted on being beside him as he told his tale. He kept reaching out to make sure she was there. Once he thought he saw her moving through the crowd, but he must have been mistaken. She wasn't speaking to him now. He had no idea why. It was a typical problem in marriages. Somehow, he was expected to read her mind.

After more than a year with only Jane and doctors to talk to he had a lot to say. "Do I just start? How much time do I have? If you want me to keep talking, I'll keep talking. I have nothing better to do, not at my age."

Somewhere a fire was burning. He could smell it although he couldn't see the flames. It seemed too warm for a fire; he supposed it was for the atmosphere. Or maybe it wasn't a literal fire, but simply his sense of the world burning. So many wildfires had raged this past year—Australia, California, his home state of Colorado—they'd left this acrid remainder in his nasal passages he couldn't shake. Climate change gets worse by the day. One more thing to make him feel helpless.

"I've never been to Arizona before, so I'm not used to the heat. Yet here I am wearing my sweater. Old men depend on their sweaters. When you're old that icy hand is always trying to slip in and steal your heart. My Jane," he gestured in her direction, "used to say we should move here when we got old. I tried to laugh off the idea, because I couldn't bear the thought of living somewhere with so much empty space."

There was movement in the crowd. He couldn't pinpoint its location because of all the shadows. He hadn't realized so many were in attendance. They moved little, which made them good listeners he supposed. He felt self-conscious being the center of attention, being overweight, being old. His CKD caused him intermittent pain and would probably end his life prematurely.

"I can't drive anymore, not with my vision, and Jane's been too ill, so we had to take the bus from Denver to get here. I spent a lot of time going to the bathroom on the bus. I worry I might smell like pee. Is that too much information? With all our scientific advances, you'd think they could help people like me."

Sometimes he had accidents and he wanted to cover his face and weep like a small child. He shouldn't have brought it up. Jane had to be embarrassed, but she didn't say anything.

"It's a long trip with a whole lot of nothing to see. Even less for me, I guess. So, I must use my imagination. Someone points at something in the distance and says 'Ain't that a beautiful mesa!' I always agree, because in my mind's eye, it *is* grand. I see most things as being much better or much worse than they are. In that regard, I suppose I'm like everybody else on the planet."

His cellphone started ringing from inside the small backpack on the bench beside him. He stared at it. "I'm so sorry." He looked around foolishly thinking he might see the caller. "I thought it was dead. It's *been* dead. My son gave it to us for emergencies. I never charge it. These things don't charge by themselves, do they? I don't know why I brought it. I never use it. The only people who ever call me are con artists." He opened the pack being careful not to jostle the contents and pulled out the phone. There was no name, and he didn't recognize the number. The phone went dark again. He dropped it back into the pack.

"My wife Jane has always wanted to see the Grand Canyon. She's been after me for years to go. I told her I didn't want to drive all that distance and spend all that money to see a damn hole in the ground. I said it harshly because I wanted to discourage her from asking again. I told her I didn't care how big it was, or that it was prehistoric. After a while she stopped asking because she knew my mind was set." It felt strange saying this in front of Jane, but he was sure she already knew.

"It's the only time I've ever lied to her. The truth is, the idea of being on the edge of that canyon always terrified me. I've seen pictures, and I'm *seriously* afraid of heights. Once we got there, I knew I would refuse to go anywhere near it. The Grand Canyon is a place where the world is broken, where it shows its wound, so why would I want to see that?

"I've always regretted disappointing her. Then this last year, this Covid year, watching people we knew getting so sick, watching neighbors and relatives dying—when Jane's sister passed, we couldn't even attend the funeral. Her brother was the designated mourner. He took a shaky video of the barebones burial and sent it to us in an email. Jane watched it over and over, crying. I was afraid this was the thing that was going to break her. I was scared to death to go anywhere, but she still had to leave the house for doctors' appointments, tests, and treatments. If she saw someone without a mask, or buying a hoard of TP, water, hand sanitizer, she made it her mission to give them a miserable day. I understood completely, but it still shocked me. Jane is the kindest person you'll ever meet, but this last year of constant stress and disappointment has worn her down to the basics. We knew the world wasn't ending, I mean we all understand this isn't the end times, am I right? But that knowledge doesn't travel very deep. We still feel on the lip of oblivion, I can't be the only one.

"We were so grateful when your invitation came. I immediately told her we would go, *had* to go. Just to see something eternal when so many people we knew were dying, losing their jobs, fracturing inside. For the first time in a long while I experienced excitement. I hadn't taken a long bus trip since my college years.

"I'm rambling. Forgive me, but I haven't talked to other people in a while. It may take me some time to remember how. Am I the only one who thinks the world has fundamentally changed?

"Do any of you still watch the news? I stopped. I can't watch that crap anymore, all those alternative versions of reality. The deliberate lies and the stupidity, and the goddamn delusion. You don't know these people, so you don't know which it is in their case. I'm just an old man with no influence or power. Before, I was a young man with no influence or power. It seems all we can do is witness and tell the truth about what we've seen. But no one wants to do even that anymore.

"Jane complains that I tend to lecture. That's not what I'm trying to do here. Old guys like me, sometimes when we talk to people it sounds like a lecture. I'm not sure why. I'm simply trying to explain myself. Let me back up a little.

"Nine months ago, I was sitting in our back yard, trying to figure out this emergency cell phone our son Blake gave us. I've never been good with cell technology, and the screen is too small for me. Blake didn't leave us his number when he left town, so who was I supposed to call anyway, some stranger? We didn't even have an address to send him a letter. I've always had trouble connecting with our only child, and I take full responsibility for that. But Jane has been such a good mother—didn't our son want to know how she was doing?

"There was this small pile of garbage against the wooden fence on the side of our yard. Our next-door neighbor tossed it over like this was a normal thing to do. Some spoiled food, some upholstery foam, discarded mail, pieces of a doll and what used to be a stuffed toy. Something new every day, and I cleaned it up every day before Jane could see it, because it upset her so much. Our neighbor wouldn't even talk to me, said he knew nothing about it, then he called me senile. It was a smallish outrage to add to the many humiliations I've experienced the past few years.

"We used to use the backyard all the time before Jane got sick. We used to have barbecues. We would sit out there and listen to the birds. But it had begun to feel unpleasant and uncomfortable. The back fence is chain link, and you can see the yards and the trees south of our house. At one point I glanced up from that damn cell phone, and I saw this dark figure standing by the fence, either on our side or the other, I couldn't quite tell. I stared at this person, waiting for him or her to move. After a tense few minutes with no change, I assumed it was an optical illusion, or maybe just a shadow, and I turned my back and walked away. I slept poorly that night, worrying over it, and wondering how I could have left without investigating more thoroughly.

"So, the next morning I went into the back yard and checked it out. I didn't find anything, no footprints, no sign of a disturbance of any kind. But as I was going back into the house, I sensed something behind me, and I turned around. Just for a second. I may or may not have seen several more human shapes in the yard, on both sides of the fence, but they weren't there a second later. Puzzling, but easy to dismiss when you have eyes as bad as mine.

"Then a couple of days later I was convinced I saw the silhouette of a man climbing over our side of the wooden fence to get into our neighbor's yard. I should have told him, but after our disagreement, I was reluctant to knock on his door. Instead, I considered getting Jane out of the house and checking into a motel, but how could I explain why? The last thing I wanted to do was scare her. So, I did nothing. I decided to wait, thinking maybe it was just me seeing things. I thought maybe I wouldn't have seen anything if I hadn't been so upset about everything on the news.

"About a month or so passed. I was out in the yard again trying to decide if the lawn needed mowing. I don't do much yard work anymore. I usually hire a teenager if I can find one. Jane was inside resting from her chemo. She was really sick the first part of the year, then she got better, then she was sick again. Most of the summer we took a cab to get her blood transfusions every few weeks. We watched a great deal of TV together, sitting on the couch and holding hands. That's how we spent Thanksgiving and Christmas. That's how we watched the insurrection, and then the inauguration. We were sitting on that couch watching when the 500,000 deaths from Covid were announced. And we watched that George Floyd video again and again, trying to understand why it happened, and knowing it had happened many times before. We felt helpless as we watched it and feeling helpless made us feel ashamed.

"But that was ahead of us. On this day, while I was trying to decide if I could let the lawn go another week or two, and if I could just ignore the weeding until next season, I noticed movement near the top of one of the trees beyond the chain link fence. A mass of leaves obscured my view, but something was changing, shifting, and causing the top branches to bend as it began its descent. I didn't know what it might be, I just had a peek of something, and as I followed this movement down the tree, I experienced an overwhelming feeling of dread. I can't remember ever feeling so afraid over apparently nothing. I waited for whatever might appear at the bottom of the tree. But what dropped out of the lower limbs wasn't a form or even a shadow, but some sort of distortion in the light, a visual ripple which quickly dissipated.

"Now, this could have been a combination of some sort of wind through the tree branches along with some play of the light. But the presence felt undeniable. I looked at the nearby trees, and after a few minutes I was sure something was sitting in the top of a second one, and now it, too, was slowly coming down, a few leaves, some bits of branch and the negative spaces in between, descending in unison, a kind of camouflage in motion. I still had no idea what it might be, but I felt threatened, and I didn't want to be there when another one reached the ground, and so I retreated inside.

"For the next week I spent a period each morning observing the trees. That experience of a barely detectable presence followed by motion and descent repeated itself day after day, until I couldn't stand to watch anymore."

Dan paused his story to allow for questions, complaints, or any kind of reaction from his audience at all. There was none. He did notice slight movements, and he had a sense of being watched, so he assumed they were still present.

"I've read that some ancient peoples believed the spirits of the dead manifested as birds, perched in the treetops and observing the living below. Not that I believe this, but if it were true, imagine their anger over how we've handled things. All the damage we've done, all the promises broken or simply forgotten.

"I tried not to think about what I'd witnessed. I didn't need something new to worry about. I didn't tell Jane." He put his hand out, thinking his touch would let her know he was sorry for that, and for talking about her so openly, and his fingers grazed the backpack. "In fact, I've never told anyone else about this. You people, you're the first."

Since Dan began this tale, his surroundings had changed. The light from the fire was more evident, casting yellows and reds through the shadows. Dan thought he could make out a few more faces, although he couldn't see their expressions. Not knowing how his audience was reacting to what he told them was disquieting.

He couldn't be sure who or what they were. In the darkness almost anyone could have slipped into the crowd, sat down, or stood at the back. Visitors might have been among them, phantoms, witnesses, those presences crept down from the trees. Some might even have followed him from Colorado. He didn't know how any of this worked, so anything was still possible.

He probably shouldn't have told them. They might be able to have him committed. He'd heard Arizona was not a good place to be mentally ill. He should have rehearsed his story with Jane first. She could have advised him what not to say.

"It's been a strange and demanding year. I'm not claiming to understand what I saw. I'm just putting it out there. I'm a rational human being trying to deal with the irrational, these phantoms at the periphery of my vision, like someone just arrived, or someone just left, or someone's waiting there, ready to do some damage, cause some mischief. I don't want to say it's related to the pandemic, but maybe everything is, if you think about it.

"People have changed so much the past few years, don't you think? Things will be fine for a while, then these pockets of—I don't know— *derangement* appear, and they spread through the population.

"I thought Jane was oblivious to it all, then one day she grabbed both of my hands and stared at me in this intense, almost scary way. 'It's that awful man they elected. People now think it's okay to say anything that pops into their heads.'

"My wife has never been a political person, so that was a lot for her to say. She wanted to go to the Women's March the day after his inauguration, but she'd been too ill. A friend gave her one of those pink knitted hats and she wore it around the house for weeks. She'd lost some of her hair, and it kept her head warm.

"We have seen so many terrible images. Those poor refugees. Children abandoned in the desert, or their bodies washed up on shore. You've seen those pictures too? Or am I crazy?"

He waited for an uncomfortably long time. Finally, someone in the distance said "yes," and another "yes, I think we've all seen them."

"I think of those children as another kind of arrival. Like the entities up in the trees, like the reminders from history. Welcome them or try to keep them out, it doesn't matter. They're still going to come. It doesn't matter how angry you are, how unpleasant, it's a matter of physics. The true facts of history are going to rise to the top however deeply you try to bury them. If people's houses are burning, they're going to find somewhere else to live. The way I see it, fires are burning all over the world.

"I've had difficulty sleeping for months. Has anyone else lost sleep?" A murmur travelled through the crowd. "Underneath everything were my worries over Jane of course. But laid over those were the soft whispers, the sensation of something touching the hairs on my arms, and I'd feel around for insects on my body which were never there. More than a few nights I listened to the sound of tree limbs brushing across the roof of our house, and then I remembered we had no trees in our yard.

"Then sometimes there was this faint crackling within the walls. Sometimes a rhythmic pulse of something moving through the rooms.

"I was relieved to have this opportunity to escape the house, to travel somewhere I'd never been before, where I knew no one. We were both so eager, so ready to go. Jane could hardly contain herself. She planned for this trip for months.

"But then on the morning of departure I couldn't make myself walk out the door. The taxi was waiting, horn blaring. It was the trip we'd been looking forward to so much, and yet I couldn't budge. For some reason I could not imagine ever returning from this trip. I felt as if I were about to go to my own funeral.

"Jane had a grip on my arm so tight it ached. She kept whispering in my ear that I'd promised her, that I'd made a commitment. So I hurried down to the cab before I could change my mind again. I held it together pretty well on the ride into downtown Denver.

I'd packed light—a few changes of clothes in a single backpack because I couldn't carry more. I'd loaded the pack with lots of brochures for every place we were going to or through. I love brochures, don't you? I'd already read them once and I planned to read them again on the bus. I'm a planner, always have been. I always refer to a map even when I've been to a place a dozen times.

"Jane kept whispering words of encouragement, bits of poems and song lyrics, anything to distract me from my anxiety. Gazing out the window I felt out of place, watching people walking around so close to each other, some with masks and some without. I wasn't even sure what the current rules were, although I knew masks were required on buses.

"I looked for those visitors and found them, those other presences crossing the street, sitting on porches, stepping out of bushes. They manifested mostly as color shifts and staggered outlines. For me this was confirmation the phenomenon wasn't restricted to our neighborhood.

"I hadn't been downtown in years. But it was much as I remembered, vast concrete stretches with little green, a few shiny new buildings and fewer of the old gray ones. Shabby figures pushed their grocery carts from corner to corner. At first, I thought these might be the visitors, but they were too crisply defined, and I realized they were homeless people. We passed an entire encampment arranged along a parking strip: a variety of small tents, carts, boxes, and trash bags filled to overflowing.

"The driver said something crude. It was brief and offhand, and I could have let it go, but it angered me. 'So, what's your solution?'

"The driver stared at me in the rear-view. 'Don't have one, I just know it's wrong to let them live in a public area. Isn't that why we have elections? To put people in charge who know what to do?'

"I felt Jane's hand on my arm. I said 'I wish the ones in charge would do a lot of things, but they don't. The economy leaves lots of folks behind. On top of that the climate's changing. We pretend there's nothing we can do. Pretty soon it will be our own family members, moving, trying to find safety. Maybe you. Maybe me if I live that long. We need to do better if we want to save ourselves. We could start with those folks out there.' Okay, not those exact words, but something like it. Yeah, sometimes I lecture people. I guess I don't mind if it's important.

"When we arrived at the bus station, we had to wait a little while before boarding. I kept stalling. Jane had to push me. I was afraid once I left on that bus my life would never be the same. It increasingly seemed a terrible idea, leaving the safety of home to go somewhere completely unknown.

"Some people were being cautious in the station and on the bus, and some people not. There were a few who behaved as if the pandemic had never occurred. Before we got to the interstate ramp the bus driver slowed down and parked on the side of the street. A few yards away the police had pulled a man out of his car and were talking to him forcefully. Some of the passengers stood up and held their cellphones up to the windows on that side. Others beat on the glass. One of the officers glanced over, then turned away. Jane kept telling me I should do something, so I got the dead cellphone out of my pack and held it up to the window. I felt uncomfortable doing that—a few years ago I would never have imagined such a thing, but the world has changed, hasn't it? I don't know if the officers were going to act inappropriately; maybe they were just doing their job. These days you can no longer assume the best, can you? Eventually the bus started up again and everyone sat down.

"Signs on the bus reminded everyone that masks (except when eating and drinking) and social distancing were required. Seats and hand surfaces were regularly sanitized. Another sign had a diagram explaining how cabin air was continuously replaced every 5 minutes. It looked very scientific, as if NASA had been involved in the engineering. These details and more were described in colorful brochures. I added one to the large collection in my backpack.

"The first four seats behind the driver were taped off so no one could sit there. These measures reassured me at first, then I saw that although many passengers wore their masks, many did not. Some had pulled their masks down in order to complain to each other about the *arbitrary* rules. One of those complaining with his mask down was a preacher, presumably. At least he had a bible in his hand which he continuously quoted from.

"The driver wasn't enforcing anything (except for that no-sit space directly behind him.) I understood—the man wasn't paid to be an enforcer and it would probably be dangerous for him if he tried. They expect people to cooperate and be on their best behavior during a crisis, but that's not how people act.

"I pulled Jane closer as we escaped the southern limits of the city and the bus headed for Colorado Springs and points beyond. The foothills grew closer, then fell away again. The stretches of flatland increased their spread, and even though there was a great deal of development south of metro Denver, I was impressed by all the emptiness. Some people like that sort of environment, the wide-open spaces with your nearest neighbor miles away. I never have.

"Although I had a definite destination in mind—this place, and the canyon beyond—I wasn't convinced we'd actually arrive here. I imagined the driver taking us as far as possible into nothing before the fuel ran out.

"I was still conscious of those ghostly visitors, but there was no evidence of their presence on the bus, and although I looked for them out in those dry, burning stretches, I didn't see any indication they were there.

A silhouette standing and watching from a distant house doesn't count—it could just be some curious resident—although I saw quite a few more of those than I expected. I attempted to see into the windows of passing cars. Of course, you can't see much unless they're travelling at the same speed. Sometimes I'd see some shadows in a back seat, but those could have been anything.

"Maybe we were too far away, traveling too fast, but I suspect their preference is to manifest within the company of human beings. By themselves I imagine they must behave quite differently. But around us, it must be like visiting a foreign country, getting used to the culture, trying to understand customs which to us feel quite strange. I have no evidence for any of this. We human beings shouldn't develop convictions and beliefs based on feelings alone, but that's what we do. The human animal is a fiction machine.

"We made ourselves a little island, Jane and I, there in the middle of the bus. All around us people were chatting. It seemed no one was travelling alone, or if they were they'd made conversational friends with a speed I could only envy. I've never been good at talking to strangers, not ever. It's not that I don't like people. I just feel separated from them, and that attitude has only deepened as I've grown older. Even on this long trip with Jane she did most of the talking. I listened, and occasionally offered some perspective, usually a negative one. Jane was used to that and mocked me playfully for my grumpiness.

"We whispered our conversations. We didn't want to disturb the other passengers, and we didn't want them to hear the secrets we shared only with each other.

"Occasionally people would turn and stare at us, even though we were whispering. Maybe they wondered what all the whispering was about, or they'd forgotten there was such a thing as privacy, or that it is considered rude to stare. There were several children on the bus, and they stared the longest, until their parents made them turn around. This was usually followed by whispered conversations of their own. I didn't try to listen. At least I know how to respect people's privacy.

"Since I've gotten old, I've noticed sometimes children point and snicker at me. I think it may be because none of my clothes fit. They haven't fit for a long time. I don't know how to make them fit or even what *fitting* means. Now I can't seem to make myself care. About either the fit or the snickering. I try not to judge.

"If I've learned one thing from this past year, it's that I'm not a bad person. I'm a good person, just not a great one.

"To be honest I felt ill the entire trip. I still feel a vague sickness throughout my body. It's *chronic*, I suppose. My lower abdomen, my chest, my constant trips to the bathroom. The bus bathroom was horrid, as I expected it would be, but I had no choice. I had to spend a lot of time in there. Each time I returned from the cramped bathroom I looked for Jane, and if I didn't see her immediately—and sometimes I didn't—my anxiety surged.

"When the stress became too much, I took a nap. This has always been my go-to solution. Once I opened my eyes and saw a much younger version of myself sitting in the seat across the aisle. He blinked, obviously alarmed. He was from long before I met Jane.

"Another time I awakened to see insects crawling through the bus, and even a rat or two. I thought I should tell someone, probably the driver, but what could he do? We were in the middle of a trip. I kept my mouth shut and went back to sleep. When I woke up again, I wasn't there. It was past my sell-by date, and I was a shadow staining the seat.

"I woke up again, now confused about where I was. Then I felt Jane's hand on my arm and saw her leaning over me. 'Have a good rest?' She must have said that same line hundreds of times during our marriage, and it was always comforting.

"I get confused a lot these days, and it sometimes takes me awhile to realize I'm confused. I always have more questions than answers."

Dan had been talking a long time. He stopped and took a slow drink from his water bottle. He worried this might have been a mistake. He might develop an urgent need to go to the bathroom. Were they allowed to take bathroom breaks during the middle of a story? 'Allowed' probably wasn't the right word—there was no coercion here, except the need to avoid embarrassment.

He was so tired of this, having to schedule his life around his unreasonable bodily needs, the toilet, his fatigue, his bouts of worry and anxiety. It was humiliating. None of those had been considerations when he was young.

It was almost pitch black. None of the parking lot lights were on, and the fire had burned out. A thick mass of variegated darkness hung in front of him. He assumed people were inside the darkness ready to hear the rest of his tale.

He turned his head to look for Jane. He couldn't see her, but he heard her whispering to him. He couldn't make out all the words, but he knew they were of love and encouragement. Fortified, he continued.

"Northeastern New Mexico is dominated by a broad region of volcanic fields. Capulin, an extinct volcano, is well east of I-25, so we bypassed it. But I still had brochures. It's strange to think about volcano activity in the US, especially near one's home. Ancient cinder cones and petrified lava flows, and the land itself looks burnt and alien. There was volcanic activity in New Mexico during the time of the Paleoindians, can you imagine? Not being able to trust the ground beneath your feet or the sky over your head? Yet maybe that's not so different from now.

"There's something vaguely romantic and emotionally familiar about the apocalyptic landscape there, but it made me uncomfortable. A smoky mist eased down the highway, soon enveloping the bus. A charred stench drifted in through the vents until the driver shut them. Unable to see past the windshield the driver pulled onto the wide shoulder. We all stopped talking and stared out the windows.

"I saw several thin, upright shadows wandering the cloudy plain across the road, appearing and disappearing as a pale yellowish film slowly drifted through. They looked like people walking away to some unknown destination. When the bus started up again, we passed a few empty parked cars a hundred or so yards down the road. I heard someone say we should stop and check if anyone needed help, but the driver ignored the suggestion.

"I saw a few animals along the road, both small and large, several rabbits and prairie dogs, and something which looked like a small antelope. I couldn't identify the rest. They might have been anything, I just knew they were covered in fur, I think. It was perhaps emblematic of the boredom of long bus rides that anytime a passenger made such a sighting they called it out and we all strained to look.

"An argument erupted several rows ahead of us. A young girl accused the preacher of touching her under the cover of his open bible. There was shouting and a great deal of shoving and I leaned over Jane to protect her. A few minutes later the bus stopped, and the preacher was thrown out onto the shoulder of the road. It happened so quickly I didn't have time to think about whether this was right to handle things that way, but everyone seemed to agree, and the driver did allow it to happen. In any case I couldn't have done anything.

"We stopped in Las Vegas, New Mexico. Jane thought it funny such a small, dusty town had the same name as that glamorous city in Nevada. According to the brochure part of *Easy Rider* was filmed here and in the old days outlaws like Billy the Kid walked the streets. I thought it would be an interesting place for us to spend the night and catch another bus the next day. I was exhausted. I wouldn't have thought sitting on a bus could be so tiring, but it did me in. Jane, who was the sick one, who had been reduced almost to nothing, never complained. I felt ashamed of myself, but it couldn't be helped. I couldn't bear to be on the bus another minute.

"We walked a short distance from the bus stop to a small motel. It was depressing in its adequacy, but it was close by, and I didn't have the energy to find another. I strapped on my backpack, and Jane and I walked around a little before having dinner at a small western-themed café. She chattered the entire time, but I couldn't really follow what she was saying. I guess I was too tired. I had a strong feeling others were walking with us but explorations into my peripheral views revealed no one. So, I assumed this town had visitors too. This was strong confirmation these phantoms were everywhere, as far as I was concerned. Witnessing, perhaps judging, because why else would they be here?

"Despite decades of living in Colorado I've never felt like a westerner. People at the café were watching me eat, at least I think they were. Jane kept telling me to ignore them. I told her I couldn't stand it anymore. I paid up and left. I've always thought we should have retired to a small town like that—it didn't matter where—I thought we'd feel safer. Jane says small town people aren't necessarily better. I guess there are no safe places anymore.

"In the parking lot of the motel a shadow stood beside an old dusty automobile. It looked like it had travelled miles and years to get there. The figure was still standing there when we walked away from the motel the next morning. The bus stop was more of a truck stop—trucks were parked everywhere, and I walked cautiously between them to get to a place where we could wait for the next bus. It wouldn't do to be run over now. I don't dread death, but I don't want to die because I've acted stupidly.

"A large open air flea market filled the block across the road. Not all the sellers had protective awnings, and they looked miserable in the hot sun. I worried that maybe I'd read the schedule incorrectly and we'd be stuck with no way to either continue our trip or to get back home. Sometimes I think worrying is my job, and it's Jane's job to reassure me and calm me down. Within a few minutes a line of waiting passengers formed behind me and the bus arrived. It looked identical to the previous bus, but I felt good about facing a new set of passengers. I noticed a man staring at us from the middle of the flea market as we boarded the new bus. I couldn't see the man's face, and I couldn't make myself stop looking at him.

"The new bus was already crowded. After we settled in a man came up to me and asked me if I would slide over so the man could sit down.

"I was bewildered by this. I kept looking at Jane, thinking she should say something, but she just stared at the man with a big smile. I finally said, a little shakily I'm afraid, 'But there are only two seats here!'

"The man kept looking at me, scowling. I began to feel panicky. Where was the misunderstanding? I pulled Jane closer to me. The man looked back toward the driver, sighed, and much to my relief found himself another seat toward the back. Maybe I should have been more patient, more understanding. He might have had some sort of mental problem, some emotional issue. We all need to be patient during times like this.

"I noticed one man on the bus had a bloodied face. For a while I watched him. He acted as if nothing was unusual about his appearance. Other people stared, but no one asked what happened, or if he needed medical attention. I overheard someone say they shouldn't allow certain kinds of people on the bus, and I wondered if we were going to have another incident like the one with the preacher. I guess people don't take chances these days, on planes, or anywhere else. Jane whispered that the man deserved his privacy.

"For long stretches the other passengers were quiet, but now and then everyone seemed to be talking at the same time. It confuses me when too many people speak at once, and this inability to distinguish conversations happens to me all the time now. There are times, it seems, Jane is the only one who will talk to me or bother to wait for my answer.

"Several passengers had canes, both young and old people, and sometimes they'd tap them on the floor when they were unhappy. I heard a lot of cane tapping on this trip. I also own a cane. Sometimes it helps me get around. I forgot it at home.

"The air conditioning went out for a while. It became extremely hot, and my nose began to bleed. I was so embarrassed. I didn't know what to do. The next time I went to the bathroom I used up all the paper towels trying to clean myself up. I felt terrible not to have left any towels for the next passenger who needed one. I thought I saw someone staring at me from the bathroom mirror, but once I focused the figure was gone.

"It turns out it's only about 125 miles from Las Vegas New Mexico to Albuquerque, where I'd planned for us to spend our second night. I thought it would make the trip much more interesting for Jane. But I'd always thought the two places were further apart. When I realized my mistake, I felt overwhelmed. I thought I'd ruined our entire trip, and this was probably the last trip Jane and I would ever share. I had to lie down. I don't know what I was thinking. I guess I wasn't thinking. I stretched out on the floor in the center aisle of the bus."

Dan couldn't see anything now, not the audience in front of him, not the parking lot, not the motel, not Jane, not even the stars. Yet he still felt surrounded. He felt pressed to continue, and so he did.

"This created a great deal of excitement, as you might imagine, with concerned people bending over me and asking what was wrong. I explained I was just a little tired. A couple of nice men helped me back into my seat. One of them gave me a bottle of water, for which I thanked him so profusely it appeared to embarrass him.

"I could see that my clothes were a mess: greasy marks on my trousers, my shirt tail out, dirty and torn. I was so embarrassed. I wanted to go clean up, but I was afraid I couldn't do it properly in that small bathroom. I'd likely spill water all over myself, and maybe I'd look as if I'd peed myself. I didn't want to take that chance. I looked down at my hands and I was troubled to see my father's hands. He had this same thin skin, stained and stretched so that you can practically see the veins inside.

"How do you know when you're old? I really don't know. I guess when everybody tells you. I look at other old people—with their white hair, all their wrinkles—and I think they're a lot older than I am. But most of the time it turns out they're younger.

"Suddenly I wasn't aware of Jane being anywhere on the bus. I twisted around, I looked everywhere. I didn't see her. Had I left her behind at the last bus stop? We hadn't stopped anywhere since Las Vegas. I started to cry. I've become so like a young child. I made myself stop because I simply couldn't afford another scene. Stopping like that, holding it in—I wanted to scream.

"Then my foot kicked my backpack which had fallen to the floor in front of my feet. I picked it up and hugged it tightly, afraid to let go.

"Jane came up behind me and put her hand on my back. She often did that when I was upset. I would recognize her touch anywhere. *It's okay*, she said, and then everything was for a spell.

"In Albuquerque, the bus driver instructed everyone to sit quietly while the police came on board. I was sure they had come for me because of that incident lying on the floor. It had only been a brief episode of confusion, but I was afraid I'd be unable to convince them of that. Sometimes if you make too many mistakes someone takes charge of you. Then you have no choice but to do what they say.

"The officers wore clear face masks, but there appeared to be no face behind the mask of the female officer. They walked past me and grabbed the man with the bloody face and pulled him out of his seat. As they led him away, he gazed around at the other passengers with a disturbing grin. He appeared to fix his attention on Jane, and she tried to hide behind me.

"I like the bus station in Albuquerque. It has that early Mexican look, with modern adobe and rounded arches everywhere. But it doesn't appear to be in a great part of town. Rather than finding a place to stay for the night Jane and I waited for the next bus. No one bothered us, which was a blessing. Jane was tired and not in a good mood. She had some harsh things to say about my behavior on this trip.

"The final leg from Albuquerque to Flagstaff, and then to here was over seven hours. It was the longest leg of the trip, taking Interstate 40 north of the Acoma Pueblo, the oldest continuously inhabited community in the United States according to the brochure, and the Zuni Reservation. I would have liked to spend some time there but by that point I was focused on this destination, this meeting, telling you this story. I was honestly afraid I would give up if we stopped for any length of time. I missed home, my own chair, my own window on the world. I didn't want to be anywhere else.

"I wondered if the driver shared my sense of urgency, because right out of Albuquerque he picked up speed and seemed to be driving much too fast. As the bus began to rock ever so slightly, I could see that the other passengers were nervous as well. At one point I remember thinking we would crash. I closed my eyes. Jane knew I was in distress. She began to rub my arm.

"Eventually he slowed down, and over that long, monotonous stretch I was able to reclaim some sleep, although pieces of disturbing dreams would now and then jar me awake. I dreamed of Jane when we were younger. We're always younger in my dreams.

"Sometimes when I woke up, I wasn't sure where we were. Had I finally gotten into the taxi, or had I insisted we stay home? Did we actually receive your invitation? Then I'd recognize the interior of the bus, but I didn't see Jane and I would wonder why I would take such a long trip without her. I couldn't figure out if the bus had gotten to Arizona or if we were still in New Mexico. I've never been here before, so I didn't know if there was much difference between the two states. It's a long way if you're unfamiliar with the route. I don't really like going places I've never been before. If I must, I always bring a map. It seems safer that way. But I wasn't driving. A stranger was driving. He could have taken us anywhere. Our future was outside the bus, ahead of us, and there was no map for that.

"Sometimes I sensed Jane sleeping beside me. If I'd had a blanket, I would have covered her with it. I had nothing. I could do nothing for her.

"I remember at one point we were headed directly into the sun. The bus was rattling, and both the sky and the land outside were red. The sun was so bright I couldn't see the driver, but I could see the other passengers: dark, not quite opaque, and not quite human. They were visitors, and my companions on this journey into a frightening interior.

"I still don't know why they appeared. Maybe they didn't want to miss what's going to happen to the world. Or maybe it's just the right time for it. I wonder sometimes if the virus came because it was the right time for it."

He stopped and looked around. The world was still thick with darkness. He shouldn't have been able to see anything. And yet he did. Hundreds of forms all made identical by the shadows. From the way they held themselves he understood they were all focused on him.

"This might have been a terrible mistake coming here. I mean, think about it. I tend not to trust people I don't know, and I know nothing about any of you, but still I've come all this way based on some random invitation I received in the mail. How foolish is that? This could be a cult and I might be about to come to some terrible end." He made a half-hearted laughing noise, and it startled him, not having heard himself make such a sound before. "You're not a cult, are you?"

No one replied. He sighed. "I suppose I don't care at this stage. Jane and I, there was never anything special about us. We weren't famous people. We lived the kind of life that ends up in a thrift store. But it's the life we had. It wasn't one of those stirring romances they make big movies about, but it was the love we had.

"I remember, as a child, those summer afternoons of endless play and discovery. The way time stretched in those days, everything lasted for years. Me, and my friends, and all those potential friends I never saw again. We'd make these grand plans and talk about the great things which would happen when we got together again, until we wore ourselves out, and one by one I'd see my friends being taken from me, sometimes by means not readily apparent, and I'd wonder what had happened to them, until finally I'd be standing there alone, and needing to find my way home. I never thought I'd ever feel such things again, and yet here I am."

His dead cell phone began ringing from within the backpack. He looked around apologetically but couldn't see faces clearly enough to apologize. Finally, he opened the pack and retrieved his cell. He stared at the screen. The number displayed made no sense to him. He tapped the screen and put the phone to his ear.

There was a brief burst of static, then her voice, distant and distracted. *You were supposed to come visit, weren't you? You were supposed to be with me. Why didn't you come?*

Shaking, he put the phone back into his pack. He let his hand linger a moment, then removed the dull metal cannister from his extra clothing and set it carefully beside his feet.

"Jane died a couple of months ago. She had Covid those final weeks, but she would have died anyway. It just meant I couldn't be with her. I begged them, but I hadn't had the vaccine yet. I have it now, in time for this, but too late to hold her hand. That's the one thing I promised her, that I would be sitting there holding her hand at the end.

"There are so many things I regret, thoughtless things I said to her, and other things I should have said but didn't. Marriages are built on things unsaid as much as anything else.

"She never told me what she wanted done afterwards. She always changed the subject. Then I couldn't ask her anymore, and she couldn't answer. I think her mind had already travelled a far distance ahead.

"I didn't know what to do. I didn't have her to tell me what the right thing would be. But I knew she hated missing this trip, and I figured both of us could still go. Every place along the way I told her what things looked like, as best I could imagine. I whispered, but maybe sometimes I whispered too loudly. We didn't travel much during our marriage, and that was my fault.

"I'm going to scatter her ashes at the canyon. She would have liked that. It will mean—oh Hell, I don't know what it will mean, but that's what I'm going to do. I hope no one objects."

No one said anything. Dan didn't know what he would have done if they did.

"It's too bad we can't leave our sorrows there, isn't it? If everybody drove to that giant wound in the earth and could toss their sadness inside, and walk away to get on with the rest of their lives, wouldn't that be a great thing?"

He pulled one of the many brochures out of his backpack. "It says here if you threw the body of every human being who ever lived into the Grand Canyon, as if it were one giant grave for all of human history, you'd fill less than point two percent of it. Isn't that, isn't that remarkable?"

The Liberation of Brother Buffalo

By Michael Boatman

My name is William Singleton. Back when I had friends, they called me Will, so I suppose you folks can call me that too. I've noticed some of you flinching at my disfigurement, so what-say we get the first (and probably the smallest) elephant out of the room, eh? Some of my more diehard readers might call me 'handsome,' save for this big ol' scar. How I came by it is one of my reasons for visiting the Canyon. The others? That's a hell of a lot more complicated.

I've been to the Canyon once before, many years ago. I was ten years old, so this would have been back in the summer of 1973. My father was an English professor at the University of Chicago. My mother was what they used to call a 'housewife' back then. They'd been sweethearts since their college days, practically joined at the hip by their shared love of Soul music, old movies, and the "Great Outdoors." My sister, Francine, and I were usually less enthusiastic. Movies were supposed to be in color and camping was for rich white kids from the suburbs.

Francine… *Frankie,* was killed by a drunk driver when I was eight years old. She was twelve when she died. I won't go into great detail about what the death of a child can do to a family. But, to my parents' credit, or deficit, they rarely let me see them grieving. Sometimes there were bumps in the road: flashes of pain that would rip away the façade and reveal—at least to one another, that we'd been maimed by Frankie's absence.

But my parents were tough, and they expected the same toughness from me. So I did my best. After a while, I shut my sister away in a tiny room in my mind, and I turned out the light and locked the door.

Since my father was off for most of every summer, my folks had made it a yearly tradition to drag the family to one of our nation's national parks. Frankie's death had taken the spirit out of my parents, and for the next two years we'd stayed home; three strangers who'd lost the element that made us a family.

We were only three weeks into that summer vacation of 1973 when my father, during dinner one night, announced that we were getting out of Chicago. One week later, they'd packed us up, and the three of us headed west.

We'd barely left the house and I was already pining for Frankie. She should have been sitting on the other side of our '71 Grand Safari station wagon with her arms crossed and her eyes squeezed shut, so annoyed by the prospect of the endless miles she'd have to spend entertaining me with games like "Let's Count the Red Cars," or "Find the Black People in These Postcards!" (There were never any Black people in the postcards my mother collected at every rest stop.)

That summer, however, we'd begun the journey saddled by the weight of Frankie's absence. As we pulled out of our driveway, I saw my mother staring out her window, her forehead pressed to the glass as she wiped away tears, as if she didn't want me or my father to see what was plain to all. However, by the time we were out of the city and heading west on Interstate 80, the mood in the car had lightened. My father even took on the responsibility of supplying the appropriate road games.

Time and memory seem to distort themselves these days; old age I guess, but I can't recall much more of that outbound trip; mostly because it's been overshadowed by the events that happened on the fourth day.

We arrived at the Canyon and set up our campsite on the banks of the Colorado River. Six families would spend the next five nights at the site below the Canyon's South Rim: Angel Campground. Our hired guides had patiently advised us while we selected horses. Then our group descended the Bright Angel Trail.

At the halfway point I looked back from the front of the line, past my mother's distracted smile and my father debating politics with a businessman who was also from Chicago. The long line of sweaty city-folk peppered the air with gasps of wonder or shouted questions as we passed groves occupied by flora native to the Canyon: white fir and blue spruce, ponderosa pine and Utah juniper trees.

I was dazzled by the infinite shades of red and gold, and how the play of sunlight seemed to animate the stone walls all around us, making faces or animal shapes. To say that I was bewitched would be an understatement.

On that fourth morning all the interested kids, about twelve in total, were allowed to venture away from the campsite on the condition that we stayed together and in sight of the river. Armed with long, pointed sticks in case we encountered rattlesnakes, we headed out along the glorious Colorado River.

We'd barely been walking for five minutes when I lost sight of the tall girl in front of me; a pretty Jewish brunette from Milwaukee named Eileen. I was following her; about six paces behind—she walked fast—while behind me trudged five younger kids and the two thirteen-year-olds who formed the rear guard. I was ambling along, happily dumbstruck by the sights and sounds, when I noticed Eileen was gone. I stopped, looked behind me and saw that the other kids had also vanished. I was alone.

"Will Singleton. That's a nice name."

I turned toward the sound of that voice and saw the oddest thing: *There was a woman standing in the river.*

She was Native American, her long black hair free and falling nearly to her waist. She was dressed, oddly, in a silver, form-fitting bodysuit that covered her from her neck to her ankles. Only her brown hands and feet were bare. Red gems sparkled at the shoulders and down the sides of the silver suit. The gems reflected sunlight so that the woman appeared to inhabit the eye of a whirlwind, a tornado formed from concentrated sunshine.

Somehow, the woman was standing *on* the water.

I turned to alert Eileen and then remembered that she was gone. For a moment, I thought I heard her yelling my name, but then the sound was disrupted by the glowing lady's voice.

"Don't be afraid," she said. "I want to show you something."

Her voice was strong, airy, like a steady breeze blowing through a forest of wind chimes. When she smiled, the sunlight seemed to coalesce around her until she was cocooned in living flame.

But I wasn't afraid. Something about the glowing lady's eyes seemed to cloak me in assurances. The feeling of welcome that radiated from her reminded me of the dizzying Christmas dinners we'd spent at the home of my aunt Charlotte, my mother's bosomy best friend.

"Folks around here call me Silver Woman," she said in that ringing wind chime voice. "It's time to go. We've already lost the day."

At the mention of time, I tore my eyes away from Silver Woman and was amazed: Night was falling over the canyon. My position on the riverbank hadn't changed, but now she was *standing next to me*. From somewhere, I heard people, Eileen, my parents, shouting—

"Will!" "*William!*"

I felt a vague sense of movement, as if the world was turning *around* me, and I saw the red sun sink below the bluffs to the west. The distant howl of a coyote startled me, and then I found myself gasping at the shock of freezing water rushing over my naked skin.

I was looking into Silver Woman's eyes. They were vast, and black as the space between stars. She held me in the roaring current, tracing my cheeks and forehead with icy fingers, bathing me in the glacial flow as she sang:

"This river is our blood. This land is our body."

Then the entire canyon was plunged into darkness and silence. But there was movement in that darkness, something that felt like... a *presence*.

"A soul," Silver Woman whispered. "A very big soul."

This shadow soul felt enormous as it shouldered its way into my awareness. I felt its hot breath, and heard its deep, rumbling growl. Its tread shook the ground beneath my feet.

The soul was filled with rage, or sadness so vast, that to my childish perceptions it felt like rage. Terrified, I squeezed my eyes shut and willed myself to become invisible.

"I have to go now," I whispered.

"Remember, little brother," Silver Woman sang.

"One day you will see my token and remember what's true."

When I opened my eyes, my father was gripping me by the shoulders. He was crying and his shirtfront was covered in blood.

We were in a small ranger's station, surrounded by a dozen older white men. Some of them were wearing park ranger uniforms. Somebody took my picture. Then someone else took another one. Then I was dazzled by a storm of flashing lights while the men shouted questions.

"Where's mom," I said. "Where's mom?"

My father was hugging me so tightly I could barely breathe. Normally clean- shaven, he was a former Air Force captain who shaved every day, even on vacation- now he looked as if he'd been hollowed out; his cheeks covered by a scraggly beard.

"What happened?" he cried. He looked feverish, like a man in the throes of delirium. "We thought... your mother thought... My God, Will! *Where were you?*"

Then someone brought my mother in and the whole crying thing started all over again. It was only later, amidst more tears, and questions from the police, that I realized I was forgetting Silver Woman. The harder I tried to recall her face the faster it receded from my memory. I was angry. I wanted to remember all of it.

Later that night, as my dad slept, exhausted, on the hotel room's spare twin bed, my mother was sitting next to me on the sofa. I'd bathed earlier, so intent on trying to hold on to my visit with Silver Woman I hadn't noticed that the bathtub was filled with red water.

"We looked all over for you," my mother said. "Dozens of people came with dogs, two helicopters.... Even family from Chicago flew out to help, but we couldn't find you."

"I'm sleepy," I muttered.

My memories of the glowing woman—

The shining lady?

—were fading, but we'd never left that spot along the riverbank, and we were together for no longer than an hour.

"That ranger opened up his station this morning and found you sleeping inside," my mother said. "You were naked, and you had… a lot of blood on you. Will?"

"Yeah?"

"Who gave you that blanket?"

"What blanket?"

"The one you were wrapped in. The ranger said it was Navajo. Hand-woven. It looked very… expensive."

"I don't remember," I groaned. *"Tired."*

"That ranger's station is in the Superstition Mountains, William," my mother said. "That's nearly two- hundred miles from our campsite."

"It was Frankie," I muttered.

"What?"

"Frankie. She gave me the blanket."

I fell asleep.

Over the next few days, I would learn why my parents were so worried. The ranger had found me on that frosty morning, naked and covered from head to toe in dried blood.

I had been missing for nearly a month.

The rest of my adventure seems like a dream to me now, like scenes from an old movie that I once loved and then forgot. I suppose that's what allows us to move on: Time. And "move on" is just what I did.

There were questions of course, but since I couldn't remember anything. I simply made things up until my answers didn't please anyone. Eventually, everyone left me alone.

College is a blur: I studied. I earned several degrees.

It was while I was working as an editor for the *Denver Plainsman* that I got the idea for the story that would eventually become the Spectre & Sparrow books.

Ah, *now* I see a few light bulbs going off.

I wrote *Book One: Spectre & Company,* the year I turned thirty: nineteen -eighty -eight. For those unfamiliar, it's the story of cyborg Commander Artemis Spectre and her intelligent starship, Sparrow. Together they battle an invading army of alien pirates from a distant galaxy.

That first book sold well enough that I was able to quit the editing job after a year to focus on writing the next one. *Book Two, The Planet Pirates,* sold well enough that Hollywood took notice. Three years later, the film version of *Spectre & Company* was a box office smash.

I was paid an equally phenomenal amount of money to write *Book*

Three: Sparrowhawk; Book Four: Hunting Spectres; Book Five: Sparrow Rebellion and *Book Six: The Veil War.* All were international bestsellers. The first three films were unqualified box office hits. *The Veil War* film was halfway through production when the 911 attacks shut down New York City.

I was in my late forties by then, and between book deals and movie rights I'd made more than enough money to call myself a successful author. I'd moved to L.A. and had been living there for ten years when I met Lisette McGee.

Now, I can't tell you much about this scar if I don't tell you about my lifelong fascination with, let's call them, "difficult" women.

We've all met people so physically beautiful they drive folks of both sexes to distraction; or romantic types, who can write love letters with one hand and pick your pocket with the other while sharpening a hatchet with their feet. Lisette McGee was such a person.

She was a coldblooded trickster motivated by unbridled ambition and her fading beauty: a weaponized sex-doll who targeted softhearted men with hardwired assets. I caught her cheating on me two months into our marriage. A month later, I filed for an annulment and avoided certain financial doom.

But the small banalities of human nature can lead us into the foulest waters, and Lisette was nothing if not banal. By far, the most annoying of her many self-contradictions was her public devotion to her "spirituality."

She'd hounded me about going to church. And no matter which of her other sponsors she may have screwed on any given Saturday night, Lisette never missed a Sunday morning sermon, courtesy of Home for The Heart International Ministries in Christ, LLC.

H.H.M. was the most recent example of the "mega churches" that had begun to proliferate around the country by the nineteen-eighties. Thanks to popular "televangelists" like Pat Robertson and his 700 Club, or Jimmy Swaggart Ministries, the mega church phenomenon had spawned a multi-billion-dollar global industry by the time I met the founder and head pastor of Home for The Heart Ministries.

I'd been separated from Lisette for nine months when Peter Scanlon, an old editor and friend, called me up.

"I'm here to moderate a writer's panel at the 'Sci-Fac' Convention," he said. "Let's get together and drink, you bastard!"

Lonely and bored, I agreed to meet Peter the next day.

I passed mostly unnoticed among the mobs of fans and Cosplayers that swarmed the Sci-Fac! (Short for Science Faction!) at L.A.'s Convention Center: By 2008 the Spectre & Sparrow films had faded from the movie-going public's awareness since their big-screen debut twenty years earlier.

The actors had aged and moved on to greater or lesser successes: none more tragically, perhaps, than the star of the original franchise.

But I'm getting ahead of myself. I'll get to the calamity that befell Vanessa Warcloud in due time.

My point is that I'd come to accept a measure of anonymity by July of 2008. Harry Potter was hot: both the books *and* the films. And with the rising popularity of warmed-over "reboots" from *Star Wars* to *Lethal Weapon* to *Batman…* the adventures of my band of intrepid space heroes had fallen out of fashion.

I'd landed a few production deals with some major studios, so I tried my hand as a "script doctor." But I quickly discovered that "punching up" other writers' work while sober was like polishing turds for an audience of monkeys. I'd pitched a few original screenplays and found that process so blisteringly dull it made me feel suicidal.

The Spectre & Sparrow books were still popular, but the place from whence I'd drawn that inspiration had dried up. When I allowed myself to be honest, I was forced to acknowledge the creeping suspicion that I was finished: washed up at forty-nine years old.

That something inside me had begun to rot.

After spending the afternoon watching my friend field questions from his devoted young fan base, we'd skipped the official meet & greet and headed to a bar I knew just up the road in the city of Santa Monica. Five hours later, after too much Jack Daniels and not enough "dinner," we were walking back to our cars when we passed an empty tennis court.

Emboldened by whiskey and feeling jealous of Scanlon's relevance, I bet him fifty bucks that I could jump over the tennis net without disturbing it. Before he could agree, I took three steps and vaulted over the net. On the way, my left foot snagged one of the holes at the top of the net. I twisted in mid-air and crashed sideways onto the court.

After I'd dusted myself off and assured him I was okay, Scanlon got into his car, still chuckling, and sped off. I took five steps toward my car before my left leg went wobbly, promptly collapsed, and dumped me on my ass again. I didn't speculate about the damage: The pain that blazed up the back of my left calf was informative.

Cursing myself for being a fool, I managed to stand on my uninjured right leg, hop the rest of the way to my car and drive myself to Cedar Sinai.

———————

"You've got a partial rupture of the left Achilles Tendon," the on-duty orthopedist informed me, some three hours later. "That big tough ligament that runs from your heel up to the back of the knee twisted when you tripped. Lucky for you it only tore. If that bad boy snapped, you'd need surgery to reconnect the torn ends."

After being fitted for an orthopedic "shoe" to restrict foot movement, I was given a pair of crutches, a prescription for pain meds and discharge papers assuring me that my ruptured tendon would heal on its own.

Feeling lower than at any other time I could remember, I rode a wheelchair through the exit to the emergency room's parking lot and into a rare L.A. rainstorm.

"You got a ride comin?" Oscar, the cheerful orderly attached to the wheelchair asked. "Can't drive all fucked up on those meds."

"No. I'm alone."

"I'll call you a taxi," the orderly said, just as a new Lincoln Town Car rolled up to the curb and stopped right in front of me. The driver's door opened and the driver, a Black man of average height and build, jumped out. He was dressed in a well-tailored black suit and wore perfectly shined black ankle boots.

The driver produced a large umbrella from somewhere inside the Lincoln. Then he ran around to the rear passenger door and opened it.

Have you ever recognized a stranger? Or found yourself driving through a completely new town, certain somehow, that you've been there before?

The woman seated in the back seat of the Lincoln was a stranger. But every one of my senses *expanded* at the sight of her. Something opened up inside of me, something like panic, or euphoria. Wet and woozy, I was immediately sobered by her: flummoxed into silence. She was the most beautiful woman I'd ever seen.

Like the driver, the woman was African American, only of a lighter complexion, with smooth reddish-brown skin. Her hair, shielded from the rain, was dark brown and straight, smoothly tied back into an immaculate bun. Full red lips complimented eyes that glinted a light honey brown. The driver handed the woman the umbrella and stepped back. Then the woman stepped out of the limo.

I imagine it was the thing about her that attracted stares whenever she entered a room; comments tossed up from bold children while their nervous parents made jokes about "the weather up there:"

The beautiful woman was tall.

Seated in my wheelchair it was hard to estimate her actual height, but I guessed she must have stood nearly seven feet tall. Her body was strongly built, with broad straight shoulders and the narrow waist of a professional athlete. She was wearing a black business suit with a white blouse, open at the collar. Her hair had been perfectly coiffed, with a single white rose pinned over her left ear.

"Will Singleton," she said. Not a question. An assertion. A *declaration*. "I'm here to collect you."

Her voice was low without being heavy, the thalassic thrum of a cello sonata played under water.

"You'd better close that or the rain'll get in."

I shut my mouth.

The tall woman looked to be in her early thirties, but her smile gave me a glimpse of how she might have looked as a teenager. As she must have looked when we'd known each other in that other life.

"I don't understand," I stammered. "I...uh...I called a taxi."

"Lisette called and asked if I would pick you up," the tall woman said. "Stan and I were on our way home from a brunch when she reached me."

"Lisette? I'm not...."

"You listed her as your emergency contact," the tall woman said. "But since you guys are estranged... well, she thought it might be better if a third party came for you."

I vaguely remembered putting Lisette's name down as an emergency contact somewhere. Now I didn't know whether to be grateful or annoyed.

"Force of habit," I said. "We were only married for a few months."

"Oh, I know," the tall woman said. "I helped her through that transition. You ought to reach out to her, by the way. She's thriving these days."

"Oh," I offered, not knowing what else to say.

"If you'll tell Stan where you parked your car, he can have someone bring it to you tomorrow morning," the tall woman said. "I assume you can't drive while you're jacked up on all that nasty old pain medication."

"I don't... I'm not sure...."

"No problem at all, Mister Singleton," the driver said. "I'm Stan Carpenter, personal assistant to the Reverend Doctor. I'm a big fan of your work. I bought Spectre & Sparrow in hardcover, and it still holds a place of honor on my bookshelf. It would be my honor to personally see to it that you and your car make it home all in one piece."

The driver laughed at his own joke.

That sense of dislocation, of *separation*, rose in me again. I was painfully aware of how I must have looked to her: foolish, middle-aged, clumsy, and I felt ashamed.

Don't, little brother, someone, probably the Vicodin, whispered. *Some things are bigger than they seem.*

The tall woman extended her hand toward me. Her fingers were long and perfectly manicured. Each of her nails had been painted the color of fresh blood, and a tiny diamond adorned the center of each cuticle.

"I'm Ursula Crusher," she volunteered, flashing that dazzling smile. "Shall we?"

That's how I fell into the shadow of the Reverend-Doctor Ursula Lee Crusher. Hell, I'll admit that *I was already in love;* too bedazzled by this deity from another reality to suspect something I wouldn't learn until it was far too late: That when I stepped into her Town Car I was stepping away from my dreams, my world.

Even my sanity.

It's not exactly cutting-edge storytelling to write about the funny nature of time; how it steals life and dulls desire; how it shatters hearts and teaches its beautiful, brutal lessons to each of us, leaving hard-earned wisdom in its wake.

We were on our honeymoon the first time Ursula hit me.

I proposed marriage to her six months after we met. She'd nursed me through my rehabilitation, driven me to my physical therapy sessions and even taught me new exercises to strengthen my injured leg.

She played basketball all through high school and college, and even played professionally for the Chicago Fire. Her greatest achievement, she told me over dinner one night, was when she'd played for the U.S. Women's Basketball team at the 1996 Olympics. Unfortunately, a knee injury ended Ursula's career. But her knowledge of physical therapy techniques was invaluable.

We'd been married for a year, but the honeymoon I'd planned was delayed because of Ursula's church commitments. I'd learned, after our yearlong courtship, that Home for The Heart Ministries was more than her life's work; it was her *calling.*

"Sometimes personal stuff has to come second, babe," she'd reply, after I'd expressed my concerns about her schedule. I was still smarting from Lisette and her betrayals. Now that I'd found real love, I had no intention of letting it slip through my fingers.

"The Devil doesn't take vacations," she said, offering me a half-smile while she punched in the next number. "God's people gotta keep it movin'."

We were driving north along the coastal route. To our left, the Pacific Ocean sprawled, opulent and endless, beneath a turquoise blue sky. But I was itching to get to San Francisco. Ursula had been shouting marching orders to her team back at church headquarters since we'd left Los Angeles.

"Pull over at the next stop," she said, ending a call. "I gotta pee."

I was happy to comply. I'd held a death grip on the steering wheel all the way from Santa Barbara. Tension had branched out from my shoulders, spread down my spine, and finally set up shop in my lower back. Nearly two years after my "tennis accident," my left leg had never regained full strength. The long drive had inevitably caused my foot and ankle to stiffen up. I needed to do my daily calf stretches.

While I was bending and twisting on a small plot of grass near the ladies' room, a middle-aged woman approached me.

"Excuse Me," she said. "Aren't you somebody?"

"Will Singleton," I said. "I'm an author."

"Oh my God," the woman drawled. "I knew it! You're the guy who wrote the books about the robot lady, Captain Spectre!"

"That's right," I said. "She's a cyborg, by the way."

"Oh, my son loves those books! And the movies too, of course! But he really loves the *books* because they encouraged him to read, and I was so grateful for *that* because before I got him those books he was practically illiterate. Do you mind if I get an autograph? It would mean so much to Brian."

"Of course." I was surprised at how good it felt to greet a fan. "Nice to know someone's still enjoying the stories."

The woman rummaged around in her purse, pulled out an ink pen and a crumpled theater program and handed them to me.

"I was looking for you," Ursula said. "Where'd you go?"

"Just took a walk to stretch my legs. Ursula this is, oh, I'm sorry, I didn't get your name."

"Elizabeth Wiley," the mother of Brian said. Then she turned to Ursula. "We're huge fans of your dad's."

I laughed. I was fifty-one that year. Ursula was only thirty-four.

"She's not my daughter," I said, chuckling. "She's my wife."

"Oh," the woman said. "My *goodness*. And tall as a Utah Juniper! I must say: you're a very lucky woman!"

Ursula's face was still, her lower jaw tightly clenched as if she were gritting her teeth. The expression was new to me.

"So nice to make your acquaintance!" Elizabeth Wiley said. "Brian is gonna shit an anvil when I tell him I met you!"

As the woman drove away, I turned back to Ursula.

"That was funny, eh?"

Ursula slapped me. There was no warning, the movement was so quick I'd barely registered it. I wasn't even sure what had happened until the right side of my face began to throb, grow warm, then hot. The slap echoed in the silence of the empty rest stop like a gunshot.

"Hey," I gasped. "Ursula, what…?"

She grabbed me by the left wrist and squeezed it.

"Shut up," she snarled, and before I could object, she slapped me again. "Shut. Up!"

Ursula wheeled around and hauled me back toward the restrooms. Stunned, it was all I could do to stay on my feet as she dragged me behind her.

"Ursula! Wait!"

It was no use: she still worked out five times a week, and she was far stronger than the average woman. And although my Achilles tendon had healed, all that physical therapy had failed to restore the strength and balance I'd lost to atrophy during my twelve-week recovery.

"Hey!" I shouted.

She dragged me behind the restrooms and up a small hill that led to another picnic area enclosed by a ring of trees.

"People thinkin', they can humiliate somebody," she hissed, so quietly that I wasn't sure I'd heard it correctly. "… let you make a damn fool outta *me* you got another 'think' coming."

She didn't stop until she'd dragged me across the picnic area and into the little copse of trees. Then, she whirled around and faced me.

"You think that's funny? What she said?"

"Ursula… I don't know what you're talking about!"

"You know goddamn well what I'm talkin' about, William," she snarled, tightening her grip on my wrist.

"Ursula, you're hurting… Owwww…that hurts!"

"You think any of this is funny?" she said. Then she threw back her head and screamed, *"Answer me!"*

I couldn't answer. I wasn't even sure I was awake. As if to prove the point, Ursula elbowed me in the left temple hard enough to knock me down. I lay there on my back seeing stars.

When my vision cleared, the woman towering over me bore little resemblance to the woman who'd spent the last year and a half nursing me back to health. I'd seen her angry before, of course. But this was different. Not anger. This was something else.

I got one leg under me and tried to stand. Ursula rushed toward me, clearing the distance in a single stride, and kicked me in the chest. I staggered back and my right hip struck the edge of a picnic table. I lost balance and fell to my hands and knees.

"Wait," I gasped. "Ursula, listen to me! I think…."

"You think," Ursula said. "You. *Think.*"

I tasted blood, swallowed a little and realized she'd cut my lower lip when she struck me with her elbow.

Ursula put her foot on my chest and pressed me down onto the grass. She was wearing casual walking shoes, but the heel was hard enough that I could feel her grinding it into my sternum.

"Now, I'm going back to the car. You are gonna stay here and *think* about what just happened. And when you *think* you got it figured out, *then* you can come out and tell me what the *fuck you find so goddamn funny.*"

She held me there, her size thirteen sneaker pressing down for another agonizing instant. Then she was gone.

I lay there, gasping as air flooded back into my body, trying to make sense of what had just happened. Ursula had never struck me before; never gotten angry enough to hit anyone that I knew of. But there I lay, bruised, busted lip and all.

I know what some of you are thinking. I should have run. I should have done a million other things than the one thing I did: I lay there in the grass.

And I thought about what I'd found so goddamn funny.

By the time I thought I'd figured it out and walked back to the car, the old Ursula, the *familiar* Ursula had returned. She was sitting in the passenger seat, checking emails.

"Have you figured out what you did?"

I should have walked into the men's room, locked myself in a stall and called the police. I should have called someone from the goddamn writer's guild. *Anything.*

"She laughed," I said. "That woman thought you were my daughter. I guess she thought it was funny."

"Did *you* think it was funny?"

"No... Ursula...."

"So why did you laugh? Were you *trying* to embarrass me?"

My brain was clicking along at a mile per second; retracing steps I'd taken in a different reality: Had I laughed? Had I flirted with the woman? What *had* I done?

"She was a fan," I pleaded, hating the tremor I heard in my voice. "Her son was a fan. I was just being polite."

"But we both know what you were *really* doing." Ursula focused on her phone. Her eyes never left its screen. "Don't we?"

She was still smiling, the smile so similar to the one that had entranced me enough to propose to its owner after knowing her for less than a year. But beneath that smile I now saw traces of *another* Ursula beneath the surface of that beautiful face, like a tiger shark lurking just out of sight beneath the waves.

"Laughing," I said, slowly. "Laughing... at you?"

"Right," she said. Then, unbelievably, she pursed her lips like a petulant toddler and her voice became the whine of a spoiled child. "You really, *really* hurt my feelings."

I bit it all back, everything I might have said about how crazy all of this was, how I was innocent. But...was I? I wasn't sure anymore. So I swallowed it. At that moment I wanted nothing more than to get in the car, drive to the nearest airport and book a flight back to L.A.

"I'm sorry."

The light from the setting sun glowed against the red-brown skin of her bare shoulders, the long curve of her neck. She seemed to shimmer in that dwindling light.

Remember what is true, I thought. Where had I heard that before? It seemed important. *Remember what is true.*

But Ursula's eyes were dead as ash. "You're sorry... what?" she said.

"I'm... sorry, honey."

"Thank you," she said. "See how easy that was? Now we can keep it moving."

Standing before you now, friends, it's easy to tell myself *that* was the moment, the surest harbinger of the horrors to come: the moment I *should* have done a thousand other things. Instead, I got into the car and drove to San Francisco.

When we arrived at the hotel, I checked my voicemail and got horrific news from my agent: Vanessa Warcloud, the Native American actress who had starred in the first three Spectre & Sparrow films, was dead, murdered by her ex-husband.

After the punishment I'd taken from Ursula, this news was too much to bear. Vanessa and I had become friends during the filming of Spectre & Company. She was a passionate advocate for the rights of indiginous women. She'd been nominated for an Academy Award for best actress for her performance as Artemis Spectre, the first Native American woman to attain that recognition.

That night, as if to seal an unspoken bargain, Ursula and I made love. Beneath her gentle hands and whispered promises, I put my concerns about her violence, and the murder of Vanessa Warcloud in a tiny room inside my mind.

Then I turned out the light and locked the door.

Apart from her regular Sunday sermons at the L.A. ministry, Ursula and I were constantly on the road: touring, doing local talk shows and radio appearances. With my tutoring she'd begun writing. She'd taken to storytelling like a natural. Of course, she was accustomed to writing her sermons but revealing her "authentic self" to her rapidly growing public through "dramatic" writing excited her.

We never spoke about the violence; or how she would vanish when the pressure became too great, so that the *other* Ursula could emerge. I was her only target and thus the sole witness to the phenomenon. Five years after the honeymoon incident I'd learned to grin and bear it. I loved her. She was complicated. She needed help.

I was eager to support Ursula's dream of becoming the first Black woman to lead an international ministry; proud to step away from the modest spotlight I'd earned writing science fiction.

In the years following the publication of the Spectre & Sparrow books the inspiration that had once sustained my creative output seemed to abandon me, swept aside by the urgency of Ursula's rise. I was happy to serve as her ghostwriter. She loved my input, and it did make her writing better. I helped her buff her own shine until it burned.

By our seventh year, Ursula was a national celebrity, speaking at universities and even dining at the White House, all without me. She claimed that my presence distracted her; that she constantly worried about my safety. I learned to embrace solitude and work "behind the scenes."

"Behind every great prophet there's always a great acolyte," she told me, during her phone call from the Lincoln Bedroom. She'd then gone on to enjoy her dinner with the President and his family.

Whenever we were in public, members of her "flock" would accost us, begging her attention, demanding her prayers. Meanwhile, at home, the beatings had grown less frequent. I doubled down on my commitment to *understanding* her. I'd come to believe my inability to "figure it out" was the cause of her frustration. So I learned to hide the occasional black eye behind sunglasses and conceal the odd busted lip with theatrical makeup. I learned to keep it moving.

On the Sunday morning Ursula was officially recognized as a "Bishop" of our denomination, she was no longer the charming woman I met outside Cedars Sinai ten years earlier.

She'd grown *austere*, smiling only when she was in public. On those occasions she could generate enough star power to charm arenas filled with her people, her passion projected from the giant television monitors we'd installed so that her image could be broadcast far and wide.

She never smiled when we were alone, as if being with me had drained her of joy. It had certainly extinguished her desire for sex.

Her personal habits had changed as well. Over the years, she'd shifted the focus of her workouts from aerobics to strength training. After an especially heavy workout, she might actually bathe. Otherwise, she might skip showering for a week, preferring to wait until Sunday morning to bathe for her sermons.

She'd taken to bringing home sacks of fast food after church. On those occasions, she'd rush into her home office and lock the door, refusing to be interrupted under threat of violence. I would stand outside her office and listen to the noises she made as she ate. It was around this time that I started to think of this new person as the Crusher.

It was during that Sunday sermon, the Sunday I came to think of as The Day of The Bishops, that I noticed something unusual was happening to Ursula. She was onstage before a packed auditorium, and she seemed to be struggling to read.

I'd written the sermon, and cribbed its climactic final beats from Psalm 23, Verse Four: "Yea, though I walk through the valley of the shadow of death, I will fear no evil: for thou art with me; thy rod and thy staff they comfort me."

It was a popular passage of scripture; one Ursula had quoted hundreds of times. But as I watched her, she lost her place and began to mumble. I sat up straighter in my seat as she began to "ad lib" scripture.

"...for thine is the kingdom, I shall not want," she muttered. "When the rockets' red glare, on Earth as it is in... ahhhh."

Looking up at Ursula's amplified face I saw her turn beet red. Her normally straightened hair had grown frazzled and plastered to her skull like a halo of black corkscrews bouncing around her head.

"I'm sorry, my dearly beloved," she grunted into the microphones. She wiped at her brow with the handkerchief I always put in the pocket of her robe. "Y'all know the work of Christ sometimes makes fools of even His brightest prophets."

The congregation laughed. When Ursula lowered her head, humbled by their approbation, the applause was thunderous. "We love you, reverend! Go on and preach!"

Ursula was crying. She mopped at her forehead and jowls with the soaking handkerchief, and then, with a grateful grin, she pointed to the ceiling, indicating that God was present.

"Thank you, beloved. What do I always say, when the Enemy tries to bring us down?"

The congregation, well trained by now, responded with Ursula's personal mantra. "Keep it movin'!"

Ursula picked up where she'd faltered. But this time she directed most of the sermon in my direction. She kept it moving.

But I dreaded what she might do when we got home.

When we met, she'd weighed one hundred sixty pounds, a healthy weight for an active woman who stood six feet, seven inches tall. Ten years later, she weighed more than three hundred pounds.

But I was telling you about the bishops.

It was customary for leaders in our denomination to welcome their new colleague with a brunch, usually held at the new bishop's home church. I'd arranged for the brunch to be held in one of the church's large meeting rooms where the eleven or so bishops in attendance could mingle with a few dozen congregants.

Many of them had travelled to L.A. from all over the country to celebrate Ursula's ascendency in the church hierarchy. The bishops were welcoming and full of praise. There were speeches honoring Ursula's service, and endless praise for the ever-expanding popularity of Home for The Heart Ministries. Ursula should have been happy.

But the Reverend Doctor looked lost, like an anxious child surrounded by adult strangers. She appeared distracted, her answers lifeless, as if recited by rote. After one of the invited bishops performed the benediction, we all sat down to eat.

It was while Ursula was demolishing her third helping of eggs, bacon, sausage, and fried potatoes that I suddenly understood what I was seeing.

Between the debacle of her bungled sermon and the celebratory brunch, that *other* Ursula had taken control. Now the Crusher was wolfing down her food, her face practically buried in her plate. She nodded at comments, paused to pray by request and pretended to listen when spoken to. I even spotted several of her colleagues eying her, curious at her rapaciousness. I watched her make excuses between helpings.

But she never stopped eating.

I sensed a storm brewing in the way she continuously gnawed at her lower lip. I saw disaster in the way she compulsively rubbed her palms against her thighs, kneading her flesh like cold clay in an attempt to contain that secret fury.

Calamity in the flex and clench of her fists.

Ursula was seated behind her big cherry wood desk when I walked into our home office. She was using her favorite letter opener to unseal envelopes containing best wishes, personal checks, or cash. The donations and prayer requests were mostly from elderly congregants who still used snail mail.

The sterling silver letter opener was a gift. A visiting pastor had presented it to Ursula on the occasion of her fortieth birthday. The long stiletto blade glinted in her hands, tossing argent flickers in the strangely harsh lighting of her office.

"You called?" I said.

"Dark in here," she muttered, unsealing another envelope. "Need more light."

Someone had removed the lampshades from her office. The big lamp on her desk and the smaller lamps scattered around the room were bare. Someone had also removed the recessed "cans" from the banks of overhead tract lighting. A dozen naked bulbs dangled from the ceiling like irradiated fruit.

I knew better than to ask why. Instead, I made a mental note to replace them in the morning.

"She called me yesterday," Ursula said.

"Who called?"

"Anya, dummy. Who d'ya think? She said she had a cancellation for her show on Friday. She wants to interview me."

I was about to reply when Ursula leaned forward and began to poke the letter opener into the expensive wood of her desktop. She stabbed at the wood, gouging at the desktop like a kid playing Whack-a-Mole.

"Ursula?" I said, "What are you doing?"

She ignored me. She thrust the letter opener into the desktop again, and again, faster and faster. Then she began dragging the blade back and forth across the desk. In moments, she'd created a hemisphere of slashes and pitted wood.

"William. Are you listening to me?"

"What?" I said, galvanized by the anger I heard in her voice. "Of course. Anya! My God, that's fantastic!"

Anya Whitlock was a force of nature even back then. The star of the immensely popular *Anya Whitlock Show*, she'd written bestselling books, acted in Academy Award winning movies and produced everything from blockbuster television programming to her own line of heart-healthy diet products.

Anya was the richest woman in America, and it was widely believed that she could run for President—she'd successfully endorsed the last three—and win. She'd interviewed kings and killers to enormous ratings success. One appearance on her show guaranteed that, for fifty minutes, the whole world would be watching you.

"That's amazing news," I said. "It's the break we've been waiting for! The chance to take H.H.M. worldwide! Did you say Friday? My God! We need to put together a list of topics she might want to cover and…."

Ursula slammed the letter opener into the desk. The blade penetrated the wood deeply enough to stand on its own: nearly a third of its length had sunk in.

"I simply can't fathom how I ever got mixed up with you." Ursula leaned forward and gripped the edge of the desk as if she were trying to gain enough purchase to flip it over. "You're so. Fuckin'. *Stupid*."

"Ursula," I said. She'd only struck me a few times in those last few months. The ministry had taken up so much of her attention she hadn't had the energy to focus on me, and I was determined to fly above the impending storm. "This is all good news."

"Oh?"

"Of course. It's a huge win."

"You already said that."

Ursula's eyes narrowed to thin slits.

"So *now* you think you know what's good for the ministry, right? You feel you know how to run things better than I do."

"Ursula, I didn't say that."

Focus, I thought. *You can fix this.*

Then, another, darker thought,

If you run, the Crusher will catch you.

The smell of French fries and pizza that had saturated her office for months seemed to enfold me in an invisible haze of fried lard and spoiled catsup.

"It's you," Ursula said. "You're what's wrong."

"Dammit, just stop!" I shouted, startling both of us. "You've got to stop."

Ursula's mouth dropped open.

"Don't you…." she began. "How dare you…."

"Ursula, shut up."

Ursula's eyes widened almost comically. Almost.

"What?" she huffed. "What did you just…?"

"Do you realize everything I've sacrificed for you?" I growled. "Do you have any appreciation for how I've bent over backward trying to make you happy? To help you move this ministry forward?"

"I never asked you to…."

Shut up!" I roared. "*I'm not even religious!* I don't believe in God or Jesus or any of it! I've gone along with it all this time: ten years of you ignoring me, humiliating me. Ten years of obliterating my fucking identity. I walked away from my fucking career! *I walked away from my life! For you!*"

I was gasping, hyperventilating. And I couldn't stop.

"Now you sit there on your ass trying to blame me? For what? Loving you? Wanting the best for you? Let me tell you something, lady: Without me backing you these last ten years, writing for you, crafting your infantile, cliché-ridden claptrap into actual adult speech, you'd be coaching basketball in some D3 college and working nightshifts at the local Piggly-Wiggly just to make the rent!"

Ursula's eyes welled up. Then tears spilled down her cheeks. "Are you finished?"

"No, I am not," I snapped. "I'm going upstairs to cool off. After that I'll be working on the next sermon. You are going to get out of this stinking office. Maybe you should go somewhere where you can think rationally about who has your best interests at heart."

Ursula stared at her desk, head down, hands folded in front of her like the hands of a Catholic schoolgirl. A steady flow of tears splashed onto the desk.

"I'm not the enemy, Ursula. I'm your husband. And despite all our... issues, I still love you. Maybe, after you calm down, you'll remember what's true, and what's not."

I left her there.

———————

We hadn't slept in the same bed for the last three years. Secretly, I'd come to appreciate the lull in our sex life. With Ursula it was easy to believe that I'd never been forceful enough to satisfy a woman of such ferocious appetites.

Even so, as I lay tossing and turning in the guest room I'd claimed for myself, a part of me still yearned for the time when she looked at me as a man, not as her assistant. But if I wasn't "The Reverend Doctor's Faithful Acolyte and Silent Partner," who was I? Who had I become?

I dreaded whatever destiny lay ahead if I chose to stay, but I questioned whether I could ever leave her. I'd reshaped myself to fit into her world. Finally, there came the thought that had begun to plague me after the Rest Stop Incident....

Just end it. Kill yourself.

I'd been miserable for so long the seed of self-loathing that had been planted at that rest stop near San Francisco had grown into a redwood.

Just drive up to the San Pedro Bridge and jump. All it takes is one small step.

Below me, I could hear Ursula moving around in the office. She was muttering to herself again. I was troubled by the memory of Ursula's tears; and the look in her eyes as she gouged that letter opener into the desktop.

"That desk was a beautiful piece of craftsmanship," one of my voices said. "Hell of a way to blow off steam."

But this voice was different.

"So," the new voice said. "You've finally come to your senses."

Someone was in my room.

I reached for the lamp beside my bed and turned it on.

Vanessa Warcloud was wearing the field uniform of the Utopian Cyborg Command: a one-piece spandex body suit and black leather duster trimmed with red piping along the sleeves. Small epaulets glittered like ruby lightning bolts at her shoulders. Red "grav-neg" boots completed the ensemble. Her bionic eye scanned the room, throwing off iridescent red pulses.

"Vanessa," I said, swallowing the sudden lump in my throat. "But… you died."

"Hard to kill what's already dead," the woman said, the wry grin revealing her trademark black humor. "Name's *Artemis*, by the way. Artemis Spectre."

My visitor was indeed Artemis Spectre. But she was also Vanessa Warcloud's *interpretation* of the character. Somehow, character and actress were one.

"This is crazy," I said. "How can you be here?"

"Easy, cadet. You're dreaming."

"Oh," I said. "Of course."

"She means to kill you, Will. But I'm thinking you already know that."

I couldn't answer. I was afraid of the answer.

"Hmmm," Spectre said, in the exaggerated way Vanessa had done in the movies. "Question is: *Are you ready to die?*"

Spectre's bionic left eye scanned my face. The movement of the techno-organic pupil trailed a lingering afterimage of red and silver motes.

"Too late for doubt, cadet," she said. "You've hidden in the belly of the beast for so long you've forgotten how it feels to be alive."

Her words hit me with the force of a slap. I *knew* those words.

"Vanessa," I said. "I mean Artemis… I don't understand."

"Wake up, Will," she said, and began to fade back into the shadows. "Time's up."

Then she was gone.

"Wait! Don't leave me!"

Someone screamed.

Then searing agony exploded my world, a pain so big it flipped my mind inside out. Suddenly I was awake.

And I was burning.

Ursula squatted above me; her knees locked tight against both sides of my head. With her right hand she held me by the throat. With her left hand she was…

"God That *HURTS!*"

…pressing the burning thing into my right cheek, my nose, and my eyebrow, pressing that scorching agony into my flesh. I smelled cooking meat and realized…

Burning

…it was me. The stink of scorched flesh, sickly sweet, like roasted pork from the luau at the end of the world.

Ursula pulled the burning thing away. I tried to push her off, but I was trapped, unable to move, to fight back. I could only scream.

"What did you do? What did you do?"

Ursula leaned down until we were practically nose-to-nose. For a moment, I thought she was going to kiss me. Instead, she placed her left hand over my mouth, muffling my screams.

"Shhhhh, darling," she said. "We're doin' just fine."

She cocked her head, like an artist scrutinizing her work.

"That's better," she whispered. "Now Anya and everyone will know you're mine. Forevermore."

Too late to understand, little brother.

The pain in my face was monstrous. As if in mockery of my agony, the left side of Ursula's face glowed red and yellow like the inside of a blast furnace. She was still holding whatever it was she'd used to burn me.

"What do you say we try a bigger one, baby?" she whispered. She reached behind her back, shifted her weight forward, and placed her hand on my testicles. "Here? Or maybe on the inner thigh?" she breathed into my ear. "How would you like...? "

I whipped my head to the right and sank my teeth into her right ear.

Ursula screamed and dropped the burning thing.

As if observing from some higher dimension, I felt it land on the bed and bounce. Something hot struck my knee, and then Ursula's scream became a roar of agony. I bit down harder, and blood filled my mouth. Ursula was flailing, howling into my ear.

"...cocksucking muthafucking asshole... hurting me!"

She hit me with her fists, her knees. I freed my arms, wrapped them around her neck and pulled her closer to me. Pain-maddened, I burrowed my face against the side of her head and bit down harder, shaking my head back and forth until I felt her ear tear away from her skull. Ursula shrieked and rolled off of me.

I whooped in a great rush of air and vomited up a mouthful of blood and Ursula's severed ear. Flames licked up the headboard, and a runner of flame smoked and crackled across the foot of the bed. A long dark object lay in the center of the flames, one end of it aglow like the eye of a vengeful god. Approximately two feet long, it was a thin black iron rod, about half the thickness of my forefinger. One end of the rod formed a circle, a handle. The other end bent at a ninety-degree angle and split into twin spikes.

A poker, I thought. *A goddamn fireplace poker.*

"You branded me," I said. *"You branded me, you bitch!"*

Ursula was blocking the doorway. Her white nightgown was covered with blood, but she seemed unaware of the damage she'd sustained. When she'd dropped the hot poker, it had bounced off her right shoulder and struck her back and buttocks. Burning strips of the white fabric she'd torn away still swirled around her like glowing cinders falling into ash.

"This is just what you wanted," she said. "You know how much Anya means to my ministry and now just *look at what you did!*"

"Let me out," I said. "Get out of the way!"

Blood from Ursula's severed ear streamed onto her shoulder and down the front of her nightgown. From that other dimension, I felt the hairs on the back of my head crisping in the heat.

"Big fancy *author*," she said. "Always thought you were smarter than me, smarter than *everybody*. You had to go and ruin everything!"

Then she charged me. I sidestepped, stuck my left foot out and tripped her. She crashed onto the burning bed and smashed it to the floor. Sparks flew as displaced air pushed the flames up the walls and across the ceiling.

I bolted out of that room, headed toward the winding stairway that led down to the front door. Smoke poured out of my bedroom now. The pain in my face was a ravaging spirit demanding my life as a sacrifice.

"We don't even own a fireplace, you stupid cunt!"

I made it to the first landing—

Ten more steps.

—I was already anticipating the cool night air as it soothed my burns, when Ursula tackled me.

Entangled, burning, we tumbled down the stairs until the back of Ursula's skull struck the marble floor. Most of her nightgown was gone, revealing pink, bubbling patches of scorched flesh along her left side. The left side of her face had melted beyond recognition. Her eye rolled in its socket and froze me with a look of naked hatred. "…Kill you," she snarled. "…Kill you for what you did!"

This is true, some voice said. *Her true face.*

Using the floor for leverage, Ursula swung her lower leg up between my thighs and catapulted me over her head. I somersaulted, crash-landed on the marble floor, and something in my pelvis snapped. My world went white, then gray.

Get up, Will. Fight.

I raised my head and saw Ursula, towering, monstrous in the glow of the spreading flames. She took three steps toward me.

Move, asshole!

Then she collapsed.

I tried to stand, but my left leg wouldn't move.

If that baby snaps you're gonna need surgery, pal!

Biting back a scream, I tried to roll up into a sitting position, but the blast of agony from my left side overruled the decision and I screamed anyway.

Keep it moving, Will, I thought. *Gotta keep it movin'!*

Ursula was on her belly, sniffing the air as if searching for some scent.

"I don't need... eyes... to find yoooouuuu," she croaked. "Jesus made you miiiine. *Forevermore.*"

Marshaling strength from some hellish reserve, Ursula began to pull herself along the floor. Her enormous strength left me no question as to which of us would eventually prove superior. She wriggled and thrashed; my beautiful deity reduced to a vast moving patchwork of scorched ruin.

In her right hand she held the black iron poker.

"Coming, baby," she rasped. "Crusher's comin'."

I scrabbled backward, sliding my butt across the marble floor, pushing with my right leg while dragging my left. It was useless. Dead weight.

Just gotta make it to the office.

The weird light from Ursula's office beckoned, ten, perhaps twelve steps down the main hall. I pulled myself along, adrenaline and fear driving me to move.

Just get to the office. Lock the door. Call the police.

"Sure," Artemis Spectre whispered. "Every sentient being in the cosmos dreams. Why shouldn't you?"

Ursula crawled toward me while I dragged myself backward. We were six feet apart.

And Ursula was closing the distance.

"Not strong enough, baby," she grunted. She swiped at me with her right hand, and the tips of her fingers brushed the toe of my left shoe. "Never were strong enough to handle...magnificent... me."

I kicked out with my right leg, air-pedaling, trying to break her nose or break her neck. Ursula surged forward, reached out and caught my right foot with one hand and twisted it. Hard. With the other hand she raised the poker and stabbed me. The iron barbs struck my right shin. They were too blunt to pierce flesh, but it hurt like Hell.

I pulled harder, fighting to free my right foot. Ursula was using both hands to twist my foot, but her hands, slick with blood, lost their grip on my shoe. I kicked down and my right heel struck her forehead. Another swing knocked the poker out of her hand. Then my right heel struck Ursula a solid blow across the temple, and she dropped to the floor.

"Someone help me!" I shouted. But all I could hear were fire alarms and flames roaring overhead. The second floor must have been totally engulfed.

Ursula lay facedown in that spreading puddle of blood, snorting, gagging, and snoring all at once.

Need to get help.

I dragged myself the last few miles.

After the fight in the dark entry hall, I was grateful for whatever weird tic had caused Ursula to remove all the lighting fixtures. That galaxy of naked bulbs blasted my eyes with white light, but at least I could see.

Fire alarms were blaring all over the house. And I heard the crackle and pop of burning wood. I crawled/dragged myself to the chair that sat in front of Ursula's desk. Whatever had snapped in my pelvis had gone numb again by the time I reached the summit of that goddamn desk.

"9-1-1. What is your emergency?"

"Fire! My house is burning!"

"What is the address of your emergency, sir?"

"7636 La Crescenta Court. Hurry…my wife…."

Ursula snatched the heavy desktop phone out of my hands and smashed it over my head. Then she hoisted me off my feet and body-slammed me onto the desk.

Her face was a nightmare mask. A flap of burned skin dangled from her forehead, revealing a preternaturally white flash of bone. Both eyes had swollen shut.

"To-ge-ther," she croaked. "Way—God meant us to… be."

Then she began to strangle me. I clawed at her hands, dug my nails into the flesh of her wrists hoping to pry her fingers off my neck, but Ursula just squeezed harder. I reached out with my left hand, trying to grasp the heavy reading lamp. Instead, my fingers grazed the handle of the letter opener.

What happened next will only make sense after I've finished the main body of my tale. For now, I can tell you this much: when my fingers touched that silver handle, *I was transformed.*

A million watts of electricity raced up my arm like a bolt of silent lightning, and suddenly, *I could see.* It was as if I were standing in that other dimension and looking down into our three-dimensional space. I saw my life play out in front of me, every love and hate, every joy, and every grief. I watched my parents' souls grow dimmer, diminished beneath the weight of my sister's death. I recognized that same dwindling in my own soul.

Frankie!

In an instant I was elevated beyond pain, beyond normal human perception. I was *exalted*, raised on high by a force I can only call godlike.

The power lit up my brain and set my body ablaze. Perhaps it was the light of Creation, or pure consciousness. Whatever it was, when that power filled me up *I knew that I could push back Death itself.*

I gripped the handle of that silver blade, and with the very last of my strength I drove the letter opener into Ursula's left ear.

I can't think of a better way to describe what happens when someone's soul vacates her mortal body, other than to say that Ursula just... stopped. Then she fell on top of me and pinned me to the desk.

Laughter: Sometimes a sense of humor is all we have to push back the night, like "a light in the darkest places," or a fireplace poker for a non-existent fireplace. I couldn't move, couldn't shift her weight off of me, so I laughed. If anyone had heard me at that moment, I imagine my laughter would have sounded more like a dying man screaming at the ridiculous horror of this world.

As the fire consumed the home we'd built together, I hugged my demon, and I wept, and I laughed.

And I waited for whatever world came next.

What came next, you ask? Well, how about a homicide investigation for starters? The detectives suspected me, of course. The spouse is always the first suspect. But my story, however outlandish it may have sounded, connected all the right dots for them.

I spent weeks in the hospital and underwent several painful surgeries. The scar? The twin "horns" that bracket my left eye and left this long trail of keloid scar tissue along my nose and cheek? I'm told, lo these five years later, that it looks like a lopsided horseshoe, or a U tilted to starboard.

On the day I was released from Cedars Sinai for what I hoped would be the last time, I was rolled out to the curb by the very same orderly who had rolled me out the night I met Ursula, ten years earlier.

"I like your scar, bro," said the now middle-aged Oscar Quineros. "Like you got *cuernos*."

"*Cuernos*?" I said.

"Yeah. Horns. From *el bufalo*. You feel me?"

Horns. From *the Buffalo*.

Or "bison," to be zoologically correct.

The house burned down. But not before fire and rescue teams pulled the two of us, still locked in that deathly embrace, out of the maelstrom. After a few hundred chest compressions they brought me back to life. For Ursula, they could do nothing.

I never learned where that other Ursula came from, or why she was the way she was. An only child, her parents had been swept away by Hurricane Katrina, never to be found. The most pedantic storyteller might suggest that the Crusher represented a part of me that needed to be confronted and defeated. I would offer a more nuanced interpretation and suggest that it was all just another example of weirdness in a life filled with weird shit.

As to what I saw the day I met Silver Woman and faced the dark beast that cast its shadow over that half-world? That's the strangest part of all.

And I only fully remembered it after a detective returned my property, more than a year after he'd completed his investigation.

I was in my new apartment, sifting through those boxes of confiscated memories when I found the implement I'd used to end Ursula's suffering, and, I suppose, my own. I'd taken it to the trash, meaning to throw it away, but some morbid curiosity stayed my hand. Instead, I tore open the envelope and examined it.

The blade was black with soot and encrusted with Ursula's blood, but that wasn't what stopped me cold. It was when I spied the model name, engraved on the handle in a decorative, looping script, clear as the clean waters of a fast-moving river: *Tatanka.*

The Silver Woman. Commander Artemis Spectre. Vanessa Warcloud. And now I could add another, forgotten name:

Tatanka.

Holding that bloodstained blade in my trembling hands, I *remembered everything.*

Standing on the riverbank with Silver Woman, I turned to face the force of nature that could cast a shadow big enough to darken the world. It was immense, with a shaggy coat and hot breath that smelled like a freshly uprooted vanilla cactus. It was a *bison,* you see, only far larger than any natural bison. It stood nearly twelve feet tall at the shoulders. The distance between its horns was greater than the span between my outstretched hands. And its coat was as white as fresh snowfall.

"He's a friend," Silver Woman said. "And more than a friend. He's my brother.

Now we were sitting in front of a campfire. Night had fallen over the river and the full moon rode a path of silver clouds. Silver Woman was sitting on the other side of the fire, feeding the flames from a small pile of dried plants.

"We were worshipped in those times. But as the millennia passed, our powers grew weak, until we were the last, he and I. Our family, who once sang among the storm clouds and danced in the guts of the Earth, was nearly gone. One day, my brother lost hope. He walked into the river and let it carry his body away. That's how I lost my beautiful Tatanka."

Sitting before that fire I remembered my dear Frankie: how the pain of her passing left a void at the center of my family that would never be filled, and I cried for Silver Woman's loss and for my own.

"When I saw your soul, it was so like Tatanka's," she said. "Back when we played together, flying between the spires, and tumbling down the white waters. I thought he had only died to play a trick on me, so I wove myself a new body to join the game. But you couldn't see me. That's when

I knew that Tatanka had lost himself. He'd forgotten what was true."

Silver Woman laughed, her wind chime voice echoing among the dark canyons far above us.

"Even the gods can be surprised: Two souls somehow made one. You're lucky, Will. Two souls means two families. I borrowed you from your human family just long enough to help you remember your other family."

This river is our blood, she sang. *This land is our body.*

We were walking out of the foothills, moving toward the rising sun. I was warm, although naked and barefoot. Silver Woman held my hand and led me upward along a rocky path. Up ahead, outlined by the brightening dawn, sat the ranger station.

"One day," Silver Woman said. "You will see my token and remember what is true."

Then, after she'd shown me an image of her token, she sent me back.

She must have been watching for him, waiting for centuries, listening for the echoes of his soul in the minds of tourists. And later, she'd been rewarded by whispers of his essence contained in the memories of people who read my books.

I believe she checked up on me occasionally, "riding the souls" of people like Elizabeth Wiley, the woman who confused me for Ursula's father.

"So beautiful," Wiley had said at that rest stop. "And tall as a Utah Juniper tree!"

That day back in 1973 our tour guides had shown us groves filled with tough, hardy plants indiginous to the Grand Canyon: white fir, blue spruce, and ponderosa pine: And Utah Juniper trees. Had Ursula sensed something about Elizabeth Wiley that spurred her to attack me?

I believe Silver Woman lent me the voice of Cyborg Commander Artemis Spectre; and that she somehow inspired the performance of Vanessa Warcloud.

When I saw the model name engraved on the handle of Ursula's silver letter opener, the pieces of my shattered soul began to coalesce.

Tatanka. The *Lakota* word for Bison.

That's the part I was keeping back. Since my memories seem to jump back and forth in time, it figures that my story should too. But I think I've put everything in its proper place now.

I'm writing again, mostly under a number of pseudonyms. I don't need fame and I've got enough money to keep me warm and dry for the foreseeable future. But so much of the Spectre & Sparrow books felt *channeled* through me, I'm still not sure how much of the story is exclusively mine.

All artists have a muse. Mine just happens to be a Native American nature goddess who sometimes keeps me from writing complete crap.

I researched them of course. References to certain gods and spirits are replete through Indigenous traditions and spoken histories from all over North America: Navajo stories of Changing Woman, or the *Mikwok* legends of Silver Fox. Other tales tell of powerful animal spirits, like the White Buffalo of the Sioux.

Or Tatanka: Sacred companion to White Buffalo Maiden.

Little Brother.

And so here I sit, scarred by love and healed by a mystery. That's another one of my reasons for returning to the Canyon. In the hospital I promised Silver Woman that I would learn her stories and pass them on. She recruited me, after all. How better to honor my personal savior than to keep those stories alive for future generations?

Do I *believe* that I'm some kind of vessel for the reincarnated spirit of a Lakota buffalo god? I'll leave that up to you, dear companions. After all, we live in crazy times, when a virus spread by a single cough can kill millions, where UFO's grace the cover of the *New York Times*, and a black man can be President of the United States.

I'll end, however, with this: My third, and most important reason, the reason I carry this silver token with me today. If you'll look closely at the *other* side of the handle you can just make out, beneath the rust and soot, the name of the manufacturer. Look closely, and then tell me what *you* believe. See it?

Silver Sister. LLC.

Tomorrow morning, I'll take this blade down into the depths of the Canyon and set up camp alongside the Colorado River. I'll offer up some silent prayers to anybody who might be listening. I'll pray for my own dear sister and reflect on how the gods suffer loss just as we do. Then I'll toss the blade into that fast-rushing current. Then, I'll light a fire and wait. Who knows? Maybe my muse will appear and show me her truest face.

Maybe Frankie will show up.

I hope for that most of all.

Think of Family:
The Filial Daughter's Tale

By Ai Jiang

If I told you this story like a regular story, would you be able to feel what I felt, imagine what I saw, want death the way I had wanted it and understand the reasons why?

Let me tell you a story, but not in the way a story is normally told, so you may live it the way I lived it only days before. You might want to slow down on the s'mores and keep your eyes on the fire, because it might be the only warmth and comfort you receive while you listen to these cold words.

Your hand moves protectively over your still-flat belly before you draw your legs up onto the couch in your parents' living room, arms wrapping around your knees.

"*Where?*" Mother, not comprehending your words, or not wanting to comprehend your words, says in Mandarin.

"Canadian, he's Canadian," you say, voice barely above a whisper.

"Chinese Canadian?" Father asks, looking up from his phone.

"No, just Canadian," you say.

"A *laowai.*" *A foreigner.* Mother chews on the word, placing a harsh emphasis that makes you flinch.

"Will he marry you?" Father asks.

"Nonsense. Even if he will, what will the elders say?" Mother tsks.

Father nods. "He'll be marrying not just you, Siyuan. You must think of what your family wants, too. Think of your grandmother—think of your grandfather watching from above."

"He's gone," you finally answer. Mother and Father know you are referring to Logan, but as soon as the words leave your lips, you can't help but feel the sharp sting of betrayal against your family as it could have also referred to your grandfather.

Mother's face blanches, matching the same expression Logan had when you first told him you're pregnant.

Your shoulders slump. The image of Logan packing his things, though not for the trip to the Grand Canyon that both of you planned to go on in a week's time, enters your mind. He left the key on the island of the condo unit you share. Your parents still don't have a clue that your roommate isn't Elumi, the only friend of yours they like—the same one you fell out with after high school a decade ago because both of you liked the same guy, or so you thought. It was really you she liked.

"Abort it," Mother and Father say at the same time, echoing Logan's exact words the night he found out.

But you want to keep the baby to remind yourself of the man who no longer loves you but did at one point, even if briefly—though six years is far from brief, you don't know just how many of those years he spent in love and how many of those years were just you holding everything together out of pure stubbornness.

You recall all the moments Logan asked when he could meet your parents and your fear of Mother and Father's disappointment. And you remember all the times you faked sick so you wouldn't have to attend Logan's family dinners, just in case your relationship came to an end, because you always knew it would at some point. But you never failed to hold onto the minuscule hope that it would last, somehow. Your parents aren't as open-minded as many of your friends'. Others always tell you that people can change, but they haven't met your parents. Stubborn—just like you.

You don't have much saved up, but you have just enough to get yourself to the Grand Canyon. Logan paid for the plane tickets and hotel, but he cancelled the whole thing before he left, even though it meant he wouldn't get all the money back.

On your bucket list sits several places you want to visit before you die: Seoul, the Leaning Tower of Pisa, the Pantheon—the Grand Canyon is last, but it is first on Logan's list. His happiness was always the most important—is the most important. Maybe if you abort the child he will come back.

You let go of the thought when you remember he blocked you from all social media platforms and your call won't go through. His friends refuse to speak to you, even though some of them have become your friends, too, over the years. How quickly people turn.

You decide the Grand Canyon will be the first and only stop you check off on your bucket list. To drop down into its vastness, lose yourself in its welcoming embrace—one you've never received from your parents since the day you no longer needed to be carried as a child, and one you will no longer receive from Logan. The smell of Logan's favorite cologne on the pullover crew you're wearing as you head to the airport with only a backpack, credit card, and handful of cash never fails to remind you of this.

Descending the stairs leading to the subway, you pull on your mask. Not many people wear them anymore, but it has become such a familiar thing. And in this chaos you find yourself in, it becomes your only comfort: a shield from the friends and family you never fail to accidently bump into and the questions they might ask because some of them know you were supposed to leave with Logan today—just the friends though, not the family, never the family. You always pull Logan in the opposite direction when you encounter family. It might be easier to just say he's a friend, in Mandarin, so you don't hurt him. But then you're the only one hurting in the end.

———————————

Just before you enter the airport, you make another call to Logan—unavailable—and decline the calls from Mother and Father, wiping the voice mails too. You shut off your phone just as a FaceTime call comes in from your aunt, the persistent one on your father's side, the one who has left China for the US but never *truly left* China. The others only leave passive aggressive messages, telling you to call Mother and Father because disrespecting your elders is a sin.

Not demonstrating filial piety is a sin. Having a child out of wedlock is a sin—simply making love and moving in with the opposite gender too. All your thoughts are sins. Everything you have ever done and will do feel like a sin, or at least the things you desire most in life because they somehow never align with your parents' ideas of an ideal child. It is nothing like the golden path that some of your cousins and parents' friends' children and your own friends have walked, are walking, or more accurately, running, while you trudge along a path you do not choose but must complete regardless of your own wants.

On the plane, the same aged girl next to you periodically glances at you from the corner of her eyes. You don't know if it's because you're crying while watching a comedy or because she's bored and wants to make conversation. But you don't give her the opening to do so, glue your eyes to the screen even when the credits roll to an end.

A tap on the shoulder. You refuse to turn. Another tap. With swollen eyes you squint at the girl. She holds out a pack of tissues without a word and places it on your lap.

For the rest of the trip, she doesn't look over. But you turn on the same comedy show and cry while her hand drifts over, patting the top of your own in silence.

When the plane lands in Arizona, neither of you speaks a word to one another or asks for each other's name. But she shows you a picture she carries of her and her daughter, and that is all you needed.

———————————

You're too tired to be concerned when you get into a taxi driven by an elderly woman who looks to be nearing ninety. Because your mask is still on, you know your swollen eyes draw more attention than usual. Like the girl on the plane, the woman glances at you from time to time through the rear-view mirror. You know she's not looking at the cars behind her because she gets honked at several intersections, seeming to be distracted by her thoughts—maybe her thoughts of you.

"I didn't want to ask, but why do you look like a raccoon?" she says.

Her lighthearted tone suggests that she is trying to make a joke. It tugs your lips upwards for a moment. She smiles. You chew the inside of your cheek. Unlike with the girl on the plane, you feel a sudden urge to pour your story into the space of this taxi.

"I'm pregnant," you say and hold your breath, not quite sure how the woman is going to react to the information.

Her wise eyes soften as she ponders.

But you don't wait for her to speak before you blurt, "But no one wants it."

Then understanding comes. At a red light, she stares at you through the rear-view mirror again. "Do *you* want the child?"

You do.

"It's not about what I want," you say.

"And why is that?"

You pause.

"This is how it should be, must be," you finally say, trying to convince yourself more than you're trying to persuade the woman.

"This is not how it has to be. You always have a choice."

The elderly woman drops you off at a motel you find with the highest Google reviews—two stars—but it's much cheaper than the hotel Logan chose. In your hand sits the slim slip of paper she closed your fingers over that holds her phone number. It has no name, but you feel like you've known her forever.

"If you ever need help, or someone to talk to."

As you walk toward the motel, you don't look back. You store the phone number among the crumpled bills, hoping you won't need it but knowing you might.

———————

By the motel, a man leans against his car clutching his satchel tight against his side, sweat beading above and below his brows. He tips his hat when you near but looks as though he regrets catching your attention, for a moment, before slipping back into ease.

"Here to see the Grand Canyon?" he asks. "This will be my sixth time." A nervous chuckle.

You notice how tight his tie sits around his neck, the worn leather of his shoes coloured in with brown sharpie, and the scars loosely hidden by the cuffs of his too-short shirt sleeves.

"Yes," you say. "It is also meant to be my last."

The man looks up, suddenly alert. "Why—?"

You caress your belly, fidget with your ringless finger. He nods.

When the man says nothing else, you head for the front entrance. But the man's sudden words stop you:

"Well, I'm glad it isn't."

You look back, first surprised, then share a smile.

Both of you pull out your phones and turn them back on. You're not sure who he is calling, but you call your parents. Father picks up after half a ring, as he usually does.

"I'm keeping the child," you say, then hang up.

Though you can't see the Grand Canyon with Logan, there is someone you will get to see it with now who is more important. And you hope when they visit alone, it will not be for the same reasons as you.

To See Her in Sepia

By Scott J. Moses

When I'm in the shower I think about death.

She slides the sizzling ham and egg plate before me with a smile. The yellow porcelain in contrast with the erratic boomerangs of the diner table. Privileged men discuss how to fix the world on the TV behind the bar, their false smiles seething beneath their just-for-show masks.

"Well?" she asks again, skin creasing at her eyes, forehead, and cheeks. "What's on your mind?"

She asked.

I sip my coffee, set it down in a cluster of boomerangs, smile. "Lately, when I'm in the shower I think about death."

Her smile ripples. "You just let me know if you need any—"

"Well?" I use her word against her, savor its taste. This peaceful exchange of power. "That all you have to say?"

She glances through the diner's storefront window, back to me. "And how does that make you feel?"

"What?"

Say it.

She sighs. "All that thinkin' on death? How's it make you feel?"

A bell dings in the kitchen window. She glances back for air.

"It makes me feel *alive*."

She smiles in her practiced way, turning back for the meaty hand still *ding-dinging* the bell.

The breakfast I can't afford stares up at me. The sweltering coffee in contrast to the briskness of the holstered pistol in my back.

Didn't come to spend money, and yet….

My rusted sedan sits obediently out front. The out-of-state plate smiling brightly in the morning sun. *Notice me*, it screams.

Perhaps it's good this place didn't take, or I didn't take to *it*. But ain't that just me—telling myself whatever I can to avoid the obvious? Forcing myself to think I didn't ruin the whole goddamn thing. Another string of empty reassurances, different, yet all the same. Like the subtle variances in tap—dependent on location, minerals, piping, etc.—it's all *water*…. Strange how something excruciatingly tasteless has multiple flavors.

Oh, the things I tell myself. That living in my car is only temporary, though it's been a month. That a membership at a nationwide gym chain is cheaper than an apartment for showering. That my savings aren't sun-bleach dry. That I'm jobless, yet they called *me* for help, her only family in the world. How, despite myself, I said I'd take care of it. How I'm having fucking breakfast like some post-quarantine elite in this hipster diner with money I don't have, while Aika lays in a hospital bed, her girlfriend worried sick. While—

The server hovers over me, sighs while setting a stack of pancakes and syrup by the ham plate. She makes a show of looking to the door. Some hipsters at the bar watch us, masks dangling from gauged ears.

She refills my coffee. "Not hungry?"

Before I can answer, she points to the pens in the pocket beneath her pinned name. *Stacy.* They're arranged by color, left-to-right, red, white, blue. "It's okay, darlin'. I'm a little OCD too. Hell, who don't have mental issues these days? My cousin eats her hair for god's sake." She nods to the cakes. "That's something from us to let you know you aren't alone. But it's the twenty-first century, hun. They have pills. Pop one and go about your day, huh?"

The gun in my back is *reeeal* convincing. Whispering it's still on, that we can take this place for all it's worth. There has to be a couple hundred in the register. Might be nice to wave a gun around in this presumptuous progressive's face. Might be enough to sate the first of many hospital bills that are headed Aika's way. Who knows what they charge the comatose these days?

"Let me know when you leave," she says, a malformed compassion coating her face. "I'll get the door for you."

A laugh crawls from my throat as she goes, and with a sigh, I scoop up eggs. *What a fucking morning*….

The sign and teal shirts displayed behind the bar boast this is the *Oldest Diner in the Town of Hallowed Ground.* As I dissect pancakes, occasionally pouring coffee down my gullet, I survey the black and white photos lining the walls.

The past is in *because the future's going nowhere.*

I swallow eggs, force a too large bit of ham in my mouth. Stacy winks at the hipsters before she disappears into the kitchen. The wooden door *swiiings, swings.*

I chug my coffee and standing, reach for my wallet (assumed the habit would've died off by now) and instead, pull the ski mask from my jacket.

Set it by my emptied mug. The greatest tip she's gotten today: *"Hey, I was gonna rob this place, maybe shoot someone if things went south. Have a nice day."*

I wipe my mouth on my sleeve and, passing the hipsters, pause at the front door.

"Pinkie, ring, middle, pointer," I mutter. "Pinkie, ring, middle, pointer…. "

Aika comatose in that hospital bed. Black ooze traveling up her breathing tube, dribbling from her lips. All eyes on me.

Getitrightgetitright.

My heart throbs in my chest. Sweat runs down my forehead. I twist the knob.

But did my pointer touch before *my middle?*

I try again, *Aika's monitor screeching, coughing up more sludge through her dislodged tube. Choking, dying. Her girlfriend shaking her, looking at me to get this right.*

Pinkie, ring, middle, pointer. I try again, *there*, push it open. The bell chimes.

Hands numb and hyperventilating, I walk through the opening, but it doesn't *feel* right.

What if you're killing her right now?

I retreat, walk through. Step back, walk—

"Sweetie, I *told* you to let me know when you left."

I wipe the sweat away, glance over my shoulder to Stacy by the register. The hipsters mutter to one another at the encore. The reason I couldn't rob this place.

"I left cash on the table," I say, and burst from the diner into cool autumn, stumbling off the curb, and *just* missing a crack in the cement walkway. My hands shake as I unlock the sedan, get in and go as Stacy lifts the ski mask through the restaurant's glass. I leave it all in my rearview, peel onto the highway. The thoughts of my sister dying sated, for now.

———————

Plastic testicles dangle below the rust-peppered bumper of the truck ahead. Black smog bellows from its exhaust as we wait out the light. *How insecure must you be to hang those on your truck?*

The driver's door opens and a gaunt man in overalls leans out, hacks into the street. The light changes, and we're off. No better to Aika than when I started south at her girlfriend's request.

"Goeken?" Naomi had said, voice shaky in my burner. Luckily, I

hadn't been all that settled in the Walmart parking lot, phone'd had a charge.

"*Uh, speaking?*"

"This is Naomi, Aika's girlfriend. We had lunch on campus? Talked about seeing The Grand Canyon? It's Aika, she's...."

She'd wept recalling it. How they'd been jumped after a frat party the night prior. How campus police had turned the corner a little too late. Aika bleeding from her head in Naomi's arms in their headlights.

And that's all it took. No matter that it'd been six months with little communication since my visit. Since spitting into that vial, back when I'd had the cash for a DNA test, to trace my roots. It's tempting for an orphan to know if they have pumping blood in the world. Turns out I did. A little sister, Aika Karimova. And from what she'd told me over Reubens that afternoon in the Arizona sunshine, the last name was the final thing her adopted parents had given her before she came out, before cutting her off altogether.

I've stepped into Hell since then. Lost my job and apartment when the pandemic hit, and with—what the government had had the decency to call—*stimulus* and savings rapidly depleting, I hit the road with gas I didn't have...but why?

Because she's a reason to get up in the morning beyond muscle memory. Because she didn't look at you the way the stray you'd let in a month before losing your home had, with lust for your bulbous eyes after you'd laid in bed twenty hours straight, too scared to move for the cracks in the floor, the door handles. Knowing something was wrong with you. Struggling to remember what the therapist said in those sessions a year ago when you were insured. Knowing you weren't crazy, though it felt like watching yourself slip down that road.

I brake as we come to a yellow light. Black smoke shrouding my view as testicles grumbles off through the fresh red.

A group occupy the median, DIY posters and signs in their raised hands. A woman, hair up, with glasses, sways her manifesto. It reads: REPENT. A balding man at her side, collared shirt half-tucked and brows furled, screams at me and those stuck at the light's sadistic timing. A young boy in a cap, twitching with each roared word and shuffling his feet, lifts a sign as well: YOU'RE GOING TO HELL.

So, the end is nigh and has been for some time, but when is it? See, most don't want to know when they're gonna die, but me? Give me the date, hour, and the minute. I *want* to know. Otherwise, we're all just lumbering around with our preferred poisons trying to forget we're gonna pass. Wouldn't it be a gift knowing the instant you were gonna bite it? You could plan, live accordingly. I like to think we'd make better use of our time if we knew when it ran out. I—sorry, I have an affinity for tangents, and it's not what I was put on this earth to do. Though, I'm not sure I was put on this earth to do *anything*. Put on this earth *at all*.

We need a task, something bigger than ourselves. *That's* why I'm here. Because a woman I didn't know a year ago is my blood and needs help. She's incentive to inhale, exhale, not that I *want* to die, not all the time anyway, but I sure as hell need more reasons to live. Aika's done more for me than she can ever know. Because that's too much pressure on someone, being the only reason you get up in the morning, and though I can't be sure of much, I'm positive of that.

———————————

I'm tapping the wheel, parked near an alley of this run-down part of a town I don't know. I blew it at the diner, but this guy? In his shining suit and tie staring up at the sky, slack-jawed? Glimmering in the sun like some attractant laid by God or the universe in the throat of the alley?

Can't fuck this up....

I kill the engine and open the door, unholstering the pistol from my back as I exit the sedan. A pair of women, mid-thirties, in masks, and dressed casually, jolt when the gripped steel meets their gaze.

We lock eyes, and I allow them to decide how this plays out. They one-eighty, retreat at a brisk pace.

We cross paths all the time, you and me. Our universes brushing one another. Cold and alone, we avert our eyes to the clouds or our phones. And we mind ourselves because God knows that's all we have the nerve for. All of us acting like we aren't consciousness trying to understand itself.

Other than the women, this seems an avoided part of town. No pedestrians. A few parked cars. The nearest of which—black paint, black rims, and black tinted windows—sits idle. I eject the revolver's cylinder, give it a look-see, click it back in place. I'm not cut out for this, whatever this is. But love drives us to stupidity. I roll my shoulders. The alley swallows me.

If the man sees me, he doesn't let on, and it's only when I close in beneath the shadows of the decrepit buildings, that I truly see him—smell him.

He stands on the toes of shined dress shoes. The acrid stench of urine rife in the air. The blotch over his crotch dark, foul. He sways, hyper-focused on the sky. His face is a stroke's aftermath. The side facing me drooped like melted prosthetic. Drool coats his chin, throat, and collar.

I inhale and he lifts a hand to the ether. I clock the Rolex on his wrist. Divine providence. I raise the gun.

"I found god here," he says, his quivering finger denoting divinity. His stench unbearable.

I click the hammer back. "Your watch, wallet, everything you have."

His mouth hangs open, head tilts my way. "You feel it? That pull beneath your feet, boy? That's the earth's center. A sphere of hungry magma. Gravity its outstretched hands. Those fingers grasp us, drag us down. Hell wants us real bad...."

He brings a red plastic jug to his lips, the sweet abundance drenching his chin, suit.

Gasoline...?

His tongue licks the excess from his lips and his head lolls back, though his gaze remains on the sky. "But if I stay tethered here, obedient, He holds me. We're always so high up...waiting for gravity to grow bored of toying with us."

This guy's left the herd.

"I said everything you have. Now."

His eyes find mine for the first time, void of anything. As if drowned in milk. His voice...different.

"I found God here...you find Him somewhere else."

He's levitating, and as he pivots toward me, the tips of his shoes brush a crack in the pavement.

Aika. No.

I barrel into him. The breath shoots from his lungs as we hit the pavement. Straddling him, I bring the butt of the pistol down hard, againagainagain, possessed by some violent bout of inertia-driven rage.

I sit back and gorge on air, taste blood in my mouth. He speaks through the wreckage of my toil, his teeth cracked or gone entirely between those bleeding, gasoline-drenched lips. "See...." he groans. "Man will kill you, but God's the one who'll keep you alive."

I rise, my hand and the pistol one entity. The boy's sign flashes through my mind.

"The Lord says go to hell."

The white drifts from his eyes before the lids close. He exhales, and the loosed breath claws its way up my nostrils, eviscerating my face and lungs. I stumble, raking my face, and—rise on my toes. As if cords cast down from Heaven suspend me. A ventriloquist's dummy waiting for manipulation. My limbs twitch as an iced-numbness spreads from the base of my skull. The alley ripples as I'm turned where the man stared. A sliver in the slate sky. A tear in the ozone. It blinks.

A landscape in sepia. A grand canyon, *The* Grand Canyon. The sun sunk low just over the horizon's maw, bathing the rock, sand, and stone orange-yellow. The warm breeze on my face. Naomi and Aika at the cliff's edge, opting not for the manufactured skywalk, but the more rugged overlook. Aika's head finds Naomi's shoulder and she strokes my sister's hair, minding the bandage fastened there. The day's events swarm my weary mind.

How when I arrived, Naomi sat me down before the ruin of my half-sister. The pungent scent of bleach lining the floors. The white on white of it all. Aika in that hospital bed, the trauma worse than Naomi had let on: face-swollen in purples and blues, IV in her arm, tube down her throat. The nurse leaving as Naomi slumped forward in her chair, crying. How the doctor wasn't sure if Aika would have permanent brain damage from the assault. How after he'd left, Naomi took her head in her hands, sucked in her snot and tears, said what she had: "We don't know why we're here or where we go after...who the fuck cares who you love?"

I'd admired her for that, everything, really. How she loved my sister. I always hoped she'd be that type of partner to her.

The sky permeates orange as nature exhales over the valley. The still perfection of it all. The medley cistern of life's whispers around us. I raise the iPhone, zoom in on them. This perfect day.

Naomi's lips part near Aika's ear. "I'm glad you came back." She looks to me, tears welling. "To us."

Aika winces, pecks Naomi's cheek. "Well, sure," she says, nuzzling into her. The purple-streaked hair seeping out from beneath the bandage. "I figured I'd walk in this meatsuit awhile longer, 'least until the muscles atrophy, bones turn to dust."

Naomi nudges her. "Well, gravity kills us all, some slower than others." She sighs. "I'm just happy to die over time with you again."

They don't care that I'm a fuck-up. About my mental illness, my joblessness...that I'm living in my car and brought nothing to offer but my presence when they needed more...they'd accepted me. Just how I'd...hoped.

You feel it? That pull beneath your feet, boy?

I lower the phone and its sepia filter. The sky an amalgamation of color I never thought possible. We'd talked at lunch months ago of coming to The Grand Canyon one day. How a fool's part of me had hoped we'd get the chance despite Aika's attack. Despite not knowing if she'd wake up.

My stomach drops, hands numb. The phone's camera unsteady in my trembling grasp.

They'd cleared Aika to leave, completely healthy, fully functioning.

Aika's in flames again, despite me seeing her now. Why am I doubting...? This is what I wanted more than anything. To see them in sepia how I hoped I would. The Grand Canyon exactly how I thought it'd be. How is it this warm in autumn...?

The melting pot-stench of an alley on the air. Piss, gasoline, misted rain....

I relish the smell, and another world calls to me, reminds me—

My shoulders tighten, and pressure swells at the base of my neck. The lurid rush of something within the walls of my skull. The nerves of my corporeal form raging. Euphoria. Everything I'd hoped for, here.

But the doubt.

That feral fear.

How, though I'm seated on the dirt not far from the pair, I'm on my toes, dangling from heaven.

I inhale. Wet brick. Gasoline. Gun oil.

My lips move of their own volition, and I wave with hands not mine. The girls reciprocate.

A sad side of town. An alley to nowhere. That's what this is, nowhere. A phone in my hand, no, a gun.

Aika twitches, and the skin of her face peels from the bones and flesh beneath. As if held by tacks.

The sky undulates green, yellow, blue.

I stand, or do I? Place my hand on the boulder, bricks, nearest me.

Whatthehellwhatthehell?

I'm primed for panic, though my body doesn't allow it. My heart beats the same. My breath no more strained than before.

A whisper on the wind:

"...notice how the serum bars his fight-or-flight. Forces calm. Some, if you believe it, actually dissociate when they get exactly what they want."

My lips part as they stand, turn toward me in unison. I glimpse the Alkaline Trio tattoo on Aika's forearm.

A commonality, a talking point, somewhere to dig in and commiserate... how I'd hoped.

The sound of an unseen vehicle passing over the void of the canyon's mouth.

The hum in my head. The rigidity forcing my throat outward. The minute blemishes of the bricks kiss my fingertips.

And though my hands grip a phone, waving to the girls so in love, another pair finds the base of my neck, grips the thick, humming cords protruding there. I pull with all I am, and Naomi's knees buckle. Aika's bandage blooms crimson. A tooth in her frozen smile falls to the dirt.

My heart beats faster, the cord pulsing hot in my hands. The sky ripples, sheening white. Naomi stumbles off the cliff, and Aika smiles, toothless. The whites of her eyes like wax down her cheeks. Nature screams and the wind roars, splitting the sky in two. Rain caresses my face.

The appendage, more tendril than tether now, wriggles in my grasp, and teeth gritted, I feel its hold weakening. Thick warmth crawls down my back.

The ground trembles. Rocks skip like lemmings from the ledge.

"You're the first to resist," the voice says. "What, don't want to stay?"

Electricity torrents through me, forcing my gaze to that sky torn asunder, and in the gap between space and all else, Aika and Naomi hold hands in love, there's a dog, kids. The wind fierce as her smile on some shore. Somehow, I know if I stay, she'll be fine. *And who am I to deny her that?* I start to smile, bite my tongue, and tasting blood, yank the dream from me altogether.

———————

My lids open to stacked brick. My vision swims, head throbs. I sit forward, vomiting what I ate at the diner between my legs. The man who stared nowhere, gone. The gun still in my hand. I rub my neck, feel the staples, the incision there.

Not a dream…. or was it the best of all?

An old fear: Am I crazy? Have I been cognizantly losing my mind for decades?

My bones cry as I rise from the pavement. Something glimmers at my feet.

The Rolex. A cream business card in the space void of an unwell man's wrist.

No crazier than believing God watches over you. No more than alien abduction, astral projection, Chakras, Astrology, reincarnation, other dimensions, government conspiracies. How one feels here, yet somewhere else too. How you can't reconcile a dream from reality, which might well be some dream altogether.

I pull the card from its place.

"Don't you deserve some reward for suffering reality?"

I flip it. A number. Something scrawled beneath.

"You'll call. They always do."

And it all crawls back. The uncertainty and doubts of this world. Knowing Aika's in that hospital comatose and there's nothing I can do but go to her. That there's no escaping how *useless* I am. And what else is there to say, other than some days you just wanna die?

But not today.

So, upright on my withering form, I pocket the Rolex.

And while there's only so much a soul can take; it can take a whole hell of a lot.

I skim the card again, knowing uncertainty's a gift because it allows for hope. We need the chase, and that's all there is. Hell, I'm not even sure we could handle knowing. I don't *know* if I'll wake up tomorrow. Who's to say she will either? But if I have this chance to live this waking unknown, I'll seize it by the throat, breathe, and live whatever this is with you, Aika.

I pause, shoe hovering over a crack in the asphalt, and breath held, heart slamming, I step down.

Aika vomiting blood, convulsing.

My phone quivers in my jacket. The numbers beckon from the card still in hand.

I toss it where the man who stared stood, holster the gun.

I'll see the canyon for myself, with or without them... Rewrite the pseudo-memory with something real.

And as I walk back to my car, I step on every crack. *All I can do is be there for her. All we can ever do is* be there.

The sun peeks out from a stretched mess of clouds as I brush the car door's handle. My ring touched before my pinkie. Panic stirs, though I ride it out. Remembering, that's key.

How do you honor life while it lives? You show up. And whatever happens, *happens*. You win some and you lose some. Mostly, you lose some, but you win some, too. Aika isn't burning, or so I tell myself.

Or so I *told* myself. But I wanted to come here anyway, you know? Not only for her, but now—for me as well.

The Preditor's Tale

By Terence Taylor

I'm a storyteller by trade.

My medium's video, so most of my work was done from home long before Covid came to town. I'm what the industry calls a "preditor"—a producer-editor—shooting and editing commissioned videos to make a living. Until lockdown. Fortunately, my editing system kept me employed cutting remotely. I was sure I could breeze through a year stuck inside, had work to do and stayed in touch with friends as always while Big Science toiled to create an effective vaccine ASAP.

Then body hunger started to sink in.

Loneliness had simple online solutions, but horniness was another matter. After almost a year and a half, I cracked. I'd become jaded, bored flaccid by nightly visits to porn site after porn site in search of fresh thrills before bed. Desperate, I remembered a news story about the rise of video chat rooms, interactive sites where you could make new friends around the world.

Reporters raced to sites and came back smirking to tell us that what they found were mostly dicks. Hard and soft, all ages, sizes, and colors, but mostly dicks. Everyone had a good laugh before they moved on to the next story. I'd considered checking it out, but never followed up since actual sex was still an option then.

That had changed.

My first visit was to a site called *DirtyChat*… *"Random free live cam chat with strangers,"* where they not only allowed sexual activity, but warned anyone not okay with it to stay out. I sent the computer's feed to my big screen TV so I could fully enjoy the live view, kept some porn playing beside it. Below the site name was the number of users who had created accounts and I was shocked to see *"over six million joined!"* The idea of even a hundred thousand members active on any given night was both humbling and validating. As Sting once sang, *"Seems I'm not alone at being alone…."*

I had the option to sign in as male, female, transgender, or a couple, and chose "I am Male." There were two blacked out video panes on the left of the site window, one above the other. To their right was a text message pane for those with no microphone or a need for discreet silence. Once my gender was set, I clicked the banner that said, *"Start Chatting."* Blank faces and bare bodies began to flash by in the top box.

I was obviously the empty black lower window. My webcam was off, but of course no one stayed connected for that, so I had to turn it on. Before I gave the site access, I pointed my lens down to only show me from my chest to my thighs, clothed, but still acceptable to most. With my face off-screen, I could play but stay anonymous.

I sat back and didn't have to wait long.

A pale body popped up above my image, seated, a naked old white man seen from the knees up. In his late sixties, his face and hairless body sagged in places mine would too, one day, but he seemed not to care if anyone saw him here or what they thought. I had to respect that, but whatever he wanted wasn't me. He disappeared with a click of his finger, promptly replaced by the torso of a skinny young guy who stood in front of his camera in a blue tiled bathroom. I could see him from his collarbone to smooth balls below a long slender cock, creamy skin hairless except for bushy brown pubes.

More interesting.

He vanished, replaced by a young brown hand cupping a small penis, and then an athletic naked male body on its back in bed, rapidly working up a presentable erection. A darkened room came after that, with a hairy belly and chest barely visible above a soft organ. He gave way to a rigid hard-on poking out of a pair of blue briefs, then an uncut average cock seen from above, bathroom floor visible beneath it. A nicely built adult torso showed off a semi, classically Grecian in his proportions from the nipples to nuts, then a collegiate fellow slapped his soft dick around a fluffy ginger bush to stimulate it—the news had been right.

It was a lot of cocks.

I kept watching. Sex partners, live or online, are like porn in that there's only so much variety. Those I saw on the site quickly fell into categories. Gender was fluid, mostly male, but with a few straight women, some looked professional from the care they took to look like porn stars. I saw cross dressers of all degrees, from boys in panties to men in full high heel and stocking drag, as well as trans men, trans women, and non-binary players whose unique appeal was partly in their ambiguity.

There were assorted fetishes, for feet, leather gear, rubber, drag, piss, scat, and the occasional diaper. I met guys who wanted their penis made fun of and got harder the smaller you said it was, and the opposite who needed their enormous endowments admired to expand. They were all punctuated by the black screens of those only online to see the sights like me. I skipped them as soon as they popped up.

While many spoke, others only texted so as not to wake roommates, parents, or partners. Some wanted to hear dirty talk, others to be verbally abused or the abuser. Some used the site as a playground, grinned happily if they showed their mouths or faces, and made sexual jokes in the text box. For them it was just fun.

Just as there was a wide range of bodies and types, all races and sizes, light to dark, fit to fat, there was a spectrum of reactions. Teen virgins in their rooms eagerly whispered how they wanted their first time to be rough. I was surprised, until I realized they'd learned it from too many hours of too much porn. There were a goodly number of bi-curious guys who'd left their girlfriend in the other room after sex to be called cocksucking whores to get off. Married men begged me to do their wives in front of them or do them in front of their wives. Couples got off being watched, older daddies treated me like their boy, men my age acted the way they would at a bar or club.

It didn't take long for me to realize that most showed off their best features as well as they could. I quickly learned to stop asking for shirts to be raised or bedding pulled away. When someone popped up you saw them at their best, available assets arranged in bright light or shadow as meticulously as a store window display designed to sell goods as soon as you saw them.

It was like a carnival sideshow with infinite attractions, every booth eager for your attention. Potential partners came from all over the world, locations displayed at the top of their text box—Pennsylvania, Catalonia, Minnesota, Ankara, Jalisco, New Jersey, Campania—names from the familiar to faraway places I didn't know. What everyone had in common was a desire to be desired. Everyone came for validation of one kind or another, for their hot bodies or ability to arouse. Horny older men made skinny teenagers ignored by their peers feel like sex gods. Sculpted muscle bottoms were assured their massive bodies more than made up for what they lacked elsewhere. Old men found younger men horny for daddies, and vice versa. With literally millions of members in rotation as possible partners, I was sure everyone found someone eventually, no matter what they looked like or what they wanted.

I got dizzy watching the endless parade of passionate people seeking arousal, and before long my hand wandered south to add its own entry to the phallic display. I rubbed my crotch, gently at first, and then harder. I slid my sweats down until the pertinent parts protruded from my waistband to salute my sins as they paraded before me on review.

It was judged a successful enough debut, applauded by standing ovations before I left the stage for the night, lauded as a "Hot Daddy with a BBC." That meant Big Black Cock, a valued commodity in some circles, but what I'd soon discovered was a select sexual niche. Whoever saw it either clicked away immediately, more often than I liked, or stayed. Those who did more than made up with their vigor and enthusiasm for those who didn't.

I was almost embarrassed by how quickly all the loudly expressed racial politics of my youth protesting how artists like Mapplethorpe and Haring objectified Black men's bodies went out the window as soon as a diverse assortment of fit young guys almost half my age offered to put on a live strip and stroke show as long as they could call me a Black Daddy.

I was hooked.

There was suddenly easy access to a global bathhouse with room after room of occupants who changed daily, if not hourly. I could stay as long as I liked, night after night, almost never seeing the same body twice. Combined with my porn collection, I was sure this would help me endure my solitude for another year at least.

After months online I started to recognize other regulars and developed the kind of casual friendships I'd had with bar buddies, with rambling late-night conversations that went beyond sex to anonymous friendships. That's what Billy was to me, just another web buddy whose name I knew, but not much else. We talked about his life, certainly more than we discussed mine. I gave him advice but didn't know where he lived other than one of the Red states. There was no way for me to contact him, I just randomly ran into him on the site now and then. He was a beautiful babe in the woods, with no idea of what he was getting into, and I'll never know if what I saw happen to him was real or a dream. Not a dream.

A nightmare.

Billy. My silly Billy....

I called him Billy Budding, a reference he was too young and clueless to get, even if he'd had Herman Melville in his curriculum, my reason for the joke. Along with generous bowls of weed my nocturnal encounters helped me wind down after a day pumped up on caffeine to get work done. We met when I was nearly done one night, as I looked for someone to finish me off after an hour of edging so I could get some sleep.

Most times, just when I was about to give up hope at the end of the night, an exceptional guy from 18-24 would show up, a porn category that had appealed to me since I was 18-24. He'd be as happy to see me as I was to see him for whatever reason, and we'd come to a mutually satisfying conclusion. I called them my Angels, as they were a minor miracle every time.

I had just clicked away from a skinny naked guy lighting up his glass meth pipe over a limp dick to see a super cute young guy come on. He had a tight firm little body with just a hint of baby fat at the waist, short dark hair, and large brown eyes like a Disney deer. He looked as sweet and innocent as one of *The Brady Bunch*. His jaw dropped when he saw what I had clenched in my hand, hungry for release.

"Wow! That's the biggest one I ever saw!" he gasped, drooled like a biker admiring a shiny new hog he wanted to ride.

"You must not have seen many, then," I said, with a smile he couldn't see with my face off camera. I chuckled, flattered, but knew my place in the size spectrum. I'd never disappointed but had enjoyed better over the years. Sometimes significantly. He had a lot to learn, and I was sure he'd found plenty of volunteers here ready to teach him. His sheet was pulled up to just below his naval. He reached under it to enjoy himself more.

"Naw man, I've...." He fell silent, his eyes glazed over as the tented sheet bounced up and down. His camera started to swing up to the ceiling, and his image slid off screen until he pulled it back down to face him. "Sorry, old laptop, weak hinge."

"What's that you're hiding?" I asked coyly, and he slid down his sheet to reveal a cute pink cock of average size, but exceptionally hard as only a teenager can be. He was evidently extremely impressed by me, and I couldn't help responding to his attention. We got caught up in a sexual feedback loop, each reaction increased the other's response. As I drank in every inch of him, I looked more closely and started to question whether or not I should be so quick to engage.

"Hey, boy, daddy's forty-one," I said. "How old are you?"

"Nice, I like older guys," he murmured, kept busy.

"You didn't answer me."

"You like younger guys?" he asked, hesitant.

"They like me," I replied, evaded his question as much as he had mine. He paused, with an embarrassed grin.

"Promise not to tell?"

"Who would I tell, the site manager? Your parents?" I said with a laugh. "Don't know either or how to reach them."

"Sixteen," he whispered and covered his mouth with a hand.

I flinched, awkwardly aware how erect I was, and pulled a throw blanket that was over my legs up to my waist. He leaned forward.

"No, don't do that," he begged, but I resisted his sweaty entreaties.

"You shouldn't even be here! Technically, you're committing a federal crime." He frowned and looked at me, puzzled. "You're a naked minor putting on a live sex show. Kiddie porn!"

"Come on!" He laughed.

"I'm serious!"

I told him the story of a fourteen-year-old kid who'd started showing off his skills online to older men in chat rooms like the one we were in. They'd convinced him to let them set up a way to pay him to do requests. After he started racking up some major bucks they wanted more, pressured him to meet in person. Some said they wouldn't take no for an answer, repeated it more emphatically each time until he panicked and went to the FBI.

They told him they'd have to charge him with soliciting sex with a minor, a heavy charge with serious time, and he freaked out. A reporter picked up his story and cut a deal with the Feds to let him off if the kid turned over his client list. The two of them went on *The Oprah Winfrey Show* to tell his story. At the end she turned to the camera and said, "This is why no child needs to have a computer with a webcam behind a closed door!"

We both laughed at that, since Billy was living proof that she was right. As the conversation continued, I got more protective, warned him not to take any bus or plane tickets from strange men he met online who wanted him to come for a visit.

When he asked why, I told him I didn't want him ending up in some creep's freezer. He didn't understand what I meant by that, so I told him about Jeffrey Dahmer, the serial killer who lured young men to his home and tried to turn them into sex zombies by injecting acid into their brains. When they died, he cut them up, cooked, and ate the choice bits, then froze the rest.

"When they arrested him, they found the severed heads of recent victims in his refrigerator. Neighbors had complained about the smell for months, *but no one listened!*"

While I told him the story Billy had pulled up the sheet and by my ending it was up to his nose, with only his big brown eyes visible above it, wide as saucers. I had to laugh.

"I feel like a counselor telling campfire stories!"

"Tell me some more!" he pleaded.

"Next time maybe. Even though you shouldn't be here. And shouldn't come back!"

That made us both crack up, and as we said our goodbyes, he said he hoped he'd see me again. I gave him an ambivalent answer and left him behind to look for an angel to take me to heaven before bed.

––––––––––

It was months before I saw Billy again.

My bedtime ritual had quickly become sliding down *DirtyChat's* digital rabbit hole into its surreal self-generating avant-garde conceptual video sex show. It transcended simple erotica and its occupants opened far more than their pants whether they realized it or not. They exposed the secrets of their souls even as they put them at risk; the identity each wanted me to see flipped past for hours like cards shuffled by a master.

I saw Billy pop up on the screen, my body bare under the dark blue open terrycloth robe that had become my site uniform and waved. After I covered up, we chatted quietly, his parents asleep in the next room with no idea what their beamish boy really did after bedtime. He was excited and couldn't wait to tell me why.

"Listen, my friend Gail came up with this great idea!"

I was afraid to ask, had a fairly good idea of what sixteen-year-olds considered good ideas, but braced myself and asked anyway.

"She said if I get her pregnant, we can audition to go on that *Teen Mom* reality show and make big money being on TV! We used to make out before I figured out I like boys, so I think I can do it. Or we use a turkey baster, right?" He laughed. "That's what they always do in sitcoms. We'll make a turkey baster baby and sell it to MTV! Oooh! What if it was *twins!*"

I winced, slowly and firmly pointed out how awfully inconvenient it would be if they weren't picked, that a human life is not something to make lightly, even if prime time's the prize. Especially for a gay teenager and his best girl friend?

That seemed to sink in, and we discussed at length what life after a baby in high school would be for them if they weren't on MTV. Once I was sure I'd reduced his urge to increase the local population, I moved on, went from protector back to predator. My online Black Daddy persona took charge as my voice dropped to a low growl with my next encounter.

I could regale you for days with tales of my digital dalliances of all varieties, quite a saga I assure you. The sad truth is that over time online sex, as in real life, even with an endless stream of anonymous partners, loses the ability to surprise or entertain. It wasn't long before I found myself sliding back into the same state of malaise that had driven me from porn to chat rooms. I grew desperate for a way to somehow heighten the experience, to return me to a state of excitation. As my mind flailed about looking for answers a high school interest in sex magick floated to the surface.

I'd almost forgotten all about it.

I was an avid reader as a child, devoured science fiction and horror as fast as it came out. In high school I binged second-hand bookstore copies of Montague Summers' gory histories of vampires, werewolves, and witchcraft; Sir James George Frazer's *The Golden Bough*; the *Jungian-Senoi Dream Manual*; and *The White Goddess*. Those led me to Aleister Crowley's writings on sex magick, the art of focusing erotic energy to manifest your desires.

A solitary summer vacation was spent engaged in deeper studies of the subject; purely in the interests of research that gave me a practical use for otherwise wasted onanistic activity. I could recall having had enough seeming successes back then to believe it worked. Invites to parties outside my social standing, birthday gifts I actually wanted, and other random advantages that could have only been coincidence, but at the time seemed significant enough evidence of more. Why not take those early experiments further to see how real they were? The idea seemed inspired.

I learned the likely source of that inspiration too late.

My first attempts were laughable.

Any attempt at magical concentration was lost as soon as the first wave of orgasm hit, whether ripple or tsunami. Something small and specific always caught my attention and made me forget all about my intentions. Focus would drift to my porn windows or partner, distracted by some texture of skin, turn of a head, or lock of hair that had triggered my climax.

I kept at it, dug out and re-read some of the old texts, worked on sigils and rituals, determined to rediscover the same highly sexed state of mind I'd mastered that distant summer. I was already practicing nightly, it was simply a matter of putting that time to better use and I did, like an eager acolyte, constructing consistent rules and rituals to give my ceremonies an air of authenticity. There were a few random instances of what felt like improved luck online and off, but I decided I had to be more specific in my desires to be sure. I bought a lottery ticket as a test and pictured myself showered with bills when I came, for weeks, the image clearer and more believable each time.

Then I won.

Not a life-changing amount, just $250. No fortune, but still transformative in that it was enough to convince me I was on the track of something potentially more substantial. I felt I'd reached the same level of expertise I'd achieved as a teenager and worked harder to build on the foundation I'd laid back then.

I increased my time on the site, my use of pot, and ordered poppers online, something I hadn't used since my sex club days. That association only added to the sensual space I was shaping to inhabit, one beyond mind or body, a state of pure sensation that could produce erotic energy directed to any purpose I chose. It could only be described as sorcery, possibly even black magic. Now that I had my methodology down, I needed to pick a new purpose and decided I wanted to start with getting hotter partners on *DirtyChat*.

There was a class of members I saw there only in glimpses, the A listers, model perfect men who only played with each other, as they had in bars and bathhouses. They flashed away as soon as they saw I wasn't one of them, their splendor still arousing me in their absence, like the afterimage of a bright light that takes time to fade. They were the site's equivalent of the cool kids whose parties I'd wanted to crash in high school, symbolic of every door in life closed to me that I wanted to kick open.

I wanted in and now I had the power.

Was it wrong to pray to unknown pagan gods for better online sex? I knew it was, despite myself. My Catholic childhood had taught me that just to conceive of such a thing made you a sinner, even if you never did it.

"You had to *wanna*," comedian George Carlin had joked on the subject of sin, and that's all it took. What better definition of video chat room sex than wanting, pure desire, even if expressed at a distance? No one on the site had physical contact with anyone else, yet we humped each other across the sexual spectrum for hours like battery-powered bunnies. How was it not sinful?

That only made it more appealing, so I stayed the course.

Years ago, in a store on Cahuenga Boulevard called *Panpipes Magickal Marketplace* in Los Angeles I overheard the aging proprietor solemnly tell a trio of naïve young women in town for a week that there were five rules of magic.

"To want, to will, to be able, to dare, and last, but most importantly, to keep silent. That was Merlin's downfall. He told the secrets of magic to his lover, Nimue, and she used it to imprison him forever! Had he kept silent, he'd be with us still…."

They were all awed by his expertise and showed their gratitude purchasing charms. His words stayed with me, as if he'd secretly said it for me to hear, and I remembered them as I sank deeper into deviltry.

Carlin was right. I was damned as soon as I had the desire to amp up my online sex game. I'd wanted and used my will to be able, had already dared to win without repercussions. I had nothing more to lose, so why not try again? What could go wrong if I followed the rules? I kept silent, told no one of my folly, wrote down my wish for quality over quantity then followed Grant Morrison's recipe in *Pop Magic*. I pulled vowels, cut out repeated letters, followed directions until I had only a few to overlap and rearrange into a simple sigil.

That gave me an image, an icon to focus my intent on at the moment of climax. I printed it out and taped it to the wall over my big screen, tested it that night and every night for a week. My options seemed to improve slightly, but still only as far as the B list. I aimed higher, so I increased the sex, drugs, and frequency.

Then came the night it worked.

I was watching porn to the side of the site window and had just sniffed from a fresh bottle of Super Rush. As my head spun and seemed to float from my body, I looked at the *DirtyChat* window. Onscreen I saw an empty sofa. An instant later a naked college jock was sprawled across it, his lean brown limbs luxuriously wet with sweat. Long black hair hung wet from his head, dark golden eyes that shone with a feral glint turned toward the camera to stare at me, lazy, but watchful.

Predatory.

I froze like a deer on a nature show about to be chased down by a panther. My head cleared of the poppers as I stared, but I still felt a strange intoxication. The guy grinned, as if he could tell, stroked his growing uncut dark dick with one hand, then rolled onto his back and raised his legs to present his bare bubble butt. I held my breath as he teased his asshole with a finger, lifted it to lick, then went back to work. I gasped audibly. He must have heard me on my microphone because he laughed, a low sexy growl.

"Like that?" he smiled. "It's yours, all for you, daddy."

The A list. I was finally there.

We began a call and response ritual of self-stimulation, silent for a few minutes, but the more aroused I got, the more I wanted to talk. I'd discovered I enjoyed trash talk on the site. When I told hot guys how and why they turned me on it usually got us both hornier. Despite my fears, he didn't object, as some did, and kept up with me.

They speak of love being sacred or profane, but whoever they are, they're too limited in their thinking. I'd found a way to walk the fine line along the border with ritualistic magic in a pornographic setting to achieve a divine kind of sex. That accomplishment was as much a thrill for me as the sensuous sight before me.

As he rolled his athletic body from one suggestive pose to another, the student became the teacher and made suggestions I was surprised he even knew about, much less experienced. He said he wanted to share them all with me, delivered on his promises and then some, left me out of breath and dehydrated as I came.

"So, do you have a name?" I flirted, voice hoarse, hoped I'd earn another round before he cut me off and disappeared forever. "Gotta call you something while we get to know each other."

He cracked a wide toothy grin.

"Oh? Was this us getting to know each other?"

"Biblically, if nothing else." I laughed and he scowled, still sexy.

"Enough of that," he sneered, "Not a fan of the bible."

His large golden eyes looked curiously crafty, vulpine. Despite his civilized tone there was something faintly feral about him. His skin was gleaming gold, not just tanned, more like he was a mutt like me. I couldn't pin down the mix and was too tactful to inquire, afraid of scaring him off. I've often been indelicately asked what I am over the years, my ancestors remarkably eclectic in their taste in partners, but you can tell I'm mostly Black. This seductive satyr could have been almost anything, from almost anywhere. Every time I thought I had him pegged moments later I was equally sure I was wrong. He was like a carnal chameleon, as if he changed from moment to moment to match my shifting desires. His age was equally indeterminate, but he looked safely over eighteen by several years.

"I guess you're more a fan of *Dante's Inferno*?" I winced at how pretentious it sounded, but that he laughed at.

"A fan of Dante at least. A very old fan." He cocked his head with a sly smile that made it seem like a private joke between us, even if I didn't get it. "Call me anything, whatever or whoever you want me to be."

It was an odd way to put it, but most guys here liked role-play of one kind or another. I thought nothing of it at the time.

"What do *you* want to be called?"

"Pick my own name? Are you giving me permission?" His eyes narrowed as his toothy grin widened. "Names have power, you know. I'm obliged to tell you that by the Law of Laws. Whoever wields a name has power over the named. Over me."

He was so incredibly hot I was dazed by my arousal, so what he said made little sense with my brains gripped firmly in my fist. Whatever he did with his hips and pelvis made him look hotter than when I first saw him. I nodded, though he couldn't see me.

"You need to say it again. Out loud," he whispered as if he knew, golden eyes bright. He leaned forward, licked his lips.

"Sure, why not. I give you permission to name yourself."

"You freely give me power over my name and myself," he prompted. When I didn't respond immediately, he waved me on until I did. I sighed and spoke, in an auspicious voice.

"I freely give you power over your name and yourself, now and forevermore!" I padded my lines and gestured dramatically. The pseudo-grandiosity seemed appropriate to the ridiculous moment and the kid's appreciative response seemed to agree as he sat back and stroked himself again.

"Gabriel-Ernest, I think," he said. "Yes. Those are nice suitable names."

"Don't be ridiculous," I laughed. He didn't blink. I stopped laughing, chilled. "That's not your real name. It can't be."

I knew the story *Gabriel-Ernest* by Saki, one of my youthful favorites about a hapless man who meets a naked young werewolf in human form on a walk through the woods. It goes downhill for him from there. How would this kid know I loved it? He was too young to even know a story that was unlikely to be on any scholastic reading list, despite its pedigree, but the way he'd told me his name sounded oddly familiar, as if quoted from the text.

"Why not? Who uses real names here? Who's even real?"

Gabriel-Ernest laughed again, this time derisive, a sound strangely more snarl than snicker, and with an impossibly swift move he disconnected and was gone.

I couldn't get the weird encounter out of my head.

The morning after it seemed dreamlike but still haunted me all day. I tried to tell myself that Gabriel-Ernest was just another late-night freak like others I'd met online, with a weirder than usual vibe. Or maybe a bad waking dream brought on by exhaustion, stress, and too much pot. As work increased over the week, I pushed his memory aside and moved forward. My remote video editing system kept me busy between online Zoom meetings with co-workers about the project. Time I'd had to spend on *DirtyChat* was lost to late night deadlines for recuts.

By autumn the vaccines were already in test stages and looked likely to be effective. With the world a little more optimistic, a little less hysterical, when the freelance job was finally done, I decided to celebrate with a trip back down the rabbit hole to Wonderland. I put on some fresh porn, opened my robe, went online, and clicked *Start*.

Nothing much had changed on the site except the players. Otherwise, the same things always done there were still being done. I slipped back into my established Black Daddy persona, made new 'friends,' and ran into a few old ones who'd stayed on the site all this time. As I raced for the finish line hours later, pleasantly stoned, I looked for an angel to wrap up the night and found my Billy boy instead. He was boldly bare as ever, lit in a golden glow from the light of a lamp on the nightstand next to his bed, as appealing as one of Caravaggio's more sensual masterpieces.

"Hey!" he hissed, his voice low, conspiratorial.

"Havin' a good time?" I slurred, stoned and sleepy, as I flipped my robe shut. He remained in full view, left his evident enthusiasm on display. "I know you've been making trouble for dirty old men like me all night…."

I barked a short laugh, as if to say it wasn't as true as I knew it was. Billy sat up and leaned closer to his laptop's microphone so I could hear him better, the twisted sheet pooled around his hips.

"Oh, you know it! And I met a friend of yours! Super sexy! Why didn't you tell me about him? Keeping the best for yourself?"

A friend?

I'd never had a name here besides Black Daddy and couldn't imagine how anyone could say they knew me from that. Even with a physical description I was a fairly generic type here and hadn't confided my video vice to anyone I knew. While I couldn't be sure none of my real-world friends visited this site it seemed highly unlikely. For a brief moment I wondered if he'd run into one of the regulars I'd just seen, until I was struck like lightning by the only other possibility.

My blood ran cold despite the warm terrycloth robe.

"What's his name?" I tried so hard to sound nonchalant but was almost overcome by a rising feeling of profound dread, one justified by Billy's answer.

"Gabriel-Ernest. Like Billy Ray, I guess. Crazy, right?"

"I only met him once, don't know if I'd call him a friend…." My sanity wavered as Billy described his first encounter with Gabriel-Ernest and the many since then. I was mystified. There were millions of people on the site every night, what were the chances that Billy would meet someone I'd almost decided was a figment of my imagination after all this time?

Someone who was more than slightly sinister?

Billy droned on, giddy with adolescent lust, about how Gabriel-Ernest had expanded his erotic activities, excited Billy in ways he didn't think possible…. I tried to convince myself this was just a coincidence and not part of something bigger, more dangerous than I could see yet. Whatever it was, wherever it went, I'd always know that I started the ball rolling if it went downhill.

"Look, Billy," I cut in. "Baby. My horny teen virgin, I know Gabriel-Ernest is sexy as Hell, but don't forget those stories I told you. The devil wears a pretty face. Don't be fooled by anything he says."

Billy laughed.

"What? Afraid he's gonna trash you? He said nice stuff, all good! Thinks you're hot! Me too…." His hand slid under the sheet again, moved in perpetual motion. As I felt a response under my robe to the smoldering look he gave me I knew it was time to go or cross a line I'd set when I met Billy. One that Gabriel-Ernest obviously hadn't.

"Stay away from him, okay? He's bad news!"

He nodded, uttered assurances as I reached for the mouse.

I knew he wouldn't listen.

My punishment for warning Billy came the next day.

A new job had started with an ad agency I'd worked for seasonally on and off for years. Their latest project was in preproduction, so there were still daily Zoom meetings to attend as they planned the shoot I would edit. I didn't mind. I was being paid and being able to make sure they brought me footage I could cut together well was a plus for us all.

Meetings only lasted an hour each day, which left me time for other freelance work or—leisure! I suddenly had time to play again. Despite the vaccine roll out, cases were rising as a Delta variant worked its way across the sea from India. I'd gotten my Moderna shots, but still didn't feel safe out and about even with a mask. That left me with evenings free, but still trapped at home alone. Against my better judgment I returned to *DirtyChat*, used it like a staycation. I tried not to, but sex was always my most effective means of stress relief, and I had no other means available. I didn't see Billy again, but it wasn't too many nights before another familiar face popped up, with an angry scowl.

"You need to stay out of my business," he snarled.

I feigned ignorance about what Gabriel-Ernest meant and smiled back at him, guileless as I could be. He glared at me with fiery amber eyes, unblinking, but I remained steadfast, determined not to let him get the upper hand.

I knew I was right to do what I did.

"Billy's a kid," I said. "He's underage and shouldn't even be on the site. Leave him alone." It was odd to say to someone who often looked so much younger than me, but something told me nothing about Gabriel-Ernest was what it appeared to be.

"Oh? How old do you think I am?" He smirked. "Maybe I'm his age."

"No. I don't know, but I know…." I hesitated, what I really wanted to say sounded more than a little unhinged. Centuries old? Millennia? To let thoughts like that even flicker through my head was enough to make me sure I was losing my mind, so I shoved them aside. Whether Gabriel-Ernest was his real name or not, he was only human. What else could he be? Any other notion was impossible. Insane. "Let's say I know you're older than you look. By a lot."

"Do you now…?" He grinned and I could have sworn it grew like the Cheshire Cat's to fill the screen. It took me back to how I'd first seen this place as a carnal variant of Carroll's *Wonderland*. Now I felt like the rabbit hole was deeper than I'd ever dreamed, worried about finding my way out if I let Gabriel-Ernest drag me down any farther.

The creepy feeling I'd had after our first meeting was stronger now. It was the way I used to feel in gay bars when I was younger and someone across the room suddenly focused on me and me alone. I could always tell when it was because I was the only Black face in the room, that I was only what they were "into," a fetish that had nothing to do with me, but everything to do with their needs. Their desire.

Gabriel-Ernest had the same sinister aspect of a sexual predator interested only in satisfying his own appetites. Not unusual on *DirtyChat*, but there was something more there I couldn't quite define, a hunger in his eyes of a kind I'd never seen before. The closest I could come was the focused stare of a massive gray wolf I'd seen on a nature show, right before it chased down and slaughtered its prey.

"Leave the boy be," I said again.

"It's not your call or mine. He can do as he pleases."

"You mean you can," I yelled, suddenly angry. It was the air of entitlement I'd seen so many times before that pissed me off. So sure, he had the right to anything that appealed to him, or anyone. "I swear, if you don't, I'll…."

"You'll what?" His arrogance was infuriating. "You gave me power over myself as soon as you summoned me. Fool. There's nothing more you can do."

"If I summoned you, I can revoke the invitation," I said, and trembled. He laughed at me.

"That easy, is it? Always and forever, you said. Your words, not mine, a binding contract by the Law of the Law that made me my own master, and this…." He lazily waved his hands in the air around him. "All of it is *my* world now."

"This is all your *delusion*," I shouted. "I don't know what you think you're doing here, but you're no incubus, no dybbuk or djinn. You're just fucking with my head, but only if I let you."

"Is that so?" He smiled slyly, sexy, but still scary.

"Fuck off." I clicked and he vanished from my screen.

I tried not to imagine a puff of smoke and went back to my own agenda. Soon I found my angel for the night, finished off with a ripped white college jock who told me in great detail how horny he was for the black guys on his football team. He groaned about how much he lusted after them in the showers, his fantasies of being on all fours while they gangbanged him on the tile floor.

The exchange was so enjoyable I couldn't help but think of my sex spell, wondered if it was still working and had done more than merely manifest my nefarious nemesis. I put fears about Gabriel-Ernest out of mind, resolved to enjoy whatever benefits I might have while they lasted.

Rest assured that I didn't try to make any more magic.

I climaxed when the jock did, closed my eyes and pictured myself sharing the sweaty scenario he'd described. When I opened them again, I saw sunlight.

Impossible. I looked at the screen in front of me.

There was a Zoom work call in progress, everyone on the team laid out before me on my big screen in gallery view. There was a moment of sheer panic when I saw them. What happened? And how? It was night moments ago. Everyone silently stared at me as I sat naked and still hard in my chair, robe open, bare belly wet with cum. I gasped for air like a fish out of water and pulled my robe shut as they just sat there, staring at me. No one said anything. No one was appalled or horrified. No screams, no protests.

Their lack of response to my current state was more disturbing than their revulsion would be. I waited for the "shock-cut to waking up from a nightmare" moment I'd seen in so many films, but I was painfully aware I was awake. Before I started making excuses for my appearance, I looked at the screen more closely. The live video thumbnail of me was dressed for work. It wasn't a still of me, but an actual "live" video avatar that moved when I moved, lips synched to what I said when I talked.

Another impossibility. They stared at their cameras, expectant. There was no choice but to act like I knew what was happening, so I improvised.

"I'm sorry, can you repeat that?" I blurted. "A, ah… a text on my phone distracted me, sorry." I switched off my camera with a mumbled excuse in case Gabriel-Ernest dropped the glamour he'd obviously cast to mask my nakedness when he put me here. I cobbled together a suitable response to the repeated question and stammered my way through the rest of the meeting.

Mercifully, it ended shortly after that.

I sat back in a cold sweat. This was new. I'd never been blackout drunk in my life and knew I hadn't been last night. I had no idea in all that was holy how I'd lost the hours since then, much less how I'd signed on to the meeting while completely unaware of any of it.

Gabriel-Ernest had proven his point.

He had power over me, not just on the site, on screen, but potentially in real life too, enough to put me at risk of losing my job and reputation. People had been fired for doing far less on Zoom work calls. If Gabriel-Ernest could make me look clothed on screen when I was naked it stood to reason it would be a simple enough thing for him to do the opposite, when I least expected it. For as long as video was my primary connection to the outside world, if he had control of how I'd be seen online, he controlled me.

And I had nothing to hold over him.

There was no sign of Gabriel-Ernest or Billy for weeks.

Work became stressful but settled into enough regularity that I had free time before bed again to blow off steam. I was still rattled by my last run-in with Gabriel-Ernest and not eager to see him again, but online sex was my only escape from other concerns for a few hours a day. An hour or two with no lockdown isolation, no Covid crisis, no rising rates of infection around the world…. I can't stay hard with those distractions in mind so staying focused on sex erased them.

With porn clips in two windows beside *DirtyChat* to keep me going between chats I fell back into a nightly video orgy that worked for me, even if devoid of real passion. While I waited for a semblance of normalcy to return to the world it was a way to shove everything except work and *DirtyChat* out of my head.

Then my sanctuary started to erode.

It began slowly, chats that went a little south as demands got more graphic, more perverse than advertised. I thought I'd seen and heard everything, but a barrier had broken. More and more men begged for abuse, verbal and physical, whipped themselves front and back with belts, ropes, whips, golden showers drenched mattresses, self-mutilation brought up lines of blood. The wonderland I thought I'd found was turning into the second circle of Dante's Inferno, and I was certain Gabriel-Ernest was behind it all, a demonic Virgil who dragged me into the depths even if I couldn't say how.

He was an unseen tormentor, but oddly ubiquitous. I actually noticed his reflection in a bedroom mirror during a chat, his face hidden in shadows, his presence ignored by the room's frenetic occupant who lay before me. Was Gabriel-Ernest really in the room, or only on my screen's view of it? He'd said *DirtyChat* was his now. I believed it as I watched the site change to suit his will. I couldn't tell whether he influenced everyone who signed on to behave as they did, or if he simply conjured what I saw and heard out of thin air to torture me.

I thought the site's decline had reached an all-time low when one night an older white man with a thick country southern drawl stopped me, eager to engage with what he called my "juicy Black dick." I decided to indulge him, and then after we started, he began to ramble on about "young darkie pussy!"

"Yeah, found me a lil' bitch on the street one day, around eight, *pulled her into an alley and, damn, I pounded that little nigger chimpan....*" I cut him off as his voice dropped to a low hiss in my headphones and I shuddered, more than a little sick to my stomach. I'd thought that four years of Trump era news coverage had exposed the ugly underbelly of this country, shown us the worst of the racist hate buried in it, but he left me feeling that we'd barely scratched the surface.

It got worse over the next few weeks.

I stopped one night to watch a straight couple because the guy was so hot. They were young, pretty, in the way only the young and pretty can be. As she rode his cock cowgirl style their intercourse got more and more aggressive, until she wrapped a red rope around the man's neck and started to choke him.

He seemed to enjoy it at first, but when he struggled against her she didn't stop. His face flushed red, spittle flew from his lips, and she ground her pelvis down harder, faster, staring out of the screen with a ferocity that paralyzed me until I forced my finger to click away from them to something worse, that I still want to forget.

It wasn't all like that. I still found some fun, but what I saw in between got weirder, worse, even if not enough to keep me away. It wasn't until I saw a grandfatherly old man with a toothless smile put the blades of sharp shiny new steel garden shears on either side of his cock and start to squeeze the handles together that I finally signed off for the night. I was unsure if it was real or fake, and didn't care, was determined not to return. I could find other sites like it, even if this one had been the best I'd found— until I corrupted it.

What was I to make of any of this?

I could write everything I'd witnessed off as a temporary mental aberration, my minor breakdown brought on by the stress of working long hours on tight deadlines during a catastrophic global pandemic. It wouldn't be easy to convince myself of that, but it would be the safest route by far.

On the other hand...

If I'd actually cracked the code to hacking the universe, and by some miracle bent it to my will to create a sentient sexual force that existed only on video—then my mastery of sex magic was way better than I thought. I tried not to be too proud because it also meant I'd unleashed something potentially deadly, spiritually even if not physically, on an unwitting public at their most vulnerable. I couldn't bring myself to walk away from that.

True or not I had to treat the site as what it seemed to be, a Hellmouth that opened when I switched on the exit sign that pulled my dirty demon out of the pit. Unable to use the New York library's main reference branch I searched online for ways to revoke my cursed creation. Sadly, whatever I'd accomplished in the field of cybernetic sex magick was too new to be addressed in anything I found there.

Traditional exorcism was my only remaining option.

I signed onto the site, sprinkled holy water stolen from the font of a local church at my TV screen while I recited the appropriate prayers from a borrowed missal. I felt stupid. The only response I got was the faint sound of Gabriel-Ernest's laughter as it echoed under whoever was on screen. I gave up and stopped using the service again. As long as Gabriel-Ernest only existed on the site, I could avoid him, and keep him—*it*—out of my life if I stayed away.

Vaccination numbers rose, and people started going out again in New York. I had outdoor brunch with a few friends, but still didn't feel safe hooking up. A few weeks later, despite my misgivings but horny as hell, I went back to *DirtyChat*. I swore to just dip in a toe to test the waters to see if things had improved since my last visit. I reminded myself there was always a strong possibility that the whole thing had been in my head.

Still, I was relieved not to see signs of Gabriel-Ernest.

The evening was a relief in its normalcy, as the site defined it, and I put past events out of my mind. I had a few enjoyable encounters and settled into a mellow groove, stoned, hard, in a satisfied state of lascivious leisure when I bumped into Billy.

"Baby boy," I sighed.

"Hey," Billy said, a sly smile on his lips.

Somehow, he looked even cuter than usual. I covered myself up as I always did and of course, he didn't. If anything, he got more naked. I lit a fresh bowl of weed.

"How have you been? Good night?"

"Yeah, well, it's okay, but not on long, glad I saw you!"

"Getting past your bedtime?" I joked, as it was already three in the morning, late no matter where he was in the country.

"No, no, someone's coming over." He grinned. Toothy.

"Your parents away?" I was puzzled. He was too young to be left home alone by what had sounded like responsible parents.

"No," Billy chuckled. "But he said it didn't matter, he could get in without them hearing him."

"He?" A familiar chill crept up my spine.

"Yeah, well, I didn't take your advice. I still talk to Gabriel-Ernest, and…. He's great, you know? I'm kind of crushin' on him and wanted more than… you know. So he said he'd come for a visit."

I panicked even though I wasn't sure why. The expression on his face was so utterly naïve and stupidly innocent I wanted to reach into the screen and shake him by his narrow shoulders.

"Listen to me, Billy! Whatever you do, if he actually shows up, if he knocks on your door or taps on your window, please, don't let him in! Promise me!"

"You have this issue with him, I don't know what it is…."

"It's not an issue. It's… hard to explain, but I know him better than you do. He's not like us, Billy."

"Oh, he's just like us!" He barked a laugh. "Maybe more!"

I slumped back in my chair. I knew I'd lost him.

What I saw next was so extraordinary no one could say it happened and expect to be believed. As I stared at Billy tangled in his sheets, I saw another body suddenly behind him, nude, face in shadow. Heavy-lidded golden eyes opened to gaze at me over Billy's shoulder. There was no way I couldn't have seen Gabriel-Ernest before, but I swear that one moment there was a single solitary figure sprawled on the bed. The next another was right there, behind Billy.

My heart raced when I saw him.

His attitude was so suggestive of a wild faun of pagan myth I was reminded of my readings in old Greek mythology. Gabriel-Ernest caressed the boy in front of him, slowly, gently, as Billy responded. The lens of the laptop camera began to rise lazily toward the ceiling as the lid fell back. Sensually oversaturated video colors drained from the picture as it did, leaving the screen cold and grey. The fornicating couple slowly dropped but before they fell completely out of view there was the most astonishing occurrence in the last moments I saw them—Gabriel-Ernest vanished!

Not into nothing but something more dreadful.

Where seconds ago, lovers had embraced, now I saw only a blur of motion that obscured a strange unnatural shape that gripped Billy, pulled him down. As the camera kept moving up, I thought I glimpsed a brief flash of thick black fur and claws, gleaming fangs, and large cruel golden eyes as the pair dropped out of my sight. The camera came to a halt on the upper wall, the taped corner of a poster visible at the top of the frozen screen and I froze too, so sure I was mistaken. What I'd witnessed was inconceivable, even after everything else I'd seen here. The picture was otherwise still. I sat silent until there was a loud, savage snarl in my headphones.

Color returned to my seventy-inch screen as a massive spray of blood shot up to stain the poster and off-white wall paint a deep red, dripped down as another followed it, and another left the wall covered in crimson.

A pale hand shot up, arm bloody and ragged. It was yanked out of sight with a growl as I heard great jaws crush small bones. I screamed, louder than I would have thought I could.

My neighbor pounded the wall.

I clamped a hand over my mouth and quit the browser. I didn't know what else to do, or who to call. What could I even tell them? Not where to send help, much less who to help, or how. What was I supposed to believe? That an anonymous teenager I'd talked to online for months had just been shredded and devoured by a lustful digital demon I'd summoned to a video chat room with high school sex magick? *Its shape and substance from a story I'd never been able to forget, a monster with an erotic appetite that was little more than an exaggerated perversion of my own?*

I knew the deleterious effects of isolation and couldn't be sure it wasn't a mad delusion. Billy was real—I'd seen him long before the appearance of Gabriel Ernest. But when someone I know is real says he's seen someone I'm not sure is real, I don't know what to believe. What's real and what's not?

Plato's allegory of the cave has evolved from believing shadows on a wall are a real image of the outside world to believing videos on a screen. Our knowledge of the world is largely secondhand, made up of moving lights and colors shaped by their source. Is reality what we experience, or only what we can verify? Can we trust that what we see on our computers, Smart TVs, and tablets is any more real than what Plato's cave dwellers saw as truth? Do you see my conundrum? My only answer was Bill Clinton's famously evasive, "It depends on what the meaning of the word 'is' is."

What I saw was entirely impossible, beyond imagining, despite the evidence of my own admittedly addled senses. I insisted to myself that what I saw had to be the result of too much weed, too late at night, like Gabriel-Ernest himself. Yet…. Whatever it was I knew I'd never forget the sight, no matter how hard I tried.

I never saw Billy again.

Oh, I looked for him, online and off, but there had always been regulars on the site who dropped out of sight, bored or in new relationships. Occasionally, some popped up again, but most that left were never seen again. I'd always thought they went off to other sites or stayed offline altogether. Now I worry about other grimmer explanations for their disappearances, and that one in particular might be my fault.

There was no way to confirm or deny what I thought I saw happen to Billy. For months I searched news sites online for any mention anywhere about the brutal suburban slaying of a naked underage teen, slashed to death in his room at night. I found nothing. It was the sort of event you'd think would make headlines, or at least the internet, but nothing. His fate stayed silent as the grave.

I was left with only one thing that was real.

I'd touched something less than human in myself that left me scarred.

The French expression *la petite mort*, the "little death" is usually used to describe what follows the state of orgasm, the post-sex melancholy that some, mostly men I assume, seem to experience after giving up precious life force, whether to partner or pillow. In fact, *la petite mort* doesn't always apply to sex. It can also describe being so deeply affected by a traumatic event it's enough to kill something deep inside you. I thought I'd discovered that other meaning over the last year of the Covid crisis. It wasn't until Gabriel-Ernest that I truly did. I'd stayed in and stayed safe but had only protected my body.

I see now my mistake was to leave my mind vulnerable.

Did I just get lost in a surreal sexscape with Gabriel-Ernest that showed me how many ways there are to lose your soul or suffer an isolation breakdown? Had I opened the back door to a pocket of hell by accident because I didn't really believe I could, or only hallucinated it all? Either everything I saw was real and I've unleashed an unholy host upon the world, or I am utterly and completely lost. Could my repeated focus of sexual energy over so much time have somehow built up enough power to breach a barrier I didn't know was there? It wouldn't take a big hole for a minor demon to slip through as an image and a voice living on electricity.

Just a crack, that's all.

I wept for Billy and for myself, so lost I didn't know who I was anymore, and couldn't stay there, not where it happened. Once it was safer to travel, I had to get away and found myself on the way to the Grand Canyon, the only hole in the country bigger than the one in me. I don't know if it will help.

There are those who would say mine is the tale of a sinner who paid the just price for his lust. Sinner I may be, but sex wasn't my downfall. The sex wasn't wrong, or bad. Intercourse is a series of trite ritualized actions of no lasting consequence, no matter how varied. It took a deeper stain than sex to damn me and leave me hollow inside.

The sin of pride... I made the same mistake as the reporters who led me down this path, I forgot there were people behind all the penises. It was my pursuit of power over them, who I was willing to be, what I was willing to do to get it, that scared me most. What it turned me into, but worse....

What it raised.

Maybe there are things we cast out of our world long ago that want back on the A list and used me as their unwitting tool. In a moment of weakness, perhaps I did break open their cell to bear witness to the coming of their herald, Gabriel-Ernest. Maybe it's not the first of the damned to arrive and won't be the last by far. Lord knows there are a multitude of doors to let the rest in and far too many idiots like me on sites like *DirtyChat* stupidly ready to pick at the locks for the masters of my digital demon. Seems I'm not alone at being alone. Gabriel-Ernest and its kin will find all my brothers in sin, wet dicks in hand, hungry for more than they get.

Ready and eager to play....

This is the end of my road. I came with the hope I might somehow find myself in the canyon's vast void. I still hope so.

I'm just afraid of what might find me first.

The Wife of Wrath's Tale

By John B. Rosenman

Ronnie was bound to find her, Melanie thought. And when he did, her fate was certain. He would take his revenge and kill her. It was as simple as that. She would be DEAD.

About her on the tour bus, thirty-odd passengers talked, laughed, and wrestled with their own demons as they rolled down the highway. Like her, they were making a journey—one could almost call it a pilgrimage—to the Grand Canyon. For her it had to do with the pandemic that was sweeping the world and the need to see something beautiful and magnificent, a natural, inspiring landmark free from disease. And, of course, it also had to do with the need to escape her abusive, controlling husband. Thanks to Covid, there had been layoffs at work, and they had both been forced to spend more of their time together in their cramped apartment. Ronnie hadn't enjoyed the change in lifestyle, blaming it on rich owners who didn't care about poor workers. He had taken out his frustrations on her with his belt and fists, leaving painful bruises she'd tried to conceal with long-sleeved shirts.

Fearing for her life, she had blindly fled with this hastily hatched plan, spending almost all she had on a sightseeing trip. She knew that, just as Ronnie followed her, the coronavirus followed them all. Both sought to kill, and both could follow her to the grave. Just as Ronnie was probably behind her on the highway, pursuing her with lethal intent, so was the microscopic virus navigating through some of the passengers' veins, perhaps hers as well. How slyly it would move at first, a tiny, almost undetectable invader. Thinking about it, she felt suddenly feverish, and her stomach began to hurt. She straightened her mask, trying to remember the first symptoms of the disease but was interrupted by a loud voice.

"Are you all right, Dear? You look a bit troubled."

Melanie glanced up, aware that in taking the window seat, she had left the aisle seat vacant. The woman had a sweet, angelic face, the kind designed to inspire socializing. Like most in Arizona, she didn't wear a mask, which meant she might be infectious. Of course, she reminded herself, if she wanted to stay clean, she should have avoided super-spreader modes of transportation like a bus and waited until vaccines became available.

"I'm fine," she finally said, speaking through her mask.

"Are you sure? You seem pained." The woman sat down beside her without permission and gave her a knowing look. "What's his name?"

Melanie clutched her purse and considered denial. But she'd already denied the truth about Ronnie for far too long. How many times had she accepted his tearful apologies and forgiven him? And how many times had he abused her all over again?

So she gave in and confided in this stranger. The woman's understanding smile soothed her pain, made it bearable.

When she was finished, her new companion stroked her arm. "I'm a member of Women Against Abuse, a domestic violence organization that can help you. Your story could help to empower so many women."

Women Against Abuse? The last thing Melanie wanted was to be recruited to some cause. All she wanted was for Ronnie not to beat her anymore and to show her a little affection like he had in the wonderful early days of their marriage. "What's your name?" she asked.

"Oh, I'm sorry. I'm Liz Coynes."

"Well, Liz, I'm Melanie Stuart, and I'd really appreciate it if you'd put on a mask."

"A mask—what for?"

The answer stunned her. What for? In the year 2020, Covid-19 had already killed over a third of a million Americans, and Liz Coynes said, "What for?" Glancing around the bus, she noticed that Liz was the rule rather than the exception. In the center of the bus, four men had gathered at close quarters and were practically shouting in each other's faces. None of them wore a mask.

"I don't want to get Covid," Melanie said. "That's why."

"But you're wearing a mask," Liz said. "If you believe it protects you, why should I wear one?"

"The mask is good, but it doesn't protect either of us completely. You can still infect me."

Liz snorted. "There's no evidence—"

"Yes, there is! Unvaccinated people are far more likely than vaccinated people to get sick and die."

"That's not true." Liz glanced about the bus. "Half the people are on this bus just to get away from such lies and to see something beautiful for a change. Melanie, this is a free country and with all due respect, you don't have the right to take away our freedom."

Melanie had heard this argument so often she was sick of it. "Yes, I do. I have the right if it helps to save my life and the lives of others, including my children, if I have any. Just check the facts. There are already well over three hundred thousand deaths and it's barely December."

"You're so negative. Those facts are fake news. Besides, President Trump has assured us the virus is about to disappear."

Melanie could see the rosy relationship she had started to forge with Liz crumble to pieces. The woman had stopped smiling several sentences ago. After a few more tense exchanges, Liz rose and left for greener, less critical pastures.

Fuck you, Melanie thought and gasped. Was that *Ronnie* sitting near the front of the bus? He was wearing a mask, but it sure looked like him! If it was, how had she missed him? She tried ducking down in her seat but decided to seek refuge in the back of the bus. She rose and slipped out into the aisle, then headed toward the rear, seeing nightmarish faces everywhere. A fat man with a bulbous nose, a slender woman with a hideous wig, a man with an eyepatch and a gaping mouth. And none of them wore a mask.

As she moved, the bus rocked so much she dropped her purse and almost fell. She bent down and searched for her purse but couldn't find it. It was made of cheap, fake leather and it didn't show up well in this poor light. Oh God, where was it? She glanced desperately about but couldn't find it. She stiffened, catching a glimpse of the stark Arizona desert that stretched away on all sides.

Finally, when Melanie had almost given up, she spotted her purse between a man's feet and snatched it up. Rising, she recovered her balance and moved on, managing to reach the rear.

She crouched down on a seat, relieved she was still alive. Unfortunately, where she sat was no better than home because there was really no place to go. Once she had found a shelter two miles from their apartment, but Ronnie had found her and dragged her out, threatening her life if she ever did it again.

Melanie tried to see the man who looked like Ronnie more clearly. He had risen from his seat and stood facing her. Shadows shrouded his face and mask. She waited in terror, knowing he was about to move. As her heart thudded, she remembered her husband's incredibly fast transformation after his workplace had shut down. Within weeks Ronnie had changed from a loving husband to a monster who demanded total obedience. Slap! Slap! Slap! How he delighted in slapping her face if she showed the slightest deviance from his orders. "Covid courtesies," he called such corrective measures. In turn, she strived to protect herself and to detect the slightest remnant of the man she had once loved.

She glanced outside at the desert, wishing she were there. But no, she had stupidly trapped herself in here, and they wouldn't reach the place where they would be staying for two hours. Even worse, when she returned her gaze to the front, she saw that the man had started toward her.

He came slowly, as if to torment her. Yet she didn't think he'd seen her. She couldn't be sure, though. Ever since the pandemic had encroached on their lives, she had become less and less sure of anything as it related to Ronnie. Once they had kissed and cuddled, played games together. Now the only game he liked to play was *Get Melanie*.

After three or four steps, the man stopped and leaned down toward a woman. At least Melanie thought it was a woman. What a mess. If the clouds, so uncharacteristic for Arizona, didn't part, it would be hard to see the splendor of the Grand Canyon when they got there. She had thought to escape her misery by running and seeing something beautiful, even transcendent. Something that would help her to become reborn and give her life direction. So far, she had found only a nightmare.

The bus lurched, and she saw the man stagger, then resume his advance. Since he was wearing a mask and the poor light made it difficult to see his face, she wasn't positive it was Ronnie. After all, she had searched all the faces carefully before she had been confident enough even to enter the bus. But the pandemic had made Ronnie clever and mean and he'd always liked to play games.

The man peered at the passengers on either side. What was he looking for? Why, *her* of course. He wanted to beat and kill her for thinking she had the right to live her own life. And would anyone here come to her defense and save her? Of course not. Twice she had gone to the police for protection, but Ronnie's good boy looks and earnest, aggrieved manner had convinced them that she was hysterical, and her wounds were self-inflicted. Melanie had painfully and repeatedly learned that if she wanted help, it would have to come from herself and nowhere else.

The man stopped perhaps fifteen feet away. Shadows shifted on what she could see of his face. Melanie saw that he not only wore a mask but had put on glasses, something Ronnie didn't wear. But then, ever since he'd been laid off, Ronnie had become progressively sneaky and tricky. If it *was* Ronnie, though, she knew his real intent. Ronnie was about to kill her, and she was helpless.

The man moved to the side and sat down.

Melanie could barely make him out now in the dim light, and the overcast sky outside didn't help. She moaned in frustration, caught between the desire to run and the desire to risk everything and confront the man. Her struggle attracted the interest of a good-looking young man. "Are you alright?" he asked.

Melanie was attractive, and she had grown accustomed to being hit on by men of all kinds. This one wore a cross and a white collar as signs of faith and virtue.

"I thought I saw somebody I know," she said.

He studied her. "You look upset, like you saw a ghost."

She shook her head. "It's the virus that upsets me more than anything else."

"Covid?" he said. "Why?"

"I'm afraid I'll catch it," she replied. "It's very contagious, and right now I'm in a bus packed with people, most of them not wearing masks."

He smiled, and she realized he was even better looking than Ronnie. "There's nothing to worry about," he said. "Masks don't help anyway."

"They don't?"

"No, and there isn't a pandemic either. It's all just a lie."

"But the sick, the dead...."

"The numbers are exaggerated by liberals and Democrats." He broke into a cough. "Trust me, it's not even as serious as the common flu."

Melanie was no expert, but she knew that wasn't true. Her two best friends had already died from Covid. She stared at his white collar. "You're a man of God, aren't you?"

He gave her a boyish grin. "A pastor at New Hope Church," he said proudly. He covered his mouth as he coughed again, and Melanie saw him shiver. "Listen, don't worry," he said. "Jesus will save us. That's all we need to know."

A growing certainty about him chilled her. "I'm Melanie," she said. "What's your name?"

"I'm Luke Garrett," he said.

Luke. One of the apostles. "Well, Luke," she said, "there's something I'd like to know if you don't mind. Why haven't you and your church ever warned us about the virus and what it can do? Regardless of what you say, we have a full-blown pandemic on our hands. My God, don't you watch the news or read the papers? Why do you just shrug and blow it off as if there's nothing to worry about? When you do that, you become part of the virus yourself. You just aid the pandemic."

Melanie gasped. She couldn't believe she'd said such things, even if they were true. In response, the young preacher stepped back. He clasped his mouth as if he would vomit, his eyes bulging at her.

"My God," she said, "you have it, don't you?"

He shook his head. "No."

"You don't want to admit it, but it's just started. In a day or less you'll be flat on your ass." She reached out for him, thinking he was a young man with his whole life ahead of him. "You need to get to a hospital fast," she said.

Pastor Luke Garrett turned his back on her and staggered toward the front of the bus. He did not look back.

———————————

They reached The Tabard Motor Inn around noon. Melanie had read that the inn provided all the comforts they needed before they went on to the Grand Canyon, but she was reluctant to get off the bus. If she did, she would be in the open and Ronnie, if it *was* Ronnie, could spot her at once.

She huddled in the back of the bus, ignoring the puzzled looks of passengers. "I don't feel good," she told one of them. "I'm going to rest a while first."

When the driver returned, though, and asked why she wasn't enjoying her lunch, Melanie gave in and got up. She couldn't hide forever. If Ronnie wanted to find her, he would.

Inside the inn, the passengers were laughing and putting together a hearty lunch from a long table. It wasn't fancy, just sandwiches you built with meat, cheese, and other ingredients; as well as macaroni; beans; chips and the like. Melanie looked around for potential trouble. She saw no sign of Ronnie (thank God!), but there was the woman who had sat down beside her and the young preacher who probably had Covid. As usual, she saw that the process of sharing a meal broke down barriers and was an effective social leveler, at least temporarily. Everybody laughed and enjoyed the experience and mixed indiscriminately when they sat down at tables to eat. Forget about politics. If you want to create a democracy, establish a national meals program.

Melanie wasn't one bit hungry. Instead, she had to pee and asked some women for directions to the restroom. She went where they pointed, passing broad picture windows that faced west toward their destination.

In the bathroom, she did her business and took off her mask to check herself in the mirror. Ah, a little touching up was in order. She removed her lipstick from her purse and leaned toward the mirror. As she did, she heard the door open, and someone enter. A few seconds later the new person came to stand behind her.

It was Ronnie. The mask and glasses were gone, and he was grinning.

She dropped the lipstick. It hit the sink and clattered on the floor. Her whole body turned to ice, and she couldn't move. Damn it, why hadn't she locked the door?

"Aren't you going to say hello to your dear husband, Melanie?" he asked.

Life struggled back into her body. She gripped her purse and slowly turned around.

"Hello, Ronnie," she said hoarsely.

He tilted his head and gave her a quizzical smile. "Melanie, what did I tell you I'd do if you ever went out without my permission or tried to run away?"

Her mouth was so dry she could barely swallow. "You said you'd—"

"Yes?"

"You said you'd…kill me."

He smiled. "Yes, or at least work you over pretty good."

She glanced at the door, praying it would open. Christ, a fellow female would be a godsend right now. But the door stayed shut and she knew it wouldn't open in time to save her.

Perhaps she should scream?

Melanie opened her mouth, but he slipped close and pressed a knife blade against her throat. She smelled the cheap whiskey he liked to drink which they could not afford.

"One peep out of you, baby, and it'll be the last thing you ever say."

She stared at him eye to eye. They were so close, their breaths mingled. Husband and wife, as it was meant to be. But Ronnie had broken faith with her, betrayed her simply because he had lost his job and was filled with self-pity.

Melanie felt her anger grow and reached inside her purse. She didn't need to search long. What she wanted was right where she expected it to be.

She pulled Ronnie's .38 Special out of her purse and put a bullet right in his belly.

He grunted and staggered back, dropping the knife. His hands went to his stomach, and he stared down at his blood in disbelief.

"You selfish, whining bully," she said. "It's the last time you're ever going to hurt or terrorize me. Consider this your richly deserved reward."

Melanie raised the gun and aimed between his eyes. Just one shot and his evil brains would be splattered all over the walls. Yet she hesitated, remembering how she had once loved him and how gloriously happy they had been in the beginning. For a while, a short, fleeting period, life had been better than she could ever have imagined.

Ancient history, she told herself. If you don't kill him, he'll eventually kill you.

"No, Melanie," he pleaded. "Don't do it!" He backed away in agony, holding his bloody hand out. "Don't shoot," he cried. "Don't do it, I beg you!"

"Why not?" she asked. "You always said a .38 was a fine handgun. Let's see if it's true."

For a moment she hesitated, then hate and rage rose in her soul. Wasn't wrath supposed to be one of the seven deadly sins? Well, let's test that claim.

One by one by one she squeezed off the remaining shots, which were ear-splittingly loud in the small bathroom. Ronnie fell back against the opposite wall and hit it hard. Oddly, though, he didn't fall. Instead, he straightened and gave her a wink.

"Feel any better, baby?" he asked.

Melanie couldn't understand it. Had she shot blanks? But no, she had bought the bullets and loaded the weapon herself. She was *sure* that Ronnie should be mortally wounded.

Something else was odd, too. There were no cartridges on the floor and there was no smoky residue in the air. And where was the gun? She must have dropped it. Most of all, she was amazed that no one had come to investigate the gunshots.

Ronnie chuckled. "Remember what the young preacher man said to you? He said you looked at me as if you'd seen…."

It took her a moment. "As if I'd seen a *ghost*," she said. When she spoke, it all came flooding back. There had been no need to run away from Ronnie because she'd already killed him. She'd finally had enough of his cruelty and had made a cold calculation. Knowing he'd kill her sooner or later, she'd gone to his bedroom and put a single bullet in his heart. Though it had long since turned to stone, it had not proved immune to metal.

"What a waste of time," she said. "I already offed you."

"Yes, you did," he said, "and then you buried me deep in the closet and doused me with disinfectant so I wouldn't smell too bad. It's a shame because eventually they'll find you and you'll swing."

"Oh, I don't think so," she said. "The justice system is more lenient these days with abused wives who finally lose their temper. In the meantime, I'm going to have the best time I can before they catch me, or I decide to turn myself in. I have a cousin in Texas who'll put me up for a while. And then, who knows." She raised an eyebrow. "Perhaps another man."

His face twisted in what looked like regret. "Melly," he said, using his old name for her. "I'm so sorry."

"No, you're not," she said, and watched him disappear.

Stuffing the mask in her purse, she washed her face and dried her tears. Next, she applied some fresh lipstick, inspected the result, and left the bathroom. Returning to the dining area, she paused before the picture window and gazed west. The Grand Canyon was just twenty-five miles away, and though she'd seen movies and pictures of it, she'd never visited it personally and beheld its awesome majesty for real. She imagined it was truly spectacular, shaped and molded by God's own hand, and that it would be a great place to begin her new life. She smiled as the sun emerged from behind a cloud. And she couldn't wait to see how the sun's rays shifted and brightened on the Canyon's mighty walls.

Leaving her mask off, she turned and headed for the lunch area where diners were eating elbow to elbow without fear of Covid. And why not? How much worse could the disease possibly get?

To Melanie's surprise, she had not only recovered her appetite but was absolutely ravenous.

The Secret Place: A Knight's Tale

By Stephen Mark Rainey

"We know little of the things for which we pray."
—Geoffrey Chaucer, *The Canterbury Tales*

McKnight had been driving since early morning, and fatigue was taking its toll on him. The northern New Mexico landscape was rugged and lonely, and he saw few signs of human habitation. Occasionally, he glimpsed lights up in the dark hills, who knew how far away. But mostly, he drove in darkness broken only by the illuminated highway lines, which whizzed toward his windshield like an endless stream of fiery tracers.

He wasn't sure this was the right road. It *felt* like the right road. Hours ago, he had decided to stick to it. He couldn't very well turn back now.

At last, in the distance, he saw a small cluster of lights.

Yes, this is the road.

There it stood, just off the side of the road. A vintage 1950s-era motel, single-story, with two wings of rooms extending from either side of a tiny, central office. A neon sign bearing the image of a huge rooster identified the place as the Chanticleer Inn. Below the rooster, a pair of fluorescent tubes spelled out YES and NO to indicate whether rooms were available. The flickering YES sign suggested he might indeed find accommodations here.

As it had all those many years ago.

Only a handful of cars occupied spaces in the parking lot, but he noticed a bus parked along the edge of the lot some distance down from the office. A tour bus, maybe, for he doubted any commercial lines would actually stop over in this remote corner of the world. He pulled into a space, killed the engine, and slipped his customary cloth mask over this face. As he shoved open the door and slid out from behind the wheel, he detected a whiff of hickory smoke. Several people gathered in a small courtyard in the front of the office apparently had a charcoal grill going.

He felt a small measure of relief that they took no notice of him as he passed. He pushed his way through the office door.

Inside, a bespectacled skeleton behind a Plexiglas pane stared unblinkingly as he approached. The ancient voice sounded creakier than McKnight's aging joints. "You with that bunch?"

"No, sir, I am not. But I am looking for a room. Is it safe to assume your sign is correct?"

"Yes, sir, we have one room left. Down there on the end, number 29. It's not our best, but it's all we've got."

"Do you actually have a best room?"

"Well, no."

"I'll take it."

The old gentleman checked him in, and McKnight headed back outside with his key. Not a key card for an electronic lock, but a genuine metal key with a motel tag attached to it. This time, as he approached the milling figures, a tall, distinguished-looking man dressed in an expensive suit stepped away from the others, apparently to intercept him. McKnight would have preferred to avoid any and all of them, but the well-dressed man planted himself in his path. Unlike most of the others, he wore no mask, though he did maintain a respectful distance.

"Excuse me, sir. Good evening."

"Good evening to you."

"My name is Harry Bailey. I suppose you're wondering about all the hubbub going on at this hour."

"I wasn't really."

"Come now, of course you were. I just wish to assure you that we have no intention of creating a disturbance or keeping anyone awake. We've been traveling for three days, and on these evening stops, we take a little time to get to know each other. Listen to one another's stories, as it were."

Mr. Bailey had dark, penetrating eyes; thick, curly hair, except on top, where it was thinning; and an immaculately trimmed mustache and beard, just going gray. Everything about him spoke of wealth and social standing. Despite McKnight's distrust of strangers—especially those who so obviously put on airs—something about Bailey's manner struck him as not altogether disagreeable. His earnestness: the impression that he lacked guile.

There's something familiar about him.

"Your business is your business. It does not concern me."

Bailey smiled. "Very gracious. Our group is heading to the Grand Canyon. We hope to get there by tomorrow evening."

"I'm sure that's the destination for a lot of folks on this road. There's not much else out there if you keep going west."

"I suppose not. In any event, as you are clearly a guest at this, uh—" Mr. Bailey gave him an ironic smile—"picturesque inn, I would invite you to join us for some refreshment and good conversation."

Definitely familiar.

"That's very kind, but I don't wish to intrude. And I do have a long way to go tomorrow."

"So do we all. But we have plenty of food, and we're more than happy to share. Or have you already had an evening meal?"

"No, actually, I have not."

The aroma of roasted chicken *did* set his mouth watering.

"And you don't have other evening plans?"

"I had planned to pour myself a scotch, make a sandwich, and hit the sack."

"Bring your drink and partake of our food. Take it as an invitation from one weary traveler to another."

The sweet-spicy scent of smoke beckoned to him.

Mr. Bailey continued to gaze at him. "We—I—would be honored, Mister...?"

Against his better judgment, he found himself replying. "McKnight. David McKnight."

"It is a pleasure, Mr. McKnight."

"Very well, Mr. Bailey. I'll go stow my things, pour a drink, and join you in a few minutes."

"Excellent."

He started back toward the Tacoma. After almost two years of little contact with others, here he was about to step into an obviously tight little group, not a member of which he knew the first thing about.

But it felt right.

And if it feels right, do it.

The roasted chicken had been delicious, and now he was glad he'd brought the bottle of Glenmorangie with him. Seated in his camping chair amid this small congregation of unfamiliar souls, he relished the scotch's rich, smoky flavor as much as its calming warmth. The eyes of the group were on him, and he couldn't help but feel obliged to honor their request for his story.

Well, Mr. Bailey's request, as it were.

This was apparently what they did. This was what they wanted.

A couple of dozen souls, give or take, sitting around in the darkness, each with some story to tell. He could barely make out any faces, but they were adults of all ages and races. Many of them sad.

At least as sad as I.

Perhaps *this* was why he was here.

"I have been to the Grand Canyon before," McKnight said. "For both very happy and very sad reasons."

He felt a little tickle in his throat, but with a couple of coughs, the irritation went away. He took another sip of scotch, braced himself, and began.

"My wife, Colleen, passed away last week. She died from COVID-19. She asked that I scatter a portion of her ashes at the Grand Canyon. It was a special place for us. Well—there was one spot in particular. *Our* special spot. We called it 'The Secret Place.'"

———————————

Damn near thirty years ago....

"It's so beautiful here," Colleen said as she scanned the brilliant colors of sunset from their precarious perch above the canyon. "I can't believe it's been closed off to the public."

"So much the better for us—as long as some ranger doesn't come along and make us move on." McKnight slid his arm around her shoulders. It was getting chillier as dusk drew near.

They had found a secluded hollow at the southern edge of the canyon, accessible only by the rugged remnants of a narrow, winding road that turned off Desert View Drive—all but invisible to vehicle traffic. It was only by way of stopping for a pee break they had noticed it. On a whim, he drove down it. Judging from the rotted wooden sign he had spied a short distance back, there had once been a trailhead here.

Their little ledge overlooked a vast, dizzying space. Behind them, a crescent of craggy stone walls rose twenty to thirty feet high, giving the impression of an arena that overlooked the precipice. From here, they had a better than 180-degree view of the canyon from east to west. Before them, rows of high towers and plateaus streaked with gold, purple, and magenta marched away toward infinity. When McKnight dared to lean forward and look down, he saw a seemingly endless gulf through which a lengthening veil of shadow crept as the sun slipped beneath the distant horizon.

"There are no tracks anywhere," Colleen said. "I bet there hasn't been a ranger out here for years."

"Doesn't look like it."

"I think we should camp right here. Put up the tent and stay as long as we want to. I bet no one will ever know."

"That is why I love you. I was about to suggest the same thing."

She turned and smiled at him. Her amber eyes reflected the sun's dying rays. "A year ago, I never would have believed any of this. That we've actually come all the way out here." Her expression turned serious. "I bet you wouldn't either."

He nodded. "It's been a hard few years. Even after I got back from Iraq, it wasn't easy to adjust. But I think this trip is a kind of turning point. We've been together a year. Things have been good. Better than I ever hoped."

"For me too."

"I wasn't sure how and when to do it, but now's as good a time and place as any." He reached into his pocket and withdrew the box containing the ring. With a hopeful smile, he opened it and presented it to her. "It's not the Millennium Star. Or even the Pink Panther. But I hope you like it."

Please like it.

"Oh, David." She gazed at the silver ring, its single sparkling diamond. Then her eyes turned to his. She whispered. "Of course, I do. I love it."

"Well. Will you?"

She lifted her left hand and extended her ring finger to him.

"I will."

He pulled the ring from the box and gingerly slid it onto her finger. "I love you, Colleen."

He saw silver glistening in her warm eyes. "I love you too. I've never loved anyone like I love you."

McKnight reached for her, and they kissed, long and full of joy.

When they parted, her eyes roved around the hollow. "You know, I think I like it here. We should make this our special place. We'll come back here every year. On this date."

"Well, I don't know about every year," he said with a chuckle. "I don't know if I can deal with staying at the Chanticleer that often. What a dump!"

She laughed. Then her beautiful eyes again turned solemn. "You've always made me happy, but I could never be happier than tonight. And we couldn't be in a better place."

"Our secret place," he said. "*The* Secret Place."

As darkness swallowed the canyon, they rose from the ledge and made their way back to the car. They had a tent to pitch, a fire to build, and he had a bottle of scotch with their names on the label.

––––––––––––––––––

And almost as if overnight....

"I'm so sorry for your loss, Mr. McKnight."

He took the proffered wooden box, one side of which bore an ornate engraving of the Tree of Life. Mr. Morton, the funeral home director, had proven himself the epitome of sympathy and propriety. All things considered, Colleen's final journey, from hospice to mortuary to cremation, had been smooth. No hiccups, no unexpected charges, just a straightforward transition from corpse to cremains.

"Thank you, Mr. Morton."

"If we can be of any further service...."

"I sincerely hope not."

McKnight tucked the box under his arm, gave Mr. Morton a final nod, and went out the funeral home door into the dreary afternoon. He headed through the small parking lot to his Toyota Tacoma, settled behind the wheel, and placed the box in the front passenger seat. Colleen's usual seat, as he thought of it. It was going to be a long trip—Aiken Mill, Virginia, to the Grand Canyon—but he had chosen to duplicate the cross-country route he and his wife had taken almost thirty years before. That had been the first of many such journeys together.

This would be their last.

Four years ago, he had converted the truck to a camper. Since then, he and Colleen had spent many of their most memorable moments together in this vehicle, out *there*, gratifyingly far from humanity, even before humanity, by simple proximity, might very likely kill you.

He headed out of town, through the three stoplights—each of which naturally turned red on his approach—to the old Barren Creek Highway. At least there wasn't much traffic at the moment.

How could she be gone?

A year ago, both Colleen and he had expected that, by now, more light would have crept back into this dismal, grim, *idiotic* world. For a time, that actually seemed to be happening. Then the new COVID variants came, and the world turned awful all over again. Even the advent of effective vaccines hadn't halted the resurgence. Not because of ineffective vaccines, but because of humankind's ineffective brains. Colleen had been vaccinated, but she was diabetic. Vulnerable. *Fatally* vulnerable.

Humankind had killed his wife, six days ago.

Humankind had killed his brother, Tommy, six months ago.

Humankind had killed his mom, just over a year ago.

Humankind had killed his friends, Jay, and Myron, and Brenda.

After Iraq, and all *that* killing, back in the 90s, he had thought... believed... prayed... that humankind was done destroying the people he knew, respected, and loved.

But no.

He felt the rage building again. The rage of knowing that the worst of humankind now held the cards. The rage that only deepest grief could ignite. The rage of having watched in helpless horror as human stupidity ripped away his loved ones one by one. Now he was alone, the last of the family unit he had known all his life, bereft of his wife—his foundation— and so many friends who had made this existence not only tolerable but beautiful.

The thoughts came unbidden. But he indulged them. He could not refuse them.

"I want to be plague.

"I will be plague.

"I am plague.

"There will be no vaccine against me."

No!

He was treading too close to the edge. Too close to pure, murderous hatred. Hatred born of anger born of grief, so intense it overwhelmed his every rational counter. His visits to that brink had become more and more frequent during the past year, and with each one, he felt less inclined to retreat from the pitch-black flame roaring in the chasm beyond it.

That is not me. I am an honorable man. I have always been an honorable man.

For a few seconds, he felt an odd tickle in his throat, almost as if he'd swallowed a small, writhing insect.

He'd swallowed a bug once—an errant fly—and he hadn't much cared for it. This was very much like that. But with a couple of coughs, the tickle went away.

An honorable man.

———————

Somewhere on a little-used, two-lane highway in Tennessee, he passed one of the ubiquitous white wooden churches with a tall steeple and prominent cross up top. The sign out front read, "NOONE CAN TAKE AWAY YOUR GOD GIVEN RIGHT TO ASSEMBLE."

He chuckled. "Something tells me I'm into something good."

Next to the main sign, a hand-painted wooden placard read, "WELL DONE PASTOR GILBERT WE WILL MISS YOU GOD HAS SAT A PLACE FOR YOU AT HIS TABLE."

So, this was where that most wonderful, most humble Pastor Gilbert preached. Even in Aiken Mill, a couple of hundred miles back, McKnight had read about the fiercely anti-mask, anti-vaccine, anti-social-distancing, anti-almost-everything-except-publicity clergyman. After a lengthy decline, Gilbert had succumbed to the newest strain of COVID. At least he wouldn't be alone in heaven, since a number of his flock had preceded him there.

C'est tragique.

A few miles on, a large, printed sign in an upcoming front yard caught his eye. "MY GOVERNOR IS AN IDIOT," it shouted.

Reasonable, decent, and thoughtful, these people.

So many like that out here in these southern sticks. Fearful of vaccines and masks ("They're injecting you with microchips! You'll get carbonoxide poisoning!"), militantly pro-freedom when it came to infecting and, in many cases, dooming their neighbors. Hell, even some of their neighbors' kids. These patriotic saints rejoiced over their children's smiling, mask-free faces, caring not a whit that too many mask-free children no longer smiled. Or breathed. Or anything.

Fucking dinks.

That had always been Colleen's go-to epithet for the derision-worthy. It worked well.

There it was. The last remnant of the old road that led back to The Secret Place. As rugged and hidden from view as ever. But this time, there were tire tracks.

The tall figure wore a black cowboy hat, opaque shades, and a black mask over his lower face. With his long, leather duster, he appeared nothing less than sinister. He had been standing on the ledge that overlooked the canyon.

Our ledge.

"Howdy," the man said, his voice muffled by the mask. "Did you come to join this group?"

In the arena-like space beneath the towering stone walls, five RVs of various models and ages were parked in a rough circle. Eight or nine men and women were busying themselves among them—building a fire, putting up canvas canopies, preparing food—basically, setting up camp.

McKnight shook his head. "Personal reasons."

"Then don't mind us. We won't mind you." The man chuckled. "Well, I can't speak for all of us."

"I'm surprised to see anyone here."

"Yes, well, these folks were looking for a secluded place to unwind. A 'place conducive to therapy,' I was told. I knew about this old hollow from a long time ago, so I brought them here."

"Therapy? How so?"

The man pointed to a tall, dark-haired woman standing in front of an RV. Like most of the others, she wore a mask. "That is Dr. Bates. She's a psychiatrist. She's the one who organized this outing and hired me as a guide. That is what I do."

"Okay."

"Now, you see that short, harried-looking gentleman wearing black? The one without a mask? That is Reverend Lee. I expect—no, I'm certain—he'll want to talk to you."

"Is that so?"

"Reverend Lee is a wild card. He pays good money to accompany some of the groups I bring out to the canyon. Do you know what he does? He collects souls, Mister…uh…?"

"McKnight. David McKnight. I didn't know souls were good for so much cash."

The man laughed. "You may call me Hank, by the way. Anyway, Mr. McKnight, Reverend Lee has his ways, and whatever your reason for being here, he'll want to know about it. I don't have any real say with him, so if you plan to stay here, just be aware you may get the third degree and then some."

"I do plan to stay. At least until tomorrow. I've come a very long way to do what I've got to do." He glanced back at the group. "Forgive me for saying so, but I don't think I have much use for Reverend Lee. Or his type."

"I got that feeling from you."

"I tell you what, Hank. I'll keep my truck parked over here, well away from your group. I'll not disturb you at all. I'd appreciate the same courtesy."

McKnight couldn't see mocking eyes behind the shades, but he could feel them. "It is public land, Mr. McKnight, and, as I said, I'm not the boss of these people. They pay me to take them where they want to go, and as far as I'm concerned, that's the end of it."

"You might deliver the message—if you don't mind."

"No, I don't mind," Hank said. "I don't mind even a little bit."

Damnation.

"Hello—Mr. McKnight?"

He pulled his gaze away from the dizzying vista beyond the cliff's edge to regard the short, balding man who had come up behind him. As before, the Reverend wore no mask.

"I am Reverend Dennis Lee. How do you do?" The small man extended a hand, which McKnight took after a moment's hesitation. He had gone a full year without shaking the first hand and doing so now seemed like violating taboo. Worst of all, the Reverend's hand felt clammy and weak. He instantly regretted accepting it.

Lee clearly picked up on McKnight's distaste, for his cool gray eyes turned icy. "I understand you came to scatter your wife's ashes at this place."

He sighed. He had divulged his purpose to Hank, and—shock of shocks—Hank had informed the good reverend.

"That's right. As yet though, I don't know why you are here. Or for that matter, most of these people."

"I am here to provide counsel. To guide the wayward. To minister to the lost."

McKnight gave him a wry smile—which remained hidden behind his mask. "I wonder if this entire group is lost. To have come here, of all places."

"Hank knows every place there is to know out here. He is good enough to allow me to accompany his groups from time to time. When I deem it appropriate."

"I'm not part of that group, so all I'm asking for is privacy so I can do what I came to do without impediment."

Lee's eyes radiated disapproval. "Mr. McKnight, if I had known your purpose when you arrived, I might have asked you to leave then and there."

"Is that so?"

"Sir, the church does not countenance the practice of cremation."

"Mr. Lee, nor am I member of your church."

"*Reverend* Lee, if you please. Mr. McKnight, you are a child of God, as was your wife. At the appointed hour, God shall resurrect body and soul of all the departed. That is His plan. Intentionally destroying the body of the deceased goes against God's will."

"Every human body decomposes. Whether Mother Nature eats it, or it's burned in an oven, no corpse lasts forever. Anyway, I thought most Protestants didn't care one way or the other about cremation. I had assumed your church is a Protestant denomination?"

Lee ignored his question. "It is less the physical destruction of the body than your lack of respect for God's word. God has decreed that a body bereft of its spirit shall return naturally to the earth. And, I might add, you are shockingly flip regarding the dead, especially considering that your wife just passed away." The icy eyes burned into his. "Furthermore, God would not approve of that mask you're wearing. It signifies a lack of faith. Of reverence. It is clear to me that you, sir, are spiritually impoverished. You fear death, and you wrongly assume that your manmade face covering offers more protection than the hand of God. Mr. McKnight, only the Almighty can save your immortal soul. I fear you are perilously close to the brink of disaster."

The brink.

"I am plag—"

No.

"What's that?"

He dismissed the question with a shake of his head. "What you think doesn't matter to me, Mr. Lee. We all fall down on occasion, but to the best of my ability, I conduct myself honorably. You, however, are a fucking dink." He gave the reverend a cruel smile. "There. I fell down."

Again, he felt an odd tickle in his throat. A good cough cleared it.

It didn't mean anything. It couldn't mean anything.

Mr. Miller offered no idle warning.

McKnight had gone back to the Tacoma, poured himself a scotch, and returned to the ledge—"their" ledge, as he and Colleen considered it—hoping to sit and watch the sunset in solitude. Of course, with all these people—*these interlopers*—at the Secret Place, that was too much to hope for.

If anyone disturbed him at dawn when he scattered Colleen's ashes, they would be lucky if he didn't send them over the edge.

"Hello," came a soft, very feminine voice. "Are you David?"

He knew without looking who it must be. "Yes. I'm David McKnight."

He felt her distinctive aura from several feet away. "I wanted to introduce myself. I'm Deana Bates. It's a pleasure to meet you."

With a low sigh, he turned. She stood a few feet away, gazing at him with thoughtful, sapphire eyes. A black cloth mask covered her nose and mouth. She was slim, even willowy, with thick, dark brown hair. Very attractive. *Some psychiatrist.* "Good evening. I'm sorry, I didn't bring my mask with me." He held up his glass of scotch.

"Quite all right. I hope I'm not intruding."

He made an expansive gesture. "It is public land."

"I understand if you'd rather be alone. I think many of us who have lost loved ones—particularly a spouse—prefer considerable alone time, especially at first."

"Are you speaking as a psychiatrist, or from experience?"

"Experience. Twice over."

"I'm sorry to hear that."

"It's been a long time. My first husband was in the Navy. He died in the attack on the *USS Cole* in 2000. I understand you were in the Army. Desert Storm."

"You are well-informed."

He detected a knowing smile behind her mask. "Mr. Miller and I spoke briefly about you. He admires those who have served their country honorably."

"And what about Hank? How did you come to engage his services?"

"Oh, I met him a few years ago, when I started these group outings. They've been very effective helping people who just need recharging."

"An unconventional method, I should think."

"Not really. No, not really at all."

"What about your second husband?"

Her eyes swiveled to the vista beyond the ledge. "He died two years ago, in an automobile accident. With his mistress."

"I'm sorry."

"They were drunk." She pointed to his glass. "Don't get too close to the ledge with that."

"No worries." He took a bracing swallow of Glenmorangie. "And how well do you get along with Reverend Lee?"

She laughed without mirth. "We tolerate each other. Barely. It's safe to say he and I have little in common."

"I'm shocked."

Now, she laughed deeply. "I don't know why Hank allows him to come along—apart from the money. They don't even like each other."

"I doubt Reverend Lee likes anyone."

"No, he definitely does not. Of course, he 'loves' everyone. That special kind of love that comes directly from God. *His* God, anyway."

"I'm not fond of that one." McKnight drained his glass and set it carefully on a flat portion of rock, well away from the edge.

For a time, Dr. Bates gazed at him in silence. Then, with a slow, deliberate hand, she removed her mask. She wore a most alluring smile. "I think it's safe enough for us without this."

"You know, I don't think I—"

She held up a hand to stop him. Then she stepped closer to him. "I know you're still curious about all this. You didn't expect it—or want it. To find these strangers out here. *Here*, of all places."

"What is it you have to say, Dr. Bates?"

"You may call me 'Deana.'"

He shook his head.

"Mr. McKnight. David. This is not what you think it is." Up close now, her smile looked false, *artificial*. As if her features had been molded in wax and set slightly wrong. In that moment, he didn't think he had ever seen anything so disturbing in his life.

"If you'll excuse me, Dr. Bates. We have nothing else to talk about."

So softly that he barely heard her, she said, "But I have something to tell you. Something you've wanted to know since the moment your path crossed ours. Something you *need* to know."

She leaned close to him, placed a gentle hand on his shoulder, and whispered in his ear.

Ashes, ashes, we all fall down.

McKnight set the box bearing the Tree of Life on the stony ground a few feet from the edge of the outcropping and settled himself, cross-legged, next to it. To his right, vivid bands of azure, pink, and gold painted the dawn sky low above the horizon. He slid the box's back panel open and removed a heavy plastic bag full of gray-white powder sealed with a metal clip. He gingerly placed the bag next to the box and opened the top of the bag. With a little shiver, he slid his hand inside the bag, into the cool, gritty cremains of the only love of his life.

He had mentally prepared a few words to recite, but now they seemed wholly inadequate. *Useless.* No words he knew could express his profound, abiding love for her, to which he still clung with desperation; his newfound loneliness, which he feared would never end; his *rage* that human stupidity had reduced the most vibrant, radiant woman on Earth to a pile of gray ashes.

He scooped a handful of the coarse powder and drew his hand from the bag.

"You are the only one who has ever owned my heart. Every part of me. I have loved you above all others, and I always will. I hope that, someday, somehow, we can be together again. I do love you so."

He threw the handful of ash over the edge. A wisp of dust lingered briefly in the air and then vanished.

Inadequate.

A scuffling sound came from behind him, followed by a familiar, hated voice.

"Sadly, Mr. McKnight, your words are empty, and your hope is misplaced."

Yes, he did *hate* that voice.

And the man.

"The only eternity waiting for you and your wife is blinding darkness."

That tickle in his throat came again. He coughed a few times to clear it. It almost went away. But he could still feel a light, prickling sensation that waxed and waned. After another few moments, it began to wax more than wane.

"I wish I could offer you words of hope," Reverend Lee continued. "But the choices you have made almost certainly preclude any chance of salvation. I fear that, for you, it is likely too late."

"You are a poor ambassador for Christ. Do you know that?"

"Derision from a sinner means nothing to me."

"To *you*. It really is all about you, isn't it?"

Again, the tickling grew more intense, and this time, it truly did feel like a spiny insect crawling up through his trachea. He stood, turned around, and stared at Reverend Lee. Now, the smaller man said nothing, but his indignant expression provided McKnight a small measure of satisfaction.

A clatter behind Reverend Lee alerted him to someone else approaching. A moment later, Hank appeared from behind a nearby boulder, as ever, wearing his hat, shades, and mask.

So much for privacy this morning.

"Forgive me for intruding," came his muffled voice. "I need Reverend Lee. I'm afraid something dreadful has happened. Apparently, Mr. Miller and his wife jumped into the canyon during the night."

Reverend Lee's look of anguish appeared *almost* authentic.

"I hate to hear that," McKnight said. "I rather liked him."

That much was true.

"A terrible loss," Hank said with a sad shrug. "Reverend, if I could persuade you to come with me, there are several upset people to deal with."

"Of course."

"Again, Mr. McKnight, I'm sorry for disturbing you at such a private moment." He started to turn back toward the "camp."

"I was as done as done gets, I suppose. However, Hank, you did know exactly where to find Reverend Lee."

The tall man froze in mid-turn and then slowly swiveled back to face McKnight.

"I confess he had indicated his intent to speak to you."

He could feel Reverend Lee seething.

"I'm guessing you knew the Millers would come to a sad end. Not only that, I suspect you somehow facilitated it. And I don't believe it stops with them."

"You know, I didn't take you for the paranoid type. I wonder if I misjudged you."

"Maybe you have, maybe you haven't. With a little information here and a little information there, I've deduced a few things."

"Mr. McKnight, whatever you think you have deduced, it's safe to say you're not even close."

The scratching in his throat—no longer just a tickle—was becoming so intense he couldn't keep from coughing. A deep, hoarse cough that didn't touch whatever was irritating his throat and windpipe.

Reverend Lee took a few steps away from him, toward Hank. From behind the nearest boulder, Dr. Bates stepped into view.

She glanced at Hank. "I believe we are at that point."

He nodded, turned, and started walking back toward their camp. Dr. Bates accompanied him.

"Are you coming, Reverend? I wouldn't dally if I were you."

Reverend Lee glanced at McKnight. His eyes radiated both curiosity and revulsion.

McKnight felt pressure building in his chest, desperate for release. He coughed again, harder, but no effort could clear his airway. The prickling and scratching had become maddening. Maybe some water. He needed water.

Something far back in his throat lurched, and he coughed so hard it felt as if his lungs were tearing themselves from his chest. One more deep, powerful cough....

And something blew out of his mouth.

Something dark and spiny. For a second, he wondered if he had hacked up some kind of tumor.

But the thing didn't fall to the ground. Instead, it hovered in the air, six feet in front of him, suspended by whirring, translucent, dragonfly wings.

A cluster of black-and-yellow banded legs, like a spider's, unfolded and spread wide. Then a long, segmented tail slid from the armored black body and whipped back and forth as if questing for a target.

"Oh, my God," Reverend Lee whispered. His eyes flicked briefly from the winged thing to McKnight. "You are damned! Unclean!"

The scratching in his throat had not finished. Another cough, and a second black horror took flight from his mouth. Another, and then another.

Now, he felt very little sensation in his throat. After the first few, releasing them was effortless.

He glared at Reverend Lee.

"I am plague."

With that, the swarm of black devils fell upon Reverend Lee. He swatted at them as they swirled around and over him, but they moved too fast—until one lit on his cheek. As the thing raised its whiplike stinger to strike, he slapped his hand against his face. But when he drew his hand away, the creature clung to his palm. Its stinger drove home, and Reverend Lee's shriek drilled like a siren into McKnight's eardrums.

Again and again, barbed stingers penetrated the preacher's flesh. He spun, thrashed, and screamed amid the whirling cloud of droning plague-dancers.

McKnight returned to the ledge, resealed the bag of Colleen's cremains, and placed them back in his box. He closed it up and tucked it under his arm.

Reverend Lee had finally stopped screaming. Judging by the way he lay motionless on the rock; he had likely stopped breathing.

If he had any feelings for the man, they lay buried far too deep to reach.

He left the ledge behind and strode into the arena-like campground, heading for his Tacoma. The few remaining men and women, none of whom would have any clue what the commotion and noise had been about, scattered at his approach, as if they sensed danger. From somewhere in the air, he heard a vague buzzing and whirring, but at the moment, he saw none of the deadly creatures he had unleashed.

He wasn't sure why these people would bother fleeing the onslaught that was surely coming. Given their reasons for gathering here in the first place, they might even welcome the swarm.

Mr. and Mrs. Miller, unaware of their destiny, had simply gotten the jump on everyone else.

Oh, no, you did not.

He sighed. So, *this* was the culmination of his rage.

Emptiness. Numbness. *Witlessness.*

He reached the Tacoma and was about to tug the door open when Dr. Bates's voice stopped him. "Mr. McKnight."

He turned and saw her standing alone in the center of the hollow. "Come to see me off?"

"Simply to bid you safe travel. You have a very long journey ahead of you."

"I don't suppose I'll be lucky enough to never see you again?"

"Only time will tell."

"Where are you going next?"

"I've always enjoyed the beach. California, perhaps."

"I will be a long way from there."

"I'm sure you will. Doing what you now do best. Perhaps I'll read about it in the news."

"Why read it? You might as well write it yourself."

"Touché."

McKnight clambered behind the wheel, set the box bearing the Tree of Life in Colleen's usual seat, started the engine, and drove away.

———————

Memories return.

As Dr. Bates leaned in close to him, he could smell her perfume. Light and floral, but with a tinge of something harsher—almost like tequila, he thought with wry amusement. Her breath tickled his ear as she whispered,

"No one here has the first desire to continue living. Each and every one has suffered loss so awful it has destroyed them. You are just the same.

"Except…we have seen to it that you will cure yourself—and them. You will be *the* cure. For everyone."

———————

In the flickering light of the motel sign, an array of eyes blazed at him. For some time after he stopped speaking, not a voice rose from the "audience." At last, he heard a collective sigh. Then a soft, female voice said, "What a terrible 'tale' you've subjected us to. You turned a terrible tragedy into a gaudy allegory."

"Oh, no," came a booming male voice. "It's a poignant expression of grief and outrage. I admire your heartfelt honesty, Mr. McKnight."

Heartfelt, indeed.

"Sinful!" From the seated crowd, a figure stood up. "Your prejudice toward religion—and the word of God—is disgraceful. You, sir, ought to fall on your knees and repent."

Impossible! Reverend Lee was dead. But no. This speaker was black, tall, and dressed in a tailored pinstripe suit.

He felt a little rush of satisfaction.

Another boorish pharisee riled.

"Bravo," came the familiar voice of Mr. Bailey. The tall figure stepped forward wearing a broad smile. "I find your story moving. And strikingly… believable."

With slow deliberation, Mr. Bailey pulled a black cloth mask over his face. Slid a pair of opaque shades over his eyes. And placed a black, leather cowboy hat onto his head. "You do yourself credit, Mr. McKnight. It is very, very good to see you again, my friend."

Hank.

Another female voice from the crowd spoke. "You are the cure, Mr. McKnight. David."

Dr. Bates.

"You lied," he whispered. He gazed in stunned horror at the beaming host. "You told me this evening that you've been traveling for three days. But I left you only yesterday."

"You're confused," Dr. Bates said, stepping into flickering view. "I suppose that's to be expected, after the trauma your body has endured. You actually left us—your 'Secret Place'—over a week ago. You have been out here ever since, dispensing your 'cure' wherever it is needed." She drew a phone from her jacket pocket and presented it to him.

On the luminous screen, a headline read, "New Mexico Town Ravaged by Locust-Like Plague." Below it, a subheading read, "Scientists Baffled by Previously Unknown Species of Arthropod."

"I hope you've enjoyed your evening," Harry "Hank" Bailey said. "It has been *quite* the pleasure for us." He made a sweeping gesture toward the seated crowd. "I wonder whether any of these good people here are...ill?"

McKnight said nothing, barely able to process the chaos whirling in his brain. Soon enough, though, the bedlam softened, and he became aware of a slight tickling in his throat.

Nothing more than an irritating, insignificant tickle.

"And high above, depicted in a tower,
Sat Conquest, robed in majesty and power,
Under a sword that swung above his head,
Sharp-edged and hanging by a subtle thread."

—Geoffrey Chaucer, *The Canterbury Tales*

The Sacred Clarion

By S.A. Cosby

Hey, do you have a light?

I know, I know it's a terrible habit but shit the world might be coming to an end so we might as well smoke 'em if we got 'em right?

Thanks. I came out for a smoke, but if I'm being honest, I had to get out of my room. The bar is open but…I mean who wants to drink when you got to take your mask off every time you want to take a sip. Plus, it feels weird being around so many people. I was never a germaphobe before…all this but now I got hand sanitizer in every pocket, and I don't even fist bump people. I just sit as far away from them as I can unless I'm outside. The pandemic turned me into a misanthrope. Which is crazy because I used to love crowds. Being in front of crowds was the best part of the best job I ever had.

What kind of job was it? Guess. No, go ahead. Guess.

Wow, no not an actress but you're close. I was a singer. I was the lead singer for a funk/metal fusion band. The Delicate Beasts. I know the name is pretentious as fuck, but it looked good on the merch. We played nearly three hundred dates a year through the Northeast and Midwest. People would come to the show expecting some Nu Metal bullshit, but I didn't rap. Not that there is anything wrong with rapping but I'm not any good at it. It ain't my thing, ya know? Nah I've always loved to sing. Got it from my mama—and my daddy—but my Mama was the one that could actually sing. She was an alto but could hit soprano notes if she was feeling real good and her girdle wasn't too tight.

She'd laugh when I'd say that. My daddy would always give me a dirty look but not like he was really mad. It was like he wanted to laugh too but somebody had to be the parent and he always seemed to draw the short straw.

How are they?

They're dead.

No, no stop you didn't know. How could you? Who starts a conversation with somebody they bugging for a light? Thanks for that light—by the way my mom and dad are dead? So, is my uncle and his daughter. All of them dead and buried. Well, not really. The funeral home didn't want to handle the bodies because of the Covid. I mean I can't blame them. We don't know what the fuck this shit really does. I feel sorry for them, ya know? We come from a small town, and they got overwhelmed real quick. When my people were there, they had fifty other bodies. They strongly suggested cremation. I took that suggestion because honestly there was no money to bury them.

Insurance? Yeah, they had insurance, but my mama made Rev. Weldon their beneficiary and he felt the money was best used for the church. Not for a funeral.

"Funerals are for the living, Sherry. Your parents would want us to use this money to expand the work of the church."

Can you believe he had the nerve to say that to me? Talking about what my parents would have wanted when he was the main reason they were dead. I wanted to reach through the phone and slap the taste out of his mouth. Anyway, that's why I'm here. Gonna take their ashes and spread them at the Grand Canyon. My parents always talked about taking a vacation but when you're poor and black and one of you working fifty hours a week at a seafood plant and the other one working sixty hours a week on a construction crew and you're paying the mortgage on a house that always needs a fucking repair that's never less than four digits, vacations just don't seem to be a part of the equation.

No, it's okay. I'm okay.

Actually…I'm not. I'm sitting here looking at this beautiful sunset and thinking how my mama and my daddy should be seeing it with me instead of in a fucking coffee can in my gym bag. When we were touring, we only made it west of the Mississippi a few times but the sky in the West is different. Maybe it's all the light back home or the pine trees that can hide the stars, depending on where you stand. I don't know. But every time we ended up out this way, I'd look at the sky as it changed from a setting sun oil painting and became a Rembrandt night sky and I'd think, "If I'd been born out here would the stars in the western sky make still make me feel like crying?"

Because they do. I look at those stars and I feel like crying like a baby. Nothing should be that beautiful. That kind of beauty hurts. Because if it's an accident then there's no rhyme or reason to it. And if it is God playing with his Crayons, then where is he when he ain't doodling? Where was he when—never mind.

What happened to my folks? That is a long story.

You sure? No, I don't mind talking about it. Maybe talking about it is good. It's just so sad. So fucking sad and dumb.

Well, if you really want to hear it give me another light.

———————————

Sherry grabbed her two gym bags from the Uber driver's trunk and sat them on the ground. Then she grabbed the backpack and slipped it over her shoulders. The whole time she was struggling with her things the driver never even looked in the rearview mirror. She couldn't believe Hamilton County actually had Ubers and Lyfts, but she wasn't surprised they weren't dedicated to customer service. People in Hamilton had small minds and smaller vocabularies. Sherry knew that was harsh, but the truth often is.

No five stars for you buddy, she thought.

She turned and walked across the patio stones her daddy had put down ages ago for a walkway that her mama loved almost as much as her only daughter. Sherry did a little hopscotch step over the stones as she made her way to the front steps. When she'd been a kid, their house had seemed impossibly large. Long hallways and rooms a thousand years wide (RIP Chris), but now the house seemed almost comically small. Too small to be quaint but too big to be a tiny house that some hipster would drool over.

Sherry knocked on the door once before her mother tore it open and pulled her into a chest crushing embrace. Sherry dropped her bags and put her arms around her mama. The warmth that radiated from the older woman enveloped Sherry, wrapping its tendrils around her thin arms and legs, and caressing the gentle sweep of her neck.

"My baby!" her mother whispered intensely.

"Mama, you know we shouldn't be hugging like this," Sherry said. It came out muffled behind the bandanna she wore across her nose and mouth. Her heart wasn't really in the admonishment though. Yes, she'd been traveling and yes, she'd come from one of the worst hot spots in the pandemic, but she was religious about washing her hands and using sanitizer and she hadn't let another person breathe on her since her last night in Memphis when Tyler had kissed her after a mildly disappointing round of love making. She teased him about his name being a version of Karen for white boys, but it was a gentle teasing. The thing people with bad communication skills passed off as love language.

"Now you hush with all that. I don't want to hear none of that talk about no pandemic. I'm covered by the blood of the Lamb. Rev. Weldon said last Sunday we have to rebuke this Covid in the name of the Lord and if we— "

"Can I bring my bags in, Mama?" Sherry said. Best to cut her mother off before she really got going and busted out the Holy Dance right on the front step. Sherry didn't know who Rev. Weldon was, but if he was anything like the last two pastors at Galilee Holy Baptist Church he probably wasn't qualified to be dispensing medical advice. Mama took a step back, and Sherry crossed the threshold of her childhood home for the first time in three years. Nothing had changed, but there was peace in that stability. Her mother still had her commemorative President Obama plates on the entertainment center. There were the two pictures of Jesus on the wall. White Barry Gibb Jesus and more recently Brown Closer to What He Might Have Looked Like Jesus. The couch with its aggressively floral sofa cover sitting against the far wall. The only change was her daddy's decrepit recliner had been replaced with a fancy new electric one with a cooler on the side and cup holder built into the arm rest.

"Where's Daddy? He working that weekend overtime?" Sherry asked.

"He went over to your uncle's to help him finally try and fix that old truck," her mama said shaking her head.

"That thing been on blocks since I could tie my shoes. How they planning on fixing it?" Sherry asked.

"Jessie started talking about fixing it up strong last year. So, he bought a bunch of parts and he determined to get that thing running," Mama said.

"Should Daddy really be over there? Look, I know you don't think it's serious but people with asthma have a hard time with this thing," Sherry said.

"They're outside so your daddy says he'll be fine. And I don't think it's serious. I just don't put my faith in man. I lean on the everlasting. Now take that mask off so I can see my baby's smile," Mama said. Sherry ran her tongue over the roof of her mouth. Was this how it was going to be for the foreseeable future? Her massaging the roof of her mouth to keep from biting her tongue as her mama just ignored all the scientists and doctors in the world of man? Never mind the seven people at the seafood plant that were in the hospital or the five that had died. Never mind the twenty or so people that had died in the Lake Castor Retirement home.

Sherry closed her eyes, took a breath, pulled down her mask and forced a smile across her face.

"How much stuff I gotta move out my old room?" Sherry asked. Her mother put her index and middle finger against Sherry's lips. Sherry did her best to not recoil.

"Shhh. Your daddy moved all our junk out of there last week when you called. He set up a bed and put an air conditioner in the window."

"Mama, y'all didn't have to do all that. I could have slept on the floor. I've done it before on tour," Sherry said.

"Hush. You're our baby. I hate this old Covid mess but I'm glad you're home. I've missed you so much Sherry Berry," Mama said. Sherry Berry was a pet name her mother used exclusively. Her daddy agreed with Sherry that it was silly, but it didn't hurt anyone, so she didn't protest.

"I missed you too, Mama. Hopefully, things will…get better, and when they do, I can get back on the road," Sherry said.

Soon as we get a new guitarist and drummer who aren't suffering from what the doc's are calling long covid, she thought. Tyler was the bassist and founder of The Delicate Beasts, but he couldn't play lead if someone had a gun in his mouth. Sherry sang lead vocals and could play a passable rhythm guitar, but she didn't have the nimble fingers required for the chord progressions in most of their songs. Abe and Tammy had both come down with the ick after a show in Fort Wayne. Sherry thought that was proof of a capricious God. A show where twenty-five people showed up was the last show the original lineup of The Delicate Beasts would ever play. In a town that was not known for their love of funk or soul, which was all The Delicate Beasts played.

"I hope you will at least stay around until homecoming. Maybe even sing at homecoming service," Mama said. Sherry let her backpack slide from her shoulders.

"I don't think Mrs. Carruthers is going to let me sing lead on anything as long as her daughter is still upright," Sherry said. She collapsed across the couch. The sofa cover was soft as the fur of a newborn fawn. Her mother sat down next to her. She picked at some imaginary lint on her jeans then scratched the back of her head.

"We don't go to Galilee anymore," Mama said. That made Sherry sit up straight.

"What do you mean you don't go to Galilee anymore? When did you leave? Where are you going to church? What happened?" Sherry said. Mama turned her head slightly to the right and tucked her chin against her chest.

"They got a new minister last year around Christmas. Rev. Ellis Weldon. And Sherry, he was wonderful. He had all these new ideas, and he was reaching out to other churches, even the white ones. He was making changes, real changes that was bringing all kinds of people to the church. And then they stabbed him in the back! The congregation tried to vote him out. Can you believe it? That damn Eunice Carruthers was one of the main ring leaders, excuse my language. Anyway, he wouldn't give them the satisfaction. So, he left and started the World of Friends Church. And me and your daddy and half the congregation went with him. Now Galilee parking lot ain't hardly full-on Sunday and World of Friends ain't got enough room for all the people coming in."

Sherry stared at her. There was a lilt and a heat in her mama's voice she'd never heard before. Mama had always been religious, that was the given in the equation, but this level of passion was new.

"Wait, y'all still having in-person services?" Sherry asked. She waved her hand as if she could just bat away Sherry's concerns.

"A lot of people wear masks. And we space people out. The governor had said we couldn't have over twenty people, but Rev. Weldon got with the other churches, and they went to court. They told them that violated our religious freedoms and of course the court agreed," Mama said. Sherry frowned. The way her mama had said "of course" made her skin crawl a little bit.

"I hope y'all got lots of hand sanitizer too, "Sherry said. She wanted to say more but she was rapidly giving in to her exhaustion. Three days in a rented car that decided to die fifty miles from her destination had worn her out. Three Uber rides later and her meager savings weren't the only thing that was wiped out. She literally didn't have the mental bandwidth to get into the vagaries of Rev. Jason Weldon with her mama.

"We got hand wipes too. But you know I was telling Cathy Deininger we walk by faith not by sight. My faith tells me my God wouldn't just throw some pandemic on us without a reason."

"Like he threw the plagues on the Egyptians," Sherry said. She connected with her intellectual Wi-Fi for a moment to drop that *bon mot*.

"That was different," Mama said, just like Sherry knew she would.

Sherry was passed out on the bed when her father's footsteps woke her. Her daddy walked through life like a proverbial bull in a China shop, but he was gentle giant. She heard his big boots coming down the hall. He leaned against the door jamb and crossed his tree trunk arms.

"Well, if it ain't the prodigal daughter! Do I get a hug too? Or is that just for your mama?" her daddy said. He grinned at her, and she smiled back. She had his smile but her mama's lean legs. She got up off the bed and gave him a hug. He wrapped her in a powerful embrace. Despite the Covid and the canceled gigs and the claustrophobic haze of her mama's religious fervor, being here with her daddy felt like the best place in the world.

"How's Uncle Jess?"

"Trying to put together that piece of junk truck. It got more rust than running parts," Daddy said.

"What made him get all hyped up about that truck all of the sudden?" Sherry said. Her daddy's smile faltered.

"Your mama didn't tell you?"

"Tell me what?" Sherry asked.

"Darlene had to go in a nursing home. Her lupus got real bad last year. He been working on that truck ever since," Daddy said.

"Why didn't Mama tell me?" Sherry asked. Her daddy shook his head.

"Probably didn't want to tell you because of what happened with Rev. Weldon," Daddy said. Sherry made a "go on" gesture with her hand.

"Your mama and them World of Friends folks went down to the nursing home and tried to lay hands on Darlene. They pulled her up out her chair and tried to make her walk. She fell down and Jess bout went the hell off. She ain't said much about Darlene since then."

"You going down to this World of Friends church too?" Sherry asked. Her daddy grunted.

"Hell no. That ol' boy talk too much shit for me. Laying on hands, seeing visions, talking in tongues. But he ain't healed nobody. All his visions is about him getting money and his talking in tongues sound like Das EFX."

Sherry laughed and fell back on the bed.

"What's up with this caution tape you got for hair?" Daddy said.

"It's just some weave I braided in. It was for our shows. Made me stand out on stage," Sherry said.

"Babygirl, you don't need nothing but that voice to stand out. I'm gonna make a cheeseburger casserole for supper. You want some or you gone vegetarian?"

"Even if I was gone vegan, I'd make an exception for your cheeseburger casserole. Let me finish my nap," Sherry said.

"Alright but if you oversleep I can't make no promises. Might not be none left." He paused.

"I'm glad you're home, Babygirl. At least for a little while."

"Me too, Daddy," Sherry lied.

———————————

The aroma of her daddy's signature dish woke her up with a vengeance. She hadn't realized just how hungry she was until she smelled his homemade concoction. Sherry made her way barefoot down the hallway and turned right. Mama was making a big pitcher of sweet tea while Daddy was pulling the biscuit lined baking pan out of the oven. The hamburger meat was covered in shredded cheese. Once it melted and the biscuits expanded it became one huge cheeseburger like meal.

"Damn I was hoping you'd nod off until I finished all of this," Daddy said. Sherry playfully punched him in the arm. It was like hitting a rock wall.

"Sherry, since you're home do you think you want to come to service with me tomorrow? It would be good for you to see the church and meet

Rev. Weldon," Mama said.

Sherry considered pretending she hadn't heard her but that could only work for so long. Better to rip the Band-Aid off now. "I think I'm gonna get settled in. Maybe go online see if anyone is hiring around here. I can still make a mean eggs Benedict and hashbrowns," Sherry said. Mama stopped stirring the tea.

"You can do that on Monday. Nobody is going to be looking at applications tomorrow," Mama said. Sherry pinched off a piece of the cheesy biscuit and used it to scoop up some hamburger. She plopped it in her mouth.

"Mama, I'm just trying to get on my feet while the band isn't on the road," Sherry said.

"I understand that. We didn't blink when you called and said you needed to come home. We got your room ready."

"I got the room ready," Daddy mumbled.

"We aren't asking for any rent. No bills. We are letting you stay here as long as you need even though you didn't visit us for years. I just think it's not too much to ask for you to come to church. You could sing for Rev. Weldon. God gifted you with a voice like an angel. Like the sacred clarion of Gabriel. Maybe he stopped you from singing all that nasty stuff for a reason." She was pointing the stirring spoon at Sherry like a wand.

"My songs aren't nasty. I write songs about love. About happiness. About sex. You'd know that if you had ever listed to any of them." Daddy stopped cutting up the casserole into squares and stepped between her and Mama.

"All right, let's chill out. Joy, if she don't want to go to church she ain't got to."

"You should come too, Elliot. But you'd rather help Jess with his piece of shit truck!" Mama said. She tossed the stirring spoon in the sink and stomped into the living room.

Daddy let out a deep soul-tortured sigh. Sherry knew what was coming next. This story was as predictable as a nursery rhyme.

"Babygirl, would it kill you to go to church?"

"With Covid? Yeah, actually it could," Sherry said.

Daddy moved closer to her. His broad shoulders dropped a few inches. "Look, you go tomorrow, mask up and it'll make your mama happy for a few weeks. You don't go and she'll raise hell for the rest of this week," Daddy said.

Sherry fought the nearly Pavlovian desire to roll her eyes. "Okay. But I'm standing up in the back. I'm not sitting next to anyone," Sherry said. Daddy chuckled.

"You might change that tune once you get there. They stay in there all day like they expect Jesus to stop by and they don't want to miss him," Daddy said.

World of Friends Church was in a former Dollar General out on the ass end of Hamilton County. Sherry counted eight parking spaces. No wonder the parking lot was always full. She walked in behind her mama and immediately realized two things. One, she was the only person wearing a mask. Two, every car must have had eight occupants because the building was packed. There was one jug of what she figured was either hand sanitizer or moonshine on a small table near the entrance. Sherry got a hit from her own personal bottle in her back pocket.

"I'm gonna stay back here. I really don't want to get too close to anyone," Sherry said. Her mama didn't argue. They had reached a truce of sorts. Sherry knew the negotiations and cajoling would resume when they got home but for now, they both agreed to disagree silently.

A group of older folks sans masks walked out onto the stage behind the pulpit. Sherry recognized a few of them but some of them were strangers to her. A few white ladies and one Hispanic gentleman. She saw Sue Ann Tompkins on the electronic keyboard that passed for a piano at World of Friends Church. The small choir launched into an ear-splitting rendition of "Do Not Pass Me By" that had Sherry wincing as notes were twisted, broken, and completely missed. She thought it would be funny if it wasn't so sad.

After two more abysmal songs an older Black gentleman rose from his aluminum folding chair and went to the pulpit. He adjusted the mic and cleared his throat. Then he coughed. And coughed again. Sherry almost turned and ran out of the building. She almost believed she could see the virus floating in the air like bits of silk waiting to light on her face or in her eyes. It was crazy, she knew that but seeing the old man cough and cough and cough again made her crazy.

"Now...I present to others and introduce to some our esteemed man of God, Rev. Ellis Weldon!" the old man said. A short compact brother came from behind some cheap curtains and strode to the pulpit. Sherry guessed he was about ten years older than her so that put him around forty something. The way her mama talked about him, she had expected a combination of Idris Elba and The Rock. That was not the case. Not at all. Rev. Weldon was almost comically plain. Just a short stout Black man with a close-cropped fade and a pencil thin moustache that Sherry knew he trimmed himself in the mirror while he talked to his reflection.

"I say, I say, who is here to praise the Lord?" Rev. Weldon boomed. Even his voice disappointed. It wasn't deep or rich with the traditional southern Baptists cadence. It was whispery as winter rain. To compensate for this lack of bass Rev. Weldon tried to project from his chest but it ended up sounding like he was howling like a baboon.

This the guy that got you to leave Galilee? Sherry thought.

"So good to see all your smiling faces today! We don't need no masks in the Lord's house amen? The only protection we need is the blood of the Lamb! Jesus is my doctor, my consoler, my hope, and my divine righteousness amen!?" Rev. Weldon yelled. Sherry had to admit what he lacked in looks and vocal talent he made up in stage presence. He was running from one side of the raggedy dais with palpable enthusiasm.

"Oh no…Oh no sister, sister in the back. Can I ask you to take off that mask so we can all see your beautiful smile? That God-given smile that the Lord gave you to share with the world?" Rev. Weldon asked. Sherry shook her head but didn't speak.

"Oh, come on now, sister. I know you might have seen all the news people telling you how terrible this here pandemic is, but I know someone who can wipe away that Covid with one sweep of his hand. He's the Alpha and the Omega. He's the Lamb of God. He's the Bright Morning Star. We call him Emmanuel! We call him the Great I Am. We call him JESUS!!!" Rev. Weldon screamed.

The hair on the back of Sherry's neck rose like zombies about to wander the countryside. The entire congregation had turned to stare at her. Well, she had a surprise for them. People staring at her were her bread and butter.

Look all you want. I ain't taking this fucking mask off, Sherry thought.

They stared at her for nearly three minutes before Rev. Weldon went on with the services.

Later in the parking lot as they were about to leave, Rev. Weldon strolled over to her mama's car. He smiled at them, and Sherry noticed her mama shiver like she'd taken a shot of tequila.

"Joy, you can't go until you've introduced me to this young lady. This has to be your daughter, Sherry," Rev. Weldon said. He held out his hand. Sherry kept her hands in the pockets of her jeans.

"I've kinda took a sabbatical from hand shaking for a while, Reverend," Sherry said.

"I understand your concern, but I've found the best precaution we can take is to stay prayed up. At least take down that mask. We are outside now," Rev. Weldon said.

Sherry took a deep breath and pulled down her bandanna.

"I see you take after your mama in the beauty department," Rev. Weldon said. Mama tittered and covered her mouth with her hand.

"Take after my daddy, too. I'm tall like him. He's bigger than me though. By a lot," Sherry said. Rev. Weldon smiled and nodded like her assessment of her father had been his idea.

"Will I be seeing you at Bible study Wednesday?" Rev. Weldon asked.

"No," Sherry said. The finality of it seemed to sap the energy out of Rev. Weldon.

"Um…all right. You ladies have a good evening. I'll be seeing you at Bible study, won't I, Joy?" Rev. Weldon said.

It wasn't really a question.

———————

As soon as they pulled out of the parking lot Sherry went in on her mama.

"I know you ain't falling for that gnome's bullshit, right?" Sherry asked.

"Sherry! Watch your mouth. Rev. Weldon is an anointed man of God," Mama said.

"Rev. Weldon is a horny little bastard. I watched him. He made sure to say goodbye to every woman at church. He ain't say shit to the men. And that 'oh you're as beautiful as your mama' thing. What was that all about? He full of it, Mama, you know that right?" Sherry asked.

"I don't know anything like that, Sherry! Rev. Weldon is a good man doing good works. He is trying to start a soup kitchen with the Catholics over in Red Hill County. He's working getting a day care started at the church. And if he's nice to me once and while, well what's wrong with that? He's kind. He's a kind man. Not everyone understands that but then again snakes don't understand why everyone don't bite," Mama said.

She was gripping the steering wheel so tight Sherry thought she could hear it cracking.

———————

By Tuesday Sherry had a job at Tony's Italian Grill. Tony was doing carry out only, but he needed help. People were buying carry out dinners so they wouldn't have to go to the grocery store. A few food delivery services had popped up in town from the same seeds that had brought Uber and Lyft. Wednesday night Sherry was on her way to work when her mama was packing up to go to Bible study. Sherry was shoving a peanut butter sandwich in her mouth as her mama was putting the final touches on a chocolate cake. Sherry went to stick her finger in the luxurious icing when her mother smacked her hand. Hard.

"No! You been eating peanut butter. Rev. Weldon is deathly allergic to peanuts. You could put him in the hospital," Mama said.

"Might not be such a bad thing," Sherry said under her breath.

"Why you making him a cake anyway? Is it his birthday?"

"It's not his birthday. He works so hard for us I thought he deserved a nice surprise. A man needs to know people see the hard work he is doing," Mama said.

Sherry took in her mother's face. Her whole smooth dark face. She was wearing dark brown lipstick and nearly nude eye shadow. Sherry took a deep breath and inhaled a vanilla scent. Her Mama's favorite perfume was a cheap vanilla brand from Wal-Mart.

I'm not going to ask her. I'm not going to ask her because it's ridiculous and even if it's true I don't want to know, Sherry thought. She finished her sandwich and headed out the door.

"I'll see you when I get off tonight, Mama," she said as she walked out the door.

———————

She was done at Tony's by eleven. Her daddy let her use his truck to drive out to Route 832 where Tony's sat at the intersection of Tow Truck Lane and Pig Mouth Road. Sherry expected to see her mama's little Toyota in its normal parking spot when she got off from work smelling like salami and ham and marinara sauce.

There were only the well-worn tire tracks in the red-yellow sandy soil that covered most of Hamilton County. Sherry got out and went in the house. Her daddy was asleep in his recliner, an empty bottle of beer on the floor between his feet.

An hour later after she had roused her daddy and sent him to bed, her mother came in the door. For the briefest of moments Sherry considered how their roles were suddenly brutally reversed from her teenage years.

"That must have been one hell of a Bible study," Sherry said. Her mama didn't respond, didn't look at her. She hurried past Sherry and into the bedroom.

I'm not going to ask. I'm not going to ask her, Sherry thought. She repeated it over and over again in her mind like a mantra.

Not going to ask.

Not going to ask.

Not going to ask.

———————

Her mother started coughing a week later. At first it was a dry hack reminiscent of when you got a popcorn hull stuck in your throat. As the week wore on it got wetter, more viscous. She ached so bad she had to call off of work for the first time in five years. The factory worked on a piecemeal structure. The more crab meat you picked and packaged the more you made. You didn't work, you didn't get paid.

"Mama, you have to get tested," Sherry said.

"I'm...okay...just...a ...bad ...cold," her mama wheezed.

"Mama, you got a hundred-and-two-degree temperature. You been going to that weekly super spreader event. Please go to the doctor. Please," Sherry begged.

"Rev. Weldon said—"

"FUCK REV. WELDON!!" Sherry howled. "Mama, you are sick. You need to go to the doctor. Rev. Weldon can't help you," Sherry said. Her mama was lying on the couch. She turned her head toward Sherry. Her eyes were red as cherries.

"He...is...a good...man," her mama wheezed.

"Mama, he isn't a good man because he is nice to you. Snakes don't understand why everybody don't bite but sometimes a deer don't understand why everybody don't run for their life." Her mother turned her face toward the couch.

A week later Mama was in ICU.

A week after that, Daddy began to cough.

Uncle Jess got it next. Then his daughter, Sherry's cousin Carlene.

By the end of the month, they were all in ICU.

Sherry could talk to her daddy through the FaceTime feature the hospital set up. He had a canula in his nose and his once solid shoulders had withered from bowling balls to brittle coconuts. Mama couldn't talk. She was on a ventilator.

"You know something? I was a little jealous of you when you went off with that band. You got to see the world. I ain't never been nowhere but Baltimore a few times and a couple of trips to New York," Daddy said. It took a lot out of him to talk but he channeled all his strength into these conversations.

"When you get out of there we'll take a vacation. Go see Mount Rushmore or something," Sherry said. She breathed in and let it out slowly. That was a calming technique Tyler had taught her to calm herself down before a show. She used it now to keep from bursting into ever-flowing tears.

"Nah...not Mount Rushmore. I wanna see the Grand Canyon. I used to talk to your mama about it. It was gonna be our fiftieth anniversary trip. Guess we shouldn't have waited," Daddy said.

"You gonna go. Soon as the doctor let you out of here, you gonna go," Sherry said. Her daddy was looking at her through the tablet the nurse was holding for him. He was staring into her eyes.

"If something happens—"

"It won't."

"If something happens. Don't let Rev. Weldon preach my funeral," Daddy said.

That was the closest they ever came to talking about it.

Mama died the next day.

Daddy died two days after that.

By the end of the week Uncle Jess and Carlene were gone too.

Sherry talked to the rest of the family, and they all decided to have the memorial service at Galilee. They lined up the four urns on four separate plant stands. Sherry told the funeral home to keep it to immediate family only. She half expected Rev. Weldon to show up anyway. His slick voice moving like crude oil over the phone lines informing her that her mama had signed over all her and her daddy's life insurance policies to him and the World of Friends Church had the air of a man who'd come to a service he most assuredly wasn't welcome.

When she got up from her seat to sing the elegy, she scanned the scant crowd, but he wasn't anywhere to be seen. There were seven other funerals for members of World of Friends Church going on across the county. The good reverend must have been busy. Sherry wondered how many of those members had signed over their insurance and houses and bank accounts.

As she began to sing "Precious Lord," she decided she didn't care.

That's it.

I lost my whole family in a month. World of Friends lost a total of twenty-five members. They ended up closing up two months later. Rev. Weldon?

He died too. Not from covid though.

For a man with a nut allergy, he sure didn't seem to mind eating brownies with peanuts in them. I heard when the sheriff found him his face was so swollen, they had to identify him by his fingerprints. He'd been in some trouble up north so his prints was in the system. Ain't that some shit? A con man comes to little ol' Hamilton County thinking he gonna clean up and that's where he ends dying like a poisoned dog. Laying on the floor gasping for breath like a fucking trout on the dock just like my mama and my daddy did.

What? How do I know how he died?

You know small towns.

People talk too much. They trust too much.

Sometimes they don't even know who they letting in their house ya know?

Can I get another light?

The Tour Guide's Tale

By Anna Tambour

"No thank you. I can't stomach s'mores. but hey, you dig in. This reminds me of another group, another tour guide, if you wanna hear. He had been a colleague of mine in grad school, and could have been your guide, but for . . ."

Her pause is half-dramatic, half hilarious. She's four and half feet in hiking boots, and wears her hair in two long braids. Her cheekbones are high and sharp and honed in the dancing firelight. And her eyes, two coals under a broad brow riven by one long crease, a feature that only a hairnet worn all day can carve.

"Well, this tour guide, Pete, wasn't so lucky as me and you. He worked for a company called Bucket Travel, the meanest, skinflintiest varmint of an operator in the industry. But Bucket was good at one thing. It had cornered the intelligent market. Like you all, its clients wanted to see the sights. They hadn't been starved like you for years, but they *were* hungry. And like your tour guide in me at least, Bucket got ridiculous value. Pete and my doctorate bills need constant feeding, and neither he nor I were, *am*, in the position to get enough grant money to--sorry. You carrying on with your phones. Divorce or separate, if you aren't inviting murder, thank you. So this Dr. Pete Wittich. One fine, pre-freak-times day, he was served up a group that wasn't like you lot. This one was weird. There was one gentleman who was booked in as "B. Fullbright" but was anything but.

"Dr. Wittich had just arrived, by foot, at the Motel 4 where he was waiting at the assembly point of next group, when he was politely accosted by a man with a creased face who explained himself unbelievably with the line but lowered his shades to allow his eyes to meet Wittich's. They locked in sympathy or empathy, and it was true love when at his next breath, the gov guy uttered the words: 'Doctor Fulbright is a fake.' Standing in the sharp but dingy four o'clock shadow cast by the Motel 4 sign, Sam Cardicle, the gov guy, clued Wittich in beyond what Bucket Travel knew or cared to know. The tour guide and the bureaucrat commiserated over the fact that honesty pays cowpats as the official talked ruefully about treating them both to a Macca's *Cappuccino* at an air-conditioned table. As if he had the budget, and they had the time.

"The story Sam told Pete riled them both. B. Fullbright, PhD. was as real as the antiquities sold by Sadigh Gallery Ancient Art. What? See me later. Anyway, this Fullbright cat was really a guy related to a guy with a famous face. The famous-face guy was his great-grandfather. But Sam and Pete's guy only flashed the famous last name followed by III. That had usually been enough for him, for it had enough trimmings. Just as Sam was finishing giving the Pete the skinny on the guy, the man himself was dropped off, and Sam skedaddled, but not before spitting at the sight of the perp: 'I could live for a year on what his must hair costs a week.' 'Huh,' grunted Sam. 'You don't have to work for grants. Coming!' he yelled, waving. 'Or for this.' And he was right. I can confirm his thinking, so if you can remember this at the end of your trip . . . So in no time, tour guide Pete and his little tour group weren't gathered around no cozy campfire eating s'mores like y'all, but instead, were sitting on the patch of astroturf greening a motel that offers a coin operated massage chair and whose air conditioners could be guaranteed to keep you up all night.

"Another member of his tour group was a Mr. Palancia, a man who Dr. Wittich couldn't hardly hide his repulsion of, for Mr. Palancia was practically doubled up on the fake grass, a permanent scowl on his mug. His baggy grandpa jeans hijacked Dr. Pete's attention, for the man stunk to Pike's Peak.

"As Pete told me, the guy's crotch made his skin crawl, for it was clear that the man needed his colostomy bag emptied. He looked almost pregnant, and at every move he made, and he was a fidgeter, his lap seemed to squirm all the more baggily. And to make matters worse, this Mr. Palancia wore more lashings of Old Spice than Marilyn Monroe did Chanel, and the rumors of her and lack of underpants and ensuing smells were . . . Sir, you've only to read.

"So, to make matters even worse--this was in the mask-mandated time--Mr. Palancia's purple nose hung over the top . . . Sorry, not. We are all adults here, but if you insist.

"Mrs. Palancia wore her mask as if she was in an operating theatre, Her head was bent over a much-pawed hardback titled *Over the Edge,: Death in Grand Canyon, the gruesome collection of fatal mishaps.*

"And next to her was a hunk named something like Buck Stepp, a poor sap who introduced himself as a bounty hunter, a good line of distraction but powerless against his Mount Kilauea of a face.

"Worse still, unlike y'all who've come from near and far and can wander off any time you wish, this little group was stuck to each other for a week, because that's what they paid for, and they all couldn't afford not to get their money's worth--and they, none of them, knew if when they ended their trip, they would live to go to another. So they had a mandated story session, nothing organic like this. But the first minutes had been wasted on sniping and sneering.

" 'Come now,' Pete had to chide. 'You've all paid for this trip of a lifetime, so let's not spoil our dreams with these petty interruptions and gloom. Tomorrow, we're catching the first dawn in the most amazing site you'll ever see, prepared for you by Nature over six million years. You'll clap your eyes on Hermit's Rest and the Orphan Lode Mine. Over the next days you'll learn about the people who . . .'

"Yeah. Blah blah blah. I don't know why they give him that script. Everyone's attention didn't just glaze. It congealed. So he cut to the next part, only going off track a bit, though he wished he could order them to be air-dropped at Malagosa Crest this moonless night. Of course, they were nothing like *you.*

" 'And we'll be together,' he continued, 'for another six unforgettable morns. So let's do something different now. Let's tell each other a story.'

"He was very cheesed off by one of the guests who'd just asked him if they could make a side-trip to Tuweep, a sore spot, for Dr. Wittich's thesis had been a continuation of some seminal study done when cheesewhiz was new, on, of all things, the rodents in that neck of the woods. And he resented like hell that no one was funding his valuable research. He, we, we're not even living on minimum wage, as we work for tips. When we work. Sorry. So Pete asked the woman who'd asked to see Tuweep to tell the first story. He thought he'd have her there. But she only answered with 'A story I wrote or just something that I observed?' at which the one who loved to get under her skin for she was beautiful but not offeringly so. As I was saying. The one who had already badgered her about keeping her mask on, wanting her to take it off, the one who couldn't stop touching his hair, the fake himself, said 'Tuweep,' and laughed, looking Pete eye to eye, gauging him, then quailing.

"For something in Pete's eyes gave Pete away. And it's time you knew too. This so-called Fullbright, PhD was sentenced to the tour by a judge known for creative justice. For 'criminal arrogance' (an imperturbable pattern of speeding and not paying tickets, intimidating wait staff, and picking fights with short people) this buffalo patty earned not only to that rock-base budget tour, but to write on his return, a ten-thousand word report due within thirty days, with pictures. Title and subject: *Darkling Beetles of the Grand Canyon,* not a word of which was to be gleaned from the Internet or any online or phone communications or personal or commercial visitations, from which he had been banned until the report was received, reviewed, and approved by the judge in consultation with park entomologists and a plagiarism zealot.

"So Pete waggled a finger mischievously at the guy and said, 'Darkling,' and 'Please do tell,' to the woman who bothered them both and who furthermore mysteriously, wore a sexless shirt emblazoned with Purina. Pete was subsequently said to have said confidentially that he'd hoped she'd packed a t-shirt and would fall into the Colorado.

"But what is undisputed is that she steepled her fingers, maddeningly composed and began: 'There was a dog who belonged to the most important person in town.'

" 'Let us guess,' the privileged perp sneered. 'The mayor.' "

" 'A garbage collector, name of Fred,' she said, unperturbed. 'And his dog was a mongrel straight out of mongrel-casting school. His or her ears each had its own mind. The dog had three coats, all worn at the same time, and each as color-challenged as the next. It could demolish a turkey carcass without a single bone piercing its insides, and it was more lovable than a day is certain to be followed by another. In short, it was the most perfect dog in town, though it cost the garbageman nothing but the effort of rescuing it after the Christmas season where the scrap of bones and fur was lying close to death after being poisoned for living off garbage cans where it had been thrown away as an unwanted gift.

" '*Finally*,' said turd the third. 'She can breathe. I thought the sentence would never end.'

" 'So, the dog?' Kilauea leaned forward, having forgotten to pick at his face.

" 'The dog found its true love in that garbageman,' quipped Stinky.

" 'And they lived happily ever after," laughed turd the third, his perfect teeth flashing.

" 'If you don't shut the fuck up!' burst Kilauea. His rivuleted face glowed, the peaks of his pimples capped with white. His fists were clenched, and he rose halfway up. Only then did his anatomy show: under the pimples which covered him like a yakuza's tattoos, he was pure muscle. His butt muscles excreted a pamphlet from his back pocket. He shoved it in before Pete could see because Pete had to deal the privilege perp again--put the guy into his place for good.

" 'Sir,' he Pete, 'There is a no-refund release for us if you cannot control yourself. Please continue, ma'am.' Turd the third opened his mouth to smart-ass but shut it. Instead, he stuck out his long wrinkled-linen-clad legs as if he was lounging at the Four Seasons, the benighted Pete and the group, in another dimension.

" 'This dog,' said the woman Pete thought of as Mother Purina. 'Remember Joplin? That town flattened in 2011? Well, this town didn't make the news, partly because it was only topped like a soft-boiled egg, and partly because there was no place to get coffee.

" 'People made garbage at the usual rate, however, so the garbageman picked it up once a week and took it to the dump where the road into town should have been. The garbageman's dog was always at his side, buckled up in the offsider's seat. When not at work, they lived at the dump and would have lived happy ever after, but for the twister.

" 'It came with no warning, at least none anyone paid attention to. And every house in the place got the same treatment, save the garbageman's because he didn't have a proper house. The others had their tops blown off so clean, if the town were shrunk, they could have been playhouses, since you could easily put furniture into them, and what was there, suddenly exposed, was a sight.'

A commotion made the woman stop. It went, if I remember correctly, like this:

Mr. Palancia was more than usually wriggly seated like the rest of them, on that patch of mangy motel astroturf by the chainlinked swimming pool. 'Didn't you say to wait here for dinner?' he whined.

" 'It's coming,' Pete assured him.

" 'Please continue,' someone said to the woman in a voice that could have clipped brass nails.

" 'Pizza?' Mr. Panancia demanded.

" 'Yes,' said Pete patiently.

" 'I don't eat anchovies," said Mr. Palancia.

" 'Who does?" Pete was reported as saying.

" 'We didn't come for the food. Please,' said Kilauea to Mother Purina. This is the moment that not only Pete was reported to have noticed the spark of love.

"The Purina woman continued, however. whether acting oblivious or being so, a matter of fierce debate. 'And the problem,' she continued, 'with every house in the town being sliced open, all twenty-two of them, all built before people stopped building basements, is that every house had closets, and in those closets.'

"At this point, she put her hands into her hair had looked like a pile of stuck mud after what must have been a long day in a hairnet. And she drew her hands down, releasing a torrent of hair. In her hand were two bobby pins that she put in her mouth. She twirled her hair back up, pinning it all back close.

" 'In those closets?' asked Mrs. Palancia. Her book now lay on her lap.

" 'There's the rub,' smiled Mother Purina, smiling as if she didn't realise she looked like a madonna. 'You'd think,' she said, 'that everyone in town would rush for newsmen to infest the place like flies, drones to thicken the air with their wings, and senators and the governor fight over who's the real deliverer of the rain of government manna to come.'

" 'You *would*,' rasped Kilauea.

" 'But no,' she said. 'The town could have been the head of a frightened turtle. Except for Fred and his dog, Cat.'

" 'Kilauea's eyes were round and green and innocent as grapes. 'His real name?' he asked.

" 'Of *course*,' said Mother Purina. 'Why would I make that up? Cat was descended, like Fred, from experts in his field. Cat's jowls were as pronounced as an old-time newsman's, and his nose just as nosey. If he could've talked, Fred and him would have been all too terrifying, but the combination kept the peace, a godsend to the town for with them, there was no need to pay for police, and no sheriff to come nosing around.'

" 'Sorry,' interrupted Mrs. Palancia, 'Didn't you say this town wasn't big enough to be a town? Wasn't it too small to have anything worth reporting?'

"Mother Purina stuck up a thumb, and winked. Mrs. Palancia seems satisfied, or something. Her response was reported to be a grin that flattened into a line thin as a dried worm.

" 'So, as I was saying' said Mother Purina. 'Fred and Cat were a team, and as a team, they were first on the scene after the devastation. They didn't have a drone so couldn't have seen that the top story of every house had been sliced off, and the ground floor exposed, but with all the new fresh air whooshed into the houses, the inside breath of every one of those fine homes was suddenly released. And there were revelations in that wealth of breaths that even Fred had never suspected.'

" 'He's only the garbageman, goddammit,' Mr. Palancia exploded. 'You'd think he was a pastor.'

"Mrs. Palancia chortled. A reportedly unpleasant sound--like that of a punctured bicycle tire being put upon a winding mile from home. Just at that moment of chortle, the courier arrived. He looked hot and harassed above his mask and behind his helmet. Pete, quite irresponsibly, just accepted the order without checking anything. The courier left immediately, tipless, beaten yet tied to the clock.

"Pete's flock was, blessedly early in the tour, already tamed by their hunger. He laid the spread out on the astroturf: vegan left, meat right. Or the other way. 'They look exactly the same,' said one of the group. 'That's the art,' said Mrs. Palancia.

"Bucket knew its clients. These dug in with no room in their mouths for whining. *Promise laid-on food, but get 'em hungry enough, they're grateful for anything whenever.* That was in the guidelines, along with the reminder of the sales pitch: 'You're a *real* explorer, not some body traveling to eat.'

Pete ate bravely, as he planned to throughout the week. Bucket had a deal these "food" providers, all firms that went through staff diarrheally. Like on the savanna, within moments, the pizza had almost disappeared.

Mrs. Palancia leaned back on her hips and spread her arms out. Her husband was too busy reaching for the last slice to notice that she was looking at him as though at some rainbow.

" 'The last supper,' she said. And she was right. The photo Pete took proves it. That group's spread was a tableaux, and her husband was dead center.

" 'The revelations?' Kilauea reminded Mother Purina. Those two had finished first, he only drinking a diet Pepsi, and she, eating one slice of pizza that she grabbed absent-mindedly and ate like a cow chews cud, eyes half closed, mind somewhere else, deep.

" ' Revelations?' she said, shaking herself like a bagged chicken leg in a shake 'n bake. 'Oh, the skeletons you mean?'

" 'Skeletons!' someone cried out.

" 'In their closets!' turd the third mocked, alone.

" 'Quite unlike the one *Yomiuri Shimbun* reported in 2012,' continued Mother Purina. Pete never *could* remember her real name, and I don't know it all, but it was, reportedly, Skelton. Doctor F. Skelton. 'That skull found in Japan,' she explained, 'was partly covered by a blanket, skull resting neatly on a pillow. The skeletons Cat sniffed out weren't lying down.'

"Kilauea's eyes glowed. If only Dr. Skelton had had a scarf to throw him, he would have lassoed and jumped on a T-rex bareback, and ridden it till it had to plucked enough daisies, with its teeth, to make a bouquet for that woman, though for all he knew, she was a only a factory worker . . . at Purina's, no less, turning out dog kibble.

" ' Ohh,' he shivered, without knowing it.

"Her eyes crinkled at him. 'Yes, indeed,' she said. 'And it wasn't just one skeleton that Cat sniffed out. In fact, so many houses in the town had skeletons in closets that Cat was confused, for Fred had no skeletons for Cat. Never had. The most Fred had ever given Cat in the way of bones was the soup bone he got once a week from his trip to Piggly Wiggly. Fred had no fridge at his little lean-to at the dump, so he had to make the trip that often, for he didn't want Cat to get old bones. As for him, he ate out of cans, sharing them with Cat, of course.

"But bones are bones. They don't need meat to be attractive. And Cat had never imagined anyone having a whole closet for bones, let alone so many that were related, one to another.

"Suddenly, he felt a keen sense of something he'd been missing. He looked at Fred, old whiskery Fred who'd tried so hard to give him a good life, but who was, Cat had to admit once these new revelations tinted his appreciation of Fred's complex scent--a failure.

" 'Why else would you be just the garbageman?' he thought at Fred, shoving his nose into that oblivious hand. Fred, thick Fred, fondled his ears and massaged his head and neck, as he just thought Cat wanted a pet.

" 'It's okay. It really is,' Mother Purina, Dr. Skelton, that woman who seemed oblivious of so much, was reported to have said, patting Kilauea's hand. 'Don't worry,' she told him, pulling out a bottle. 'I'm quadruple-vaxxed and here's some disinfectant.'

" 'So what did Cat do?' demanded Mrs. Palancia.

" 'Who?' said Dr. Skelton. 'Oh, Cat. He sat in front of the house with the biggest skeleton smell, lifted his head, and howled. Now no one, not even Cat knew that Cat's great great, great grandma had lived by the Missouri River up in South Dakota. Unlike Cat, she was an unprotected gray wolf weighed down by the label *predator/varmint*. And she was a true lone ranger with no home, no companions, so she never could enjoy a good howl. Cat didn't know he had it in him till that first howl snuck up his throat and flew out.

"Then he couldn't hold them in. Fred never knew the dog had it in him. Nor did the neighbors, nor anyone on the next block. And though everyone in the town was in their own states of shock, this alarm set up by Cat made them fly to his side and barrel up to Cat sitting on his haunches at the front door of that house.

"And when they opened the door that he was pawing, a whole family of skeletons poured out, one on top of another. There was daddy skeleton, mommy skeleton, and even one of a thumb-sucking toddler. Their bones were strung together like Christmas popcorn strands, but that was nothing to Cat, whose jaws had made nothing of the joints in tossed toaster ovens, the handlebars in worn-out trikes, that solid block of ice that someone threw out one post-Christmas: a new recipe for aspic made from gravy.

" 'Skeletons!' shouted a neighbor. 'So what,' said the owner, whose hair was still festooned with pieces of wall and window. He tried to be nonchalant, but he *had* souvenired them from his faculty when he was booted out for getting to retirement age.

" 'They're teaching materials,' " he announced haughtily. 'What's your excuse?'

"But the crowd had already moved on, for For Cat had struck again. His paws this time were not so polite. The neighbor's closet under the stairs that ended at nothing gaped at top and sides now, as out sprawled not only a human head sporting a brown shoulder-length wig, but a tailor's dummy wearing a blue and white polka dress of the 1950s with an enameled butterfly pin fluttering over its capacious bust.

" 'Grandma!' screamed the neighbor, kicking at Cat.

" 'Grrrr,' " thought Cat, but backed away, yellow eyes gleaming.

"The *next* householder who kicked Cat was not so lucky, for Cat's fang caught in an eyelet, and blood dripped out onto Cat's excited snout.

"And within a half hour, everything in that known world was topsy. Fred *had* been the most important in the town, for garbage tells. He'd known, for instance, that Yisabel wasn't ND's daughter, but H's. He'd known the real reason the door-to-door donut salesman had to skip this town. He'd known who the real blond in town was, from the bagged bathroom shavings.

"He thought he knew everything, till that day of Revelation. And Cat thought himself Fred's dog, for Cat was a conservative at heart.

"If only Fred had thought to give Cat a corpse to chew on. As Fred and the town learned, it didn't need to be fresh.

" 'And that,' said Dr. Skelton to the group, rolling her fine shoulders in that shapeless Purina shirt, 'is the end of my story.'

"Mrs. Palancia perched her glasses on her nose again and took up her book.

"Mr. Palancia clutched his crotch, and Pete was just thinking how he could insist the man go to the bathroom when that terrible crotch convulsed, and . . . a ferret! Yes, out erupted a ferret, a undesexed male, the animal known to make pigs faint. He grabbed for it but it leapt with with the speed of a zit exploding. The ferret shot out over the astroturf, past the Motel 4 sign, straight onto the highway.

" 'I *told* you,' said Mrs. Palancia, dogearing a page.

"The end. Thank you for listening, those who did," says the little tour guide.

"But you didn't finish," says another guide.

"They don't wanna know."

"Yes we do!"

"I know already!" shouts a woman in a crisp pinstriped shirt. "Isn't that the tour where someone died from choking on a spine of an Arizona Fishhook Pincushion?"

"Oh my God! In his s'more."

"Now *that's* the end," said someone sitting just far enough from the fire to be a confusing silhouette.

Every Form of Person

By J. A. W. McCarthy

I've had a million opportunities to spit her out.

From the tiny town in the Cascades where her mother handed me her soul, to the northeastern corner of Oregon, to the pale, quiet fissures I cleft through Idaho and Utah, I had opportunities in every rest stop bathroom, highway diner, and motel room that dotted my journey. Instead, I held her in. Every cough, every sneeze, I clamped my mouth shut even as I feared the sickness had finally sunk hooks into me, too. I kept my words lean and relied on polite nods when I knew my emotions would overtake me. I swallowed down that gas station hotdog that repeatedly fought its way back up and delayed my trip for a day. One way or another, she could've killed me. I let the tears fill my mouth until I thought I'd choke, rather than release her.

Like the first inhale of asthma medication, I clung to Asa, willing her deep into my lungs where she would be safe, where she could disperse and flow through me. I did my job, kept my promise, and carried her. My literal ride or die.

Really, what I should've done was spit her out onto the yard in front of her childhood home. I should've let all that remained of her dry there atop the gravel and grass after what her mother said to me.

The last time I saw Asa in person was on the eve of our county's first lockdown. Sunday night, just three hours before all nonessential businesses were to shutter for two weeks, and the bar we were at was packed. Every table, bar stool, every inch of floor space was cluttered with people laughing, yelling, spit flying, breathing into each other's open mouths, eyes, and noses. There'd been talk on the news of particles, an aerosol virus, our lungs and tissues vulnerable sponges with no recourse but to welcome the invasion. Other just as loud, just as conflicting voices shrugged it off as "just the flu." I hadn't thought about it much back then, not like I do now. All I saw was Asa, and the empty seat across from her at the tiny high-top she'd managed to snag, and what I felt was relief.

"I don't know if I can wait until the fall," she said, once I was settled with a drink in hand. Though the same warm smile Asa had greeted me with still lingered on her face, her fingers squeezing and releasing her pint glass over and over again told a different story.

"They said two weeks," I assured her. "We haven't even bought the plane tickets yet. We can go in late April, early May."

"A virus isn't going to magically go away in a couple of weeks. It's not safe to get on a plane."

"Then we'll drive."

Asa's gaze abruptly darted to the bar. She squeezed her eyes shut and forced her lungs into a deep breath. All I saw were the two bartenders scurrying between rows of glasses and bottles, but I knew what she'd seen there: the same hungry shadow that had been stalking her since she was a child.

Hungry because every year it took another little bit of her, piece by piece. A little strength, a little clarity, a little of the fire that had drawn me to her twelve years ago. She'd been a painter and a jeweler then, before the shadow stole her dexterity. We would stay up all night laughing, talking, before the shadow leadened her limbs and pressed her body into her bed. Every year, the shadow bit a little harder, took a little more. It left its mark on her, forcing her fingers to scratch an endless outline of her body for every nibble it took. No one saw the shadow, so no one believed her. I needed nothing more than the wet hollow of fear and defeat in her eyes to trust what she told me.

"We will get there this year, I promise," I told her. "It'll be just the two of us in my car. Even if there's no vaccine, they'll know more by the fall. We'll know how to stay safe. We can isolate."

Asa polished off her beer and offered a small smile to her empty glass. "You know you don't have to go with me, Gilly. You've done enough. Too much. I can't ask anymore of you."

In the last six years we'd been all over the country, visiting the places that she believed might finally shake the shadow loose from her soul. She'd leaned back as far as she could over the observation deck railing at Snoqualmie Falls. She'd screamed her throat raw at the Badlands Overlook. She'd lain in the dunes of White Sands. Dipped her toes and washed her mind clean in the Great Salt Lake. At each place, she'd sent her mother a series of scenic photos without telling her the real reason we were there. I'd watched, hoped with every breath same as her, held her the next day when the shadow reappeared, its gloating maw gripping her even tighter in the wake of failure.

Each trip was carefully planned, each destination researched and confirmed as vibrating at a numerical value that matched or complimented the Chaldean value of her name. She had to go with me because my name—Gillian—was a seventeen and combined we made the most powerful number of all, twenty-two. "Together, we're a fucking master number—if that can't save me, nothing will," she would proclaim on late nights when we'd had too much to drink. Her arm around me, her face buried in my neck as the shadow weighed down on her head, she would talk about going to the next sacred place where she would not only be unburdened but be reborn. Hope diminished as the list dwindled, but she swore she wouldn't give up. We still had the Grand Canyon National Park, the last place left in the US.

I wouldn't allow myself to ask what we would do if she couldn't excise the shadow there.

"You gotta hang on, okay?" I said, trying to catch her gaze. When her eyes finally locked onto mine, I knew I had her, just like she had me all those times I had nowhere to go. "A few months. I'm with you all the way and I'll get you to the Grand Canyon. Together, we're powerful, remember? We'll take a week off work and—"

Asa's laugh was a bitter, rueful huff. "They're planning for us to be back in the office in two weeks, whether this shit is over or not. If it hadn't been for this order from the governor... I mean, I do fucking data entry. Real essential. You know I have to fight for a sick day in that place. If I say I can't come in because of a pandemic, there's no way in hell they'll let me take a vacation."

I wished she could quit her job, that the health insurance she needed didn't keep her tied to that terrible place. I wished I could offer her a job with me. But carrying the souls of the dead is more of a birthright than an occupation.

"And if what they're saying on the news is true...you'll be busier than ever," she added with another dry, joyless hum.

It was a worst-case scenario in my mind, but I knew she was right. In the few weeks since this virus had come to our attention, hundreds of people had already died in nursing homes and hospitals and other crowded places where there was no respite. I'd gotten three requests to carry the souls of the dead in the past week alone, but I'd turned them all down as the world closed up tight and the virologists warned us of what was to come. I wouldn't put myself in this kind of unknown danger, no matter how much I needed the money.

Focused on me, Asa reached across the table and pulled my hand into hers. Her skin was cool, a little wet from her glass, whorls of texture spiking against my fingers, as electric as all those nights she'd steadied my shaking shoulders in the wake of rotten boyfriends and lost jobs and every failure that was solely mine. Had we known then, deep down, the powerful number we made when we were together?

"I'll be okay. I'm just being dramatic," she said, offering a rare hopeful smile. "I've lived with this thing my whole life, so what's another few months, right? Now, can we talk about something else?"

A man bumped our table, his apology too close to my face. People threaded through the narrow channels between tables, yelling, laughing, so unbelievably open as if they hadn't seen the news reports, the shaky guidance from our local officials. Asa remained fixed on me as if I were the only thing keeping her afloat, and I scrambled to come up with a funny story from my day or a new TV show we could talk about. But whatever I had was not enough. I could tell by the set of her shoulders—hunched yet rigid—that the shadow had sealed itself to her bones, and she was steeled to carry it yet another night as she always had.

––––––––––––

When I get a job, it's a referral. Always. The souls I've carried to a favorite local beach or to ancestral land halfway across the world—months later their bereft might whisper to a grieving friend or acquaintance that I can do the same for their loved one, and I get a text or call knotted in tears and cash promises. I've kept souls in the safety of my mouth on airplanes and trains, long hikes up to vistas I never thought I'd see. In moments of fear or surprise, when I doubted my own reflexes, I've swallowed a soul like so much phlegm to protect it, then forced my fingers down my throat when I reached my destination. My gift has shown me the world and every form of person I could taste.

In my mouth, Asa tastes the way a snuffed-out candle smells: charred fibers, smoke gummed against my teeth, the bald softness of wax cracking under a dusting of soot. I first taste it after checking into the inn just a couple miles' walk from the Grand Canyon's South Rim. Asa moves from the safe pocket between my gums and the inside of my cheek, rolling over my molars before pouring into the cradle of my tongue. It's not like in the other motels that dotted this journey, the nights she coated the back of my throat in a thick film the same as a seasonal sickness that sticks your lips together, something foul and faint and just out of reach. It's not like on the road, where she nestled in my sinuses and let me enjoy the blandness of stale french fries and endless cups of drive-thru coffee. In the privacy of my room, at the end of our journey, she wants me to taste her as she really is.

I did taste Asa in life, once. I was crying in her embrace—another failure, another broken promise in a broken relationship—and as I started to speak, she shifted, the soft line of her jaw brushing my lips, my tongue. She was an expanse of flat land in mouth, and as plain as that. I remember thinking a Chaldean five like her—a person with a number that vibrated on the same frequency as some of the most sacred places on earth—would be sparks and cardamom and the divinity of lust, flavors I couldn't even comprehend. The disappointment turned to doubt then a guilt that I never quite shook. I don't know what else I should have expected.

Sitting on the creaky motel bed, I roll my tongue back and push her down my throat. She slides then catches, a lump I swallow against. I'm the vehicle, the coffin, the last and only person to know the crystallization of what once was.

The taste of charred wax lingers, a phantom of Asa burrowed into my tastebuds.

Outside the sun is setting, broad strokes of flaming orange and burnt umber, all tinged in a falling drape of violet-blue, same as every photo I've seen in books and online. As expected, it's majestic, but I close the curtains. In the dark of Room 22, surrounded by undefined and unfamiliar shapes, I can't be sure that the shadow I see moving across the opposite wall is the same shadow that stalked Asa all her life. Is this what she saw almost every day, a humanlike shape with hulking shoulders and a puffed chest, hovering in the periphery, expanding as it neared, fleshing out from hazy to opaque as it slowly, luxuriously frayed her every edge? Did it hurt—does it still hurt in this soul that I am carrying—as it gnawed at the thing it wanted most? I can't let myself think about what it means, why the shadow didn't die with her, why I now see it. I need that ambiguity, at least for tonight.

———————

Her memorial was held online. I found out last minute, via a link shared on one of her socials. A minister read bible passages that rang hollow. Pink and white lilies crowded the frame, colors Asa hated on a flower that gave her headaches. Most of the photos of her were from high school, well before I met her: flat-ironed hair, impossibly shiny lip gloss, round cheeks lifted and straining from *smiling smiling smiling*. From her living room in Asa's childhood home, her mother said a few generic words about her only child, things like "life" and "joy" and "a free spirit burdened by nothing, carried by the love she gave others." Though she shared Asa's interest in Chaldean numerology, I could tell Mrs. Lee's words were spoken for the comfort of others; there was no point in saying that despite how carefully Asa read them, the numbers failed her.

"Reeling" the wizened and bleary faces repeated in the chat afterwards. Asa had been a good daughter, so close to her mother. But no one could've known what she would do, they assured Mrs. Lee. These people were talking about a stranger, an idealized version of Asa untouched by the darkness that stalked her. When had any of them last spoken with her?

Asa had been selective about whom she told, and, as one of the few she trusted—the only one who believed her—I didn't understand why Mrs. Lee hadn't reached out to me, why the event was organized by Tricia, a childhood friend Asa had mentioned only once or twice in the time I'd known her.

The truth was, I failed Asa. There'd been our usual flurry of almost daily texting and FaceTime, but I let her "I'm okays" placate me. I sank into the relief of a smile that reached her warm brown eyes, the barbed laughter we shared lamenting the sudden dearth of toilet paper and cleaning products, "is it allergies or...?" scares, and our new status as shut ins. We doom scrolled, watched the news together, worried about our loved ones who couldn't shelter at home. She seemed to be doing okay, and I was comfortable in that delusion because I was sad and tired too. I didn't push all those times I saw the scratches along her neck and arms, the hunch of her shoulders, her posture betraying her under the shadow's weight.

"You can come over," Asa would say. "We'll keep our masks on." But I didn't. I'd carried the souls of strangers—possibly dangerous people to sometimes dangerous places—so why couldn't I risk this virus to see her?

The shadow won, and it never occurred to me that it might not die with her.

I was supposed to release Asa's soul yesterday. In the lingering humidity from a late season thunderstorm, I started the trek to Maricopa Point imagining the tourist clotted spot where I would somehow spit her soul into the golden gaping maw of the canyon unnoticed. The wind might grab her, take her all the way to the pale waters of the Colorado River. Would that be enough? Perhaps it would be better to take a shuttle to The Abyss, where I could spit her soul straight down into the canyon. She'd finally join the frequency that matched her own, the one that would shake loose the shadow once and for all.

Instead, I turned around and went back to my room, and I haven't left since. Asa's restless, sliding around in my lungs then crawling up my throat when I lie down. This time, she's not a snuffed-out candle on my tongue. When she reaches my teeth, there's an edge of bitterness, like over-steeped black tea. Once, I carried the soul of a person who'd died in a fire, and though I'd smelled smoke in my hair until I released them, they didn't taste charred as I'd expected. On my tongue they were marzipan and chamomile and bright, bright apples, the flavors of contentment. That's when I realized I was tasting the person's life, not their death.

But Asa.... Is this the shadow I taste? Is she a bitter coating of soot in my mouth because of what the shadow did to her body? When her landlord found her, Asa was in her bed, her hands and feet chewed away, her every literal edge frayed by teeth marks that the medical examiner couldn't identify. Her cheeks, her chin, shoulders, hips—all nibbled and scorched, a snack in small bites. What was left of her hair was a wet, dark rope torn from the jaws of a rabid dog.

Her mother accepted the ruling of suicide. She made it clear I never really knew her daughter.

The shadow's on the ceiling now, stretching toward me but never quite touching where my own shape begins. I'm ashamed to admit there were times—in a hug, when I'd made myself vulnerable with one drink too many, when Asa looked like there was nothing left to take—I thought the shadow might leave her and attach itself to me, but Asa knew in her bones that the shadow was bonded to only her. It follows me because she's in me, undeterred by death and searching for a body that is no more.

As long as I keep Asa in my body, she'll never be free of this thing. But if I keep her—if I wait too long and let my tissues and organs and flesh absorb her—maybe I'll finally, really know who she was.

———————————

The tidy brick rambler was nestled in a rural neighborhood thick with trees and not much else. Dark green trim and door, gauzy white curtains, the eastern corner window strung with multi-colored lights, just as Asa had described. She'd laughed about how her mother hadn't changed a thing. At every visit she'd slept in that same bed with the cowgirl print sheets, surrounded by the same books and stuffed animals that had become a bittersweet museum of her past.

Mrs. Lee came to the door before I could knock. Dressed in flow-y layers to ward off the late autumn chill, she swept me into the cozy living room and seated us in front of the fire with coffee and apologies for not having more to offer.

"Thank you for coming all the way out here," she said. "I know it was a long drive."

I wondered at what point Asa had told her mother about my job, what I can do. Had she made her mother promise to contact me, declaring her last wish, even though she knew her mother wouldn't believe her, wouldn't understand the importance of the pilgrimage? Had this been an uncomfortable conversation revisited yearly? Or was it recent, because she knew the end was near, because she knew she'd never make it to the Grand Canyon alive, because she knew I would fail her?

"I'm glad I could do it for you. For her," I said.

We chatted—briefly, awkwardly—Mrs. Lee alluding to the suicide that she was still trying to process, while I listened and was grateful for my mask covering the motions of my simmering scream. Even though I had to take off my mask, I preferred the uneasy silence that followed as we sipped our coffee. No sounds of cars, or people talking, or construction in the distance—not like in the city. The crackling fire was a murmur that might've been human if I was willing to close my eyes.

Framed photos dotted every surface, a timeline of Asa from birth to adulthood stretched from the front door to the mouth of the kitchen. Both of her parents flanked her in her childhood and preteen years; by high school it was just her mother or another teenage girl, perhaps the long-ago friend who had organized the virtual memorial. All those smiles were frozen in time, untouched by a shadow that had not yet learned to bite. I could see both why Asa ran from here and why she went back as often as she did.

"I guess I should give you my, uh…my Asa's soul now," Mrs. Lee said, rising. Her lips wavered after her words, a stoic smile determined to win.

I stood too. Asa's room was down the hall, the door open just a crack. "Would you mind…could I see her room first?" I asked.

I regretted it the moment I said it—it was an overstep; the door wasn't fully open because it had to be too painful to look into that room every day—but Mrs. Lee didn't hesitate in leading me into Asa's childhood bedroom. The bed was neatly made, vintage cowgirls with their hats and neckerchiefs peeking out over the top of the comforter. Her favorite paperbacks lined the windowsill just as she'd described, their edges stained and curled from condensation. Magazine photos of Snoqualmie Falls, Mt. Shasta, White Sands, the Great Salt Lake cluttered the scant wall space, each place we'd visited together before marking it a failure. Even as a child, she had believed these places would free her from the shadow.

The shadow must have laughed as Asa lay in that little bed, facing her every failure.

"I don't know how I'm going to fit all her stuff in here," Mrs. Lee said, glancing around wistfully. "Tricia's cleaning out her apartment and helping me put her furniture in storage, but I wanted to bring some of her clothes and personal items home. I know it's impractical, but I'm not ready to let go yet."

"Tricia?"

"Her best friend," Mrs. Lee said.

My first urge was to correct her, but I held my tongue. Parents were wrong all the time, clinging to their memories of their child as a child, not always acknowledging what they haven't witnessed. Mrs. Lee knew Tricia as Asa's childhood best friend, unaware that they hadn't kept in contact over the last twenty years. Even if Asa would've preferred that I go through her things, I couldn't be offended that Mrs. Lee had reached out to Tricia instead.

"She organized the memorial," I said.

"Yes. She's been such a great help. Tricia was trying to get Asa to the Grand Canyon. They'd been planning for months. I wish she could take her soul there—Asa would've wanted that. Tricia knew how important it was to her."

My stomach sank. The little bedroom was too crowded, too hot, Mrs. Lee's words hanging damp and bloated over my head. Though I'd always feared it, I desperately wanted to see the shadow now. I wanted to see it crawl down the wall, smear its grimy fingers over the lip-glossed, shiny-haired, *smiling smiling smiling* photo of Asa and Tricia on the vanity, reach its long fluid arms around Mrs. Lee and squeeze until her ribs splintered in front of me.

No, I wanted it to take tiny bites, to slowly, excruciatingly devour Mrs. Lee over weeks, months, years the way it had her daughter.

The coffee we'd just drank surged up the back of my throat, a bitter film that curled the sides of my tongue. "I was at the memorial," I said.

Mrs. Lee studied my face for a moment, cocking her head. "Oh, that's right. I thought you looked familiar. So, you knew my Asa?"

"A little. I'm curious...Could you tell me how you found me?"

"A friend of a friend. You carried her husband's soul to St. Augustine, I believe."

Back in the living room, Mrs. Lee gave me Asa's soul. It was a swirling orb of vapor trapped in a small jar from the funeral home, barely discernible if it wasn't for its occasional muscling against the glass. I usually asked the bereft if they could see their loved one's soul—about half could, and they often seemed to find comfort in describing the colors or textures they perceived—but I didn't care to know how Asa appeared to her mother. I was glad to get back to business, glad to drop the forced pleasantries and accommodating smile that had already been hard enough without the knowledge that I hadn't been as important a part of Asa's life as I'd thought. As hurt as I was, it was a relief to fill my mouth with Asa, to have an excuse not to talk.

The truth was, I'd intended to do it for free, carry Asa's soul to the Grand Canyon as I had promised in life. Instead, I pocketed the cash her mother handed me and slipped my mask back on. Asa rolled onto my tongue, and I wondered how she would've tasted to Tricia, if it would be the same disappointing nothing I tasted now.

"Thank you again," Mrs. Lee said as she showed me to the door. Tears choked her next words. "You're doing God's work, Gillian."

As I headed to my car, I considered spitting Asa out onto the lawn, but her mother still watched me from the doorway. There were coffee shops, rest stops, scenic points—so many opportunities to rid myself of her and go on with my life, finally unyoked from the requisites of our friendship. I considered every one on my journey to Arizona, but I couldn't do it. My car filled with the scent of charred fibers and warm wax and fresh smoke in my hair, and I kept driving.

I don't want to see the canyon. I don't want *her* to see the canyon.

I shouldn't be doing this. As a soul carrier, I should not be transporting my own loved one. Many soul carriers before me never made it to their destinations, so bereft by their personal loss that they allowed the soul of their loved one to absorb into their own bodies rather than release them as promised. They held on too tight and lost a piece of themselves to the remnants of a corpse.

Sometimes I think I should've never answered Mrs. Lee's call. I should've let Asa's soul dry out and die in that little glass jar.

I won't lie; it stings. I spent the bulk of our friendship trying to help Asa escape a monster that no one else could see. I thought she loved me the way I loved her. Instead, she kept me at arm's length from her family, her friends, a whole other life I'm just now discovering. I wasn't worth mentioning. I never existed to them.

I could spend the rest of my time in Room 22 wondering, begging this shadow that traces but never quite touches my edges if it knows why Asa never mentioned me. It knew her better than her mother, than Tricia, than anyone.

Better than me, anyway.

So I keep hanging onto Asa, thinking she'll reveal herself once she becomes part of me. The shadow crawls over the seams of this room, expanding and contracting, as restless as Asa is on my tongue. It follows me—follows her soul—until the numeric divinity of the Grand Canyon tears it from her very being.

Five. Seventeen. Twenty-two. Destiny determined by a set of numbers we had no control over. Asa and I may have made a powerful number when we were together, but I don't think we vibrated on the same frequency. Now I know the attraction was never equal.

In the bathroom, I stare into the sink drain, then the shower drain. The shadow follows, ready to chase Asa down whatever abyss I send her into. I never said I wasn't petty or cruel. I'm just doing my job, whether it's in this room or the canyon itself.

Tomorrow. I have at least a couple of days left before my body starts to absorb her. Maybe tomorrow I will want to see the canyon.

Vending Machine Girl

By Eric LaRocca

Think of it as a gift, I tried to convince myself whenever I looked at her. An opportunity to finally say all the things I was never able to.

I had already accepted the fact that Val might never return. Years of pining and grief had given way to recognizing it was for the best when I had learned of the horrible things Val had done.

What I had imagined, what once might be a precious reunion was now an unbearable burden ever since Val had appeared on my front porch like a stray cat three days ago.

I had once rehearsed confronting Val and telling her how I knew of the gruesome details of each killing. But, for some reason, I could never bring myself to do it.

All words muted, my tongue swelling as if burned, as I regarded my lover across a table littered with Chinese takeout cartons. Val's mask of pity, absent for the past thirty years, would usually soften all my resolve like sugar melting in warm water—Val's guilty eyes as wet and as shiny as exit wounds and often leaking a similar loss.

I found it ironic as both of our appearances had made it seem as though we had traded places long ago. Val—hair buzzed short like a Marine and face permanently etched with the mournful look of a virgin martyr about to be led to public execution. My face—obscured by a glistening mask of metal with ornate, homemade piercings covering every inch of exposed flesh like an extravagant masquerade disguise.

I sometimes wondered if I had misremembered Val entirely until I realized thirty years was a longer amount of time than all the five victims' lives combined.

While we ate dinner, I couldn't help but wonder if an undiscovered grain of brutality remained hiding somewhere within Val. Although I recognized thirty years had robbed most of Val's appearance—her once firm and exquisite beauty now thawed completely to form a supple visage of old age—I wondered if certain tendencies had been just as pliable.

Watching as Val playfully poked a broth-soaked dumpling with her fingernail, I wondered if Val were imagining slicing open something obscener. I pondered whether or not Val's armpits were still bruised with purple, crescent-shaped welts from the crutches she had used in her disgusting playground performances to bait the poor children.

I figured it wasn't entirely unlikely the bruises remained. After all, the interior of Val's arm remained scarred with track marks, small leathery impressions dotting the bowl where her joints meet like the undisturbed remnants of ancient ruins. More importantly, if the bruises remained even after thirty years, I convinced myself I would have to play dumb at the sight of them when—and if—we finally made love again.

Of course, I certainly wasn't going to encourage the possibility of intimacy, however. To me, a bed became as uncomfortable as a church confessional when two bodies shared it. I reasoned I would have to tell Val how one of the neighbors from the trailer park had visited while she was out for the afternoon.

The unpleasant exchange—revolving entirely around Val.

In fact, I had never seen Mrs. Petit so glum before. The old woman's somber demeanor had shocked me at first and acted as a stark contrast to the lavender highlights in her nest of white hair and her monogrammed pink velour tracksuit. With a wrinkled mouth like an open wound and a cadaver-like face caked with rouge, I had always thought of Mrs. Petit as Henley Edge's premier embalmed drag queen.

"You know why I'm here—?" the old woman had asked me, dipping a bleeding tea bag inside a Styrofoam cup of microwaved water. Her voice—so hideously brittle and hoarse that I had always thought she had sounded like a dying insect.

"I don't need to pretend to be polite like the others do," she had said. "I'm here because none of them wanted to even look at you, girlie."

I had cleared the catch in my throat. "I—thought I've always been a good neighbor to you."

"To hell with being a good neighbor," Mrs. Petit had said. "It's your fucking taste in house guests."

I recalled my body shrinking, every extremity shortening like flowers after sunset.

"It's—not for long," I had stammered. "She just needed a place to stay for a few weeks. Until she gets back on her feet."

I remembered how the loose skin on Mrs. Petit's face had suddenly hardened like cooling beeswax when their eyes met.

"I don't think I should have to remind you all the pain that woman has caused."

My eyes had lowered, fingers fumbling nervously with her hair to hide the three large cursive letters tattooed beneath my ear—Val.

"She says she has nowhere to go."

"She can't fucking stay." Mrs. Petit had punctuated the statement by slamming her empty cup on the table. "You have to tell her she's not welcome here, girlie."

"And if she won't leave—?"

Of course, I had immediately regretted asking.

Mrs. Petit's face had creased with a grotesque sneer. "We'll find some way to convince her."

I shook, the silver rings sewn into my forehead quivering like an embroidered tribal mask, when I thought deeply about what Mrs. Petit had meant. With the curtains drawn over every window and every door bolted shut, I could scarcely conceal my concern from Val at the dinner table.

"What is it—?" Val asked, spearing a wonton with one of her chopsticks.

My eyes mechanically opened and closed, breath whistling. "Why—did you come back to me?"

Val never faltered for an instant. "You're my home. Don't you want me here?"

I loathed to admit the fact that I wasn't actually sure.

———————————

I pretended to act surprised when Val knocked on my bedroom door in the middle of the night.

My rehearsed astonishment, however, gave way to unplanned panic as I watched Val's silhouette flicker against the trailer's wall while she tiptoed to the other side of my bed. My face flushed with warmth, every limb deadening with the possibility of movement, when Val slid beneath the sheets and the heat from her body drew closer. It wasn't long until I sensed Val's hairless thigh sweeping against mine in a playful act of solicitation.

Like an inexperienced participant in a bizarre nocturnal ritual, I remained without movement like a virgin to the invocation even as Val's body began to make more deliberate supplications. Val's fingers, delicate at first, began measuring the distance between my shoulders and my breasts. I soon felt all gentleness from her disappear as fingers began to instead move with much more unreserved intent, slipping underneath my bra and circling my nipples as they stiffened.

As if invited by Val's mere touch, an unpleasant thought visited my mind. I imagined Val's fingers braiding with a faceless six-year-old's as she led him toward an idling car parked near a playground. However, the thought disappeared as suddenly as it had arrived.

Careful to avoid the diamond-shaped spikes lining my lips, Val pressed her mouth against mine. She was especially cautious to evade the most lethal ornaments on my mask of piercings—long silver skewers fixed within both sides of my nostrils and fanning out in a glittering wreath to resemble a feral cat's whiskers. When our mouths finally parted, Val dragged a thread of spittle from between my lips—and with it, she pulled out the very last of my resistance.

It was then I began to sense molten cream leaking from between my thighs. As Val guided her mouth along my collar, she dragged me closer until our bodies became choked in what felt like a permanent embrace. My pleasure was short-lived, however, as I suddenly sensed teeth pressing against my shoulder, a tiny point gently stabbing me.

No longer lost and unfettered in a boundless ocean of ecstasy, I sensed my body desperately mooring against the bedpost in some futile attempt to retreat from Val. My eyes remained open, dogged in their examination of the faceless shape gently stirring in the bed beside me. I became sickened as I pressed a finger against my throat and felt a small dot of wetness begin to flower.

Val violently writhed next to me, orgasming in what appeared to be the throes of a grand mal seizure. As I leaned over the side of the bed, hand reaching for the light switch, Val threw herself at me. Predicting something far worse, I released a short cry and slashed Val's stomach with my fingernails. Val lurched back, startled enough to scream.

Surprised and immediately remorseful, I twisted the light switch and recovered my composure with a look of concern.

"I'm—sorry," I said.

Val showed little emotion, chin tucked into her throat and her eyes forced downward as she silently inspected the lines of redness heating across her stomach from where my fingers had slashed.

Guilt fluttered in my mind for a moment as I hastened to the bathroom to run a towel under the faucet. Watching Val inspect the wound with childlike curiosity, I did my best to convince myself that Val had deserved the small punishment.

I was not prepared to admit, however, that I was suddenly filled with an unbearable longing to punish her again and again.

Not long after Val left to walk down the street to pick up a pack of cigarettes and beer, I was alarmed by a knock at the door. Eyes squinting through the peephole, I was greeted with the glistening bald crown of my neighbor, Mr. Lindsey.

He was tall and slender, most of his clothing immeasurably too large for the thinness of his frame. His teeth—as dark and yellow as amber. His breath—as rancid-smelling as sun-scorched trash bags. His smile— uniquely obscene for such an otherwise kind-looking old man.

Mr. Lindsey was not smiling when I opened the door, however.

"I'm—sorry," I stammered. "I'm expecting company any minute."

"Company can wait," he said, his feet crossing the threshold and body threatening to pass inside my home invited or otherwise. "I think it's best I come inside."

Slipping past me, he reached the small kitchenette before turning on me with a look of condemnation.

"I'll keep it brief," he said, the muscles in his throat flexing. "A few of the neighbors asked me to come over here and tell you there was a meeting held last night. You can guess why."

Mr. Lindsey adjusted the glasses sitting at the tip of his nose, glaring at me. I merely nodded.

"About twenty-five of us. Trying to agree on what's to be done about—" His voice trailed off, all euphemisms lost. "The two people who did most of the talking were Billy and Martha Hoxley. You've heard their names—?"

"Yes." My voice was a murmur. "Their son was—"

"The youngest one. Five years old."

I closed my eyes, body tensing.

"I—remember when they found him," Mr. Lindsey said, the light dimming from his eyes at the grim recollection. "Inside a dumpster behind a shoe store. His little body—thrown away as if he were nothing more than—garbage."

I shut my eyes and recalled the small black and white photo they had printed in the Henley's Edge Post—a child's body, dressed in torn overalls, a plaid shirt, and dark boots, lying face down and arranged on a small bed of shiny black trash bags. I remembered reading how there was a small black thread tied about his finger and how his mother had tied it there every morning before he left for school.

"We let them talk. And, after a while, we came to an agreement."

I trembled, scared to ask. "What kind—?"

Mr. Lindsey's eyes narrowed at me with a threat. "If there was any justice, she'd be left alone in a room with the families."

I felt as if I was going to collapse. "What do you want from her?"

"Nothing from her. I'm here to see you. As a friend," he said, his voice soft at first. It suddenly became low as though his throat were filled with wet cement. "Because your time is now precious. Pack a suitcase. And leave tonight. Do you understand?"

"Why?"

Mr. Lindsey hesitated for a moment, pursing his lips. "You're going to have a visitor this evening."

I sensed vibrations working their way throughout my body until they disappeared, and every extremity became as immovable as bedrock.

"Who—?"

"A man hired for his—talents," Mr. Lindsey said. "A friend of the

Hoxley's. He's been given your address and was instructed to break in through your bathroom window."

My breath became rapid as I realized. "I'll go to the police."

Mr. Lindsey smiled as though he had expected the useless defense. "Waste of time. Bill's a retired Officer over in Kent. The police in Henley's Edge have already agreed to comply."

He turned and began inching toward the door.

I willed myself to move and hurried after him, pleading.

"Please. Don't do this."

Mr. Lindsey's face was as steadily fixed as a bronze statue. "Write a note for her and say you went out to the store so that she won't be alarmed."

Leaving me with no other options, I deflated like an untethered balloon. I felt every metal piercing on my face sink further inside, dragging my skin down until I wondered if I might suffocate from the agonizing pressure.

"I'm afraid this is what happens when you choose to be so eager to forgive," Mr. Lindsey told me.

It was nearly dusk when I finished packing.

As I dragged two small suitcases and a large bag stuffed with dirty laundry toward the front door, I heard the sound of Val's boots climbing the porch steps. My whole body stiffened as my mind raced with possible scenarios. I thought of hiding the suitcases in the pantry closet and kicking the laundry bag under the sink. But, before my body could make the decision for me, the front door opened, and Val greeted me with a look of bewilderment.

"Where are you—going?"

I kicked the bag onto the floor until my clothing confessed, spilling out in an incriminating heap. Cheeks warming with redness, I wiped the hair from my eyes.

"I—needed to run out for the laundry."

My eyes followed Val's until they arrived at the suitcases. I watched the recognition creep across Val's face until her eyebrows furrowed and lips pulled downward.

"Are you—leaving?"

I inhaled deeply as if bracing my every extremity to be ripped apart by a maelstrom.

Val blinked, eyes glittering with confusion. I imagined Val's face resembled the puzzled faces of the little ones she had coaxed to an idling car parked near the schoolyard as they were met with a strange-looking man in the driver's seat.

"You're leaving me—?"

Although I shuddered at the sound of pain breaking in Val's voice, I couldn't help but secretly delight in her despair.

"I—can't forgive you," I told her. "I don't think I ever will."

Val remained without movement, my words visibly filleting her like a fresh cadaver prepared for autopsy.

"I wanted to," I said, gathering my clothing in a pile and stuffing it inside the bag. "I wanted things to be how they were before you left. But they can never be again."

Val grabbed my arm, cupping my chin, and tilting my face until our eyes met. "Maisy. I want to have a baby with you. This—could be our second chance. Don't you want that?"

I had waited to hear those words from Val for so long. Of course, I had imagined the moment—rehearsed my every movement and word in each unfulfilled fantasy—but I had never expected it to come to be. I felt weightless, as if every ring of metal had been vacuumed from my face and I was once again as pure as the day we had first met.

"I want to show you something," Val whispered.

She pinched the rim of her lower lip, pouting, as the impression of her cupid's bow puckered slightly. Peeling the lip down until the oily flap of skin extended to her chin and exposing the pinkness of her gums, Val positioned her fingers to highlight five letters crudely inscribed on the interior of her lip. I leaned closer and covered my mouth when I recognized what the letters spelled—Maisy.

"I had it done a few years ago," Val said.

My mouth hung open in disbelief, my eyes coveting each letter of my name.

Val released her lips, secreting the tattoo once more. "I wanted you with me always. Even if I never got to see you again."

Without hesitation, I pressed my lips against Val's. My tongue stabbed her mouth, coiling inside and desperately searching as if to suck the ink from every letter. Our mouths finally parted, lips ravenous to be reunited as we exhaled deeply and inhaled the heat of one another's breath.

"We'll leave tonight," I said, the piercings on my face pressing against Val's as we leaned against one another. "Pack as fast as you can."

But Val's eyes instead hinted at the bedroom door and returned to me with a look of insatiable hunger.

The place between my legs was still damp when Val shifted beneath the sheets and stretched to the nightstand to light a cigarette. I watched as Val wiped the threads of fluid from her mouth and guided a cigarette between her lips. I clenched my thighs together while I sensed the supple cushioning of Val's breasts pushing against my backside, nipples firming like small rubber coils.

Still lost and unfettered in a seemingly endless current of bliss, I found myself sinking further into Val's embrace.

"We have to pack," I whispered, eyes closed and with no intention of opening.

Val's hands insisted on prolonging the pleasure as they circled the lips pouting with wetness between my legs.

"Everything I promised you is going to come true," she said. "You'll see."

I basked in the serenity of the moment until Val's hands abandoned me. Eyes opening, I was met with Val's gaze as if my face were an ornate jigsaw puzzle she was trying to rearrange.

Val simpered coyly and turned, beginning to rummage through the drawer to the nightstand.

"What are you looking for?" I asked, drawing the sheets around my neck like a pashmina.

"You had some thread in here the other day," Val said.

Her body finally relaxed as she found it. I watched as Val drew a small thimble of white string from the drawer and began wrapping it about her index finger. Clenching the thread between her teeth, she bit down and separated the material like some primal creature severing a newborn's umbilical cord.

My heart fluttered giant pulses as if it were going to burst through the plate of my sternum. My mind invoking the black-and-white image of the little boy found in the dumpster, I couldn't help but recall the thread tied about his finger.

I could scarcely speak at first, my throat sealed with a mere whisper. "What's—that—for?"

Val shook her finger, the thread's tail lifting like a bewitched snake. She smiled. "Just a trick to remember something. I learned it a while ago."

The question tiptoed off my tongue. "From whom—?"

Val ignored me, drawing another drag from her cigarette. "There's something I want to remember to tell you when we're finished."

Val whimpered as if her body were on the threshold of orgasm. My eyes remain glued on the small thread wrapped around Val's finger, my stomach performing somersaults as I wondered if Val enticed the more hesitant children with playful baby-talk or tiny sobs.

"I still have to come," Val panted, heating my shoulder with her breath as she kissed it.

I searched Val's face for a semblance of familiarity—the woman I had loved and remained loving for so long—but was instead met with the vacant mask of an apparition. Val's eyes slowly crept down her body until they fell below her waist and her thighs widened with an invitation for me to get to work. Every extremity now a mere servant to Val's fancy, I positioned myself between her legs. I regarded the hairless slit where Val's legs met with disdain as it frowned, winking obscenely at me.

I poked my tongue out between my lips, preparing to go to work. But I suddenly hesitated.

"My piercings," I said, exposing my tongue of sparkling jewelry. "I've—never tried it before. It might—hurt?"

"Go ahead," Val said. "I like the way it feels."

I cleared my throat, hands unsure and face whitening with uncertainty. Bowing on hands and knees as if addressing royalty, my tongue began to circle the flexing lips of Val's womanhood. Tongue curling at the bitter taste, I finally pushed deeper inside the damp sleeve until it bloomed like a rare orchid.

Raking her head back against a pillow, Val closed her eyes. "I can't wait to get the fuck out of here with you. We can begin our new life and start a family."

I withdrew my tongue, wiping the wetness from my lips. "You promise you never—hurt—any of those children—?"

Val opened her eyes, face flushed with a look of betrayal. "Why are you asking me that?"

"I just—need to know," I said. "If we're—going to have a baby. I want to know if—"

"I would ever hurt it," Val finished, devastated.

I said nothing, my mouth hanging open. I was unsure whether I wanted Val to lie or tell the truth.

Val drew in a deep breath, her eyes threatening to water. "I was going to tell you."

My body tensed, dreading Val's every word.

"There was a little girl with a strawberry print dress and Mickey Mouse sunglasses," Val said. "She was—nine or ten. I had met her at a bus stop as she was waiting for her mother. I was—wearing my crutches and I had told her my cat just had a litter of kittens and they were free if she helped me. She—started crying—when she saw—him—waiting in the car."

I winced, burying my face in my hands in disbelief.

"He asked me to watch—him with her," Val said, clearly disgusted with herself. "And when I said I couldn't, he threatened to cut me off. He told me he'd get rid of me. I would've had nowhere to go."

I covered my mouth, choking on quiet sobs. "I would've—taken you back if you came to me."

Val's entire body deflated like a puppet with loosened strings. Her voice trembled, eyes avoiding me at all costs. "So, I watched him as he— started to choke her. When he turned and saw I was crying, he told me to touch myself."

Val's hands covered her mouth, straining to stifle a scream.

"And I did," she whimpered, shivering with small sobs.

I nearly vomited at the horrible confession.

I regarded the plump whiteness of Val's naked body as if she were nothing more than a slug. Becoming distracted by the hairless pearl of tissue gloating at me, I grimaced and imagined Val's sex becoming moist at the mere sound of a child's sobbing.

Grunting like a feral animal in heat, I pressed my mouth against Val's labia and began devouring. Val's whimpers soon turned to moans as I stabbed the cleavage of tissue with my tongue, snaking inside and massaging the velvet walls of her womanhood. The motion of my tongue slowed to a steady throb as I finally uncovered what I had been searching for—the small gemstone of Val's clitoris. I teased it gently and it began to harden like a small bead.

When I was certain Val was in the throes of climax, I tilted my head slightly so that one of my long metal piercings softly teased her. Before another moment of hesitation, I lurched forward and speared the skin like a skewer stabbing a morsel of meat. Val let out a soft cry, as if confused. As her vulva opened, sprouting thick curtains of tissue, I buried my face between Val's legs and dragged the sharp tips of my piercings through until my face was sprinkled with red.

Val began to squirm like a pinned rat, but I held her legs down as my tongue pushed deeper inside her until I once again came upon her clitoris. Steeling my resolve one final time, I pushed the rubbery knob between my teeth and bit down.

Val screamed as I grunted, teeth clenching as they worked to separate the clitoris from its cushion. Finally, the small coil—a fleshy diamond jeweled in a bassinet of silk—tore from its root with a squelching sound as I drew it out between my teeth. I sensed Val's womanhood squeeze tight, warm fluid squirting from the opening and spraying my face with a geyser of blood as black as ink.

Val screamed as I lifted my face from between her legs—the rings and hoops of my piercings now dripping wet with blood. As more blood flooded between her legs, Val lunged off the bed and scrambled onto the floor with palsied limbs. I spat the oily tissue out and leapt after her, shrieking like a livid chimpanzee.

Val's arms raised across her face could only protect her for so long before I weakened all of her resolve, slamming my fists into her skull. Finally, in a blow that decided the matter, I grabbed the lamp from the nightstand and slammed it against Val's head. Val twitched like a puppet, her body crashing against the floor with a vulgar thud and slowing until it was finally without movement.

As silence returned to the small room, I inhaled deeply as if awakening. When I found Val was still breathing, I rolled her over until she was lying on her backside.

Arranging her body so that she could be carried, my work was far from finished. I ripped the seashell-print shower curtain from its metal rod with fumbling hands and wrapped it about Val until her body disappeared. Leaning close to where I guessed Val's mouth was beneath the curtain, I heard the faint murmur of her breath creasing the plastic material. I gripped the curtain and began dragging the body toward the front door. A line of Val's blood followed me, smearing the floor, like the trail of a boat left behind on the surface of a lake.

A blast of cool air greeted me, stiffening the hairs in my nostrils, as I opened the front door. Slipping on a coat and wrapping a scarf about my neck, I slid my fingers into a pair of black leather gloves. After making certain the street was empty, I pulled Val over the threshold and dragged her down the steps while the dim hum of the flickering porch light serenaded me. Opening the door to my car, I slid Val's body into the backseat. Val squirmed beneath the curtain like a fussy newborn.

I lurched into the passenger seat and slammed the keys into the ignition, shifting the car into reverse.

Ambling down the row of trailers, the engine humming, I knew for certain that I could never return. Although at first surprised sadness was absent from me, I sensed my foot leaning on the gas pedal with urgency, as if I were being beckoned by something far beyond where the lights in the tiny houses could reach.

———————

I drove until I saw the sky begin to break open like a piece of ripe fruit and wash the horizon with streaks of lavender and gold. I sensed my eyelids becoming heavy as I noticed the English words written on the highway signs giving way to French, nearing the Canadian border. Eyes darting from the road to the rearview mirror of the backseat, I heard Val whimpering as the curtain rustled like an insect cocoon. My eyes narrowed at the sight, thinking Val was no better than larvae.

Pulling off the highway, my car crept down the ramp and slowed as it pulled into a small parking lot situated near a collection of basketball courts. There were a few teenage boys dressed in matching navy tracksuits running the length of the caged area, passing the ball to one another and shouting. After I parked, both of my hands remained fastened to the steering wheel as if they were glued there.

My attention soon drifted to a small concrete building with signs posted for public bathrooms, a vending machine marked with neon lettering situated near the entrance. I couldn't help but wonder if Val had been here before.

Glancing in the rearview mirror, I noticed a line of blood trickling like spilled honey from under the curtain and down the leather seat. I climbed out of the car, tucking my chin into my scarf as a gust of wind swaddled me. My eyes searched the branch-veined canopy of leafless trees and empty stretch of roadway beside the parking lot and courts.

Coiling my fingers around the passenger door handle, I pulled and the curtained bundle lying in the backseat unfurled as if it were wrapping paper. Val was without movement, her eyes as vacant as a doll's. Her hands were clasped together like the front legs of a praying mantis, and I wondered if Val had prayed before the life had drained from between her legs. I hoped she had. More importantly, I hoped the prayer would go unanswered.

I grimaced, noticing the white thread tied about Val's finger. I pried her hand open until her fingers stretched as if thawing and I was able to tear the small string, pocketing it immediately.

My ears pinned at the sound of shouting. I lifted my head and noticed the group of teenagers harassing a young boy, no older than eight, dressed in a brown wool jacket and an orange ski hat. I watched as they snatched the backpack from his shoulders and began rummaging through it, showering the ground with textbooks and pencils.

The young boy shouted muted insults at them as they tore the coat from his arms and threw it on the ground, stomping on it. Then they ripped the hat from him as he screamed and began passing it around the small group as each took turns spitting in it. As he retaliated, one of the boys kicked him in his leg. Like animals teasing half-dead prey, the group of teenagers slammed their feet into the small boy until he was doubled over with sobs and clutching his knee.

I watched as the horde of boys left him, dragging the wool coat and hat with them, like feral creatures abandoning carrion nearly picked to the bone. I saw his little shape lift himself up from his knees and begin to collect the remains of his lunch bag. As I saw him struggle, I was reminded of myself—certain things far too irreversibly broken to ever be put back together.

Then I thought of Val.

Kneeling to view my reflection in the car door mirror, I was suddenly filled with unease at the sight of a woman I did not recognize—my face rusted brown with Val's blood, eyes dimmed of any semblance of emotion like a hospice patient in the final stages.

Not wanting to frighten him, I wrapped my scarf about my face and began to walk across the parking lot toward the boy. I rehearsed in my mind what I might say to him. Children had always been afraid of me, and I dreaded his inevitable look of bewilderment, longing for a tender expression of graciousness only common between a mother and their child.

I saw him glance up from his labor, watching as I approached. I released a deep breath of relief at the exquisite sweetness of the boy's face—his frank brown eyes, healthy pink cheeks, a smile conjuring the likeness of cherubs in Italian frescoes.

I trembled slightly, disgusted, when I recognized how much Val would have once delighted in the young boy's perfections. Hesitating for a moment as he choked on soft sobs, I gagged slightly when I imagined Val's hand circling the valve between her thighs while listening to the sounds of the boy's agony. Composing myself, I blinked until beads of tears cleared from the corners of my eyes.

"Are you hurt—?" I asked him.

He merely lifted the leg of his pants and exposed a purple bruise just above his shin.

"That's not so bad," I said, smiling.

The boy said nothing, his chapped lips trembling with soundless words. His body shuddered like a small bird with a broken wing as a gust of wind leveled him.

I shrugged the coat from my shoulders and presented it to him with a motherlike reverence. Hesitant at first, he took the jacket and slipped it on until his tiny body was swallowed by it. I watched as his face flushed with warmth, his body shifting comfortably inside the jacket until he was content. Another blast of cold air passed over us and the boy tightened the coat about his collar, shutting his eyes.

I made the decision before my hands could hesitate, removing my final protection—my scarf. Peeling it from my face like a second layer of skin and holding it out for him to take, our eyes met as I exposed my glittering veil of metal crusted with dried blood. Although I waited for the boy to scream or cry out in confusion, I was instead met with silence. The boy merely took the scarf from my hand and looped it about his throat until his neck and mouth were covered.

Finally unmasked in all my monstrous glory, the thing looking out from behind my eyes slowly crawled out from hiding and was greeted by the boy with a look of tenderness as he revered me the same way a child might look at a mother.

Remembering the thread in my pocket, I pulled it out and it fluttered between my fingers like an angry spirit. The boy's face was enchanted with bewilderment while he watched me present the sacred object. He held out his hand as I dropped it into his open palm like a sliver of ice from a tree branch.

"What is it—?" the boy asked, his face softening as he cupped the thread in his hands.

"Think of it as a gift," I said to him.

Curious about other Crossroad Press books?
Stop by our site:
https://www.crossroadpress.com
We offer quality writing
in digital, audio, and print formats.

www.ingramcontent.com/pod-product-compliance
Lightning Source LLC
Chambersburg PA
CBHW020642180626
46816CB00003B/1090